Goering's War

Book Two

Book Two

By Kim Kerr

Chapter One: September 1943

Goering sat with his head in his hands. The pain from the old wound near his groin always seemed to trouble him when he was stressed. Speer sat with him hoping the news wouldn't get any worse. Before them stood Grand Admiral Raeder and behind him, pinned to a board, was a map of the ocean between Norway and Iceland.

"Both carriers were lost, and the Prince Eugen?" asked Goering again.

"Yes, my Führer, and the Scharnhorst was heavily damaged and won't be ready for action for at least six months," said Raeder.

"And the convoy got through?" continued Goering.

"Unfortunately the weather turned soon after the battle and we were unable to find the allied ships for a number of days. Also, the anti-shipping units took heavy losses in the actual battle and the number of aircraft able to attack the convoy were few."

"How many did you sink?"

"We got their light cruiser and four merchant ships."

"This is a disaster. Our navy is gutted and we virtually have no surface fleet," said Goering.

"A battleship and a battle cruiser remain," said Raeder.

"To face the might of the Commonwealth and American fleets; that is nothing," yelled Goering.

Raeder fell silent and stood with his hands behind his back. Speer knew that besides a few extra light cruisers and some destroyers there were no big naval ships in the pipeline.

"What were the enemies' losses?" Goering asked.

"The South Dakota was damaged and later finished by U 238. Two American light carriers were hit by the guided bombs of KG 100 which had the good fortune to catch the carriers while most of their aircraft were off attacking our ships. The first six JU 290s went in low with HS 293 guided glide bombs. The enemy Hellcats went after them, allowing the following twelve aircraft to attack unmolested.

One of the carriers, the Cowpens, was hit by at least five Fritz X

bombs and blew up."

"So we lost two carriers and so did they, still the convoy got

through," said Goering, a little more quietly.

Speer could see he was consoled by the fact the Americans had at

least taken heavy losses in the battle.

"Why were we beaten?" the Führer, asked suddenly.

Raeder nodded as though this topic had been anticipated.

"They were ready for us. We didn't believe the enemy had a

concentration of carrier strength in the Northern Atlantic. No, we

knew they didn't, hence our plans to attack this convoy. Somehow,

they noted our naval concentration or information was leaked. In the

actual battle our fighters were matched by the new American

Hellcats. The ME 155s still held their own but the US pilots are now

veterans of the fighting against the Japanese. Then there was the

issue of range. We haven't solved the problem that the American

planes can fly further than ours."

"And U boat losses are still climbing?" asked Goering.

"Donitz's Wolfpacks are under constant pressure. New enemy weapon systems are proving very effective," said Raeder.

"So all we have for now are the guided bombs," said Goering.

Speer knew that these systems were vulnerable to countermeasures, and wondered how long it would be before the Allies found a way to incapacitate them.

Private Charlie Winklen sat behind the steering wheel of the M8 armoured car as it cruised quietly along the Spanish country road. He enjoyed driving the vehicle as it was similar to his dad's light truck that he had operated in Michigan. The synchromesh gear box was just an added bonus when driving the M8. Charlie wished sometimes he was in the turret where the armour was thicker, but at least the sand bags under his feet gave him added protection if they hit a mine. Sergeant Fred Renwood, commander of the armoured car, laughed at this.

"Do you think a bit of sand is going to stop a German Tellar mine blowing your balls off?"

It was alright for the Sarge. He stood up next to the gun. Charlie smiled though when he noted that his commander had placed sand bags on the floor space of all of the M8s.

The 4th Armoured Division, to which he was attached, was advancing slowly on Madrid, coming down from the north towards the town of Arevalo. The US forces were still a good twelve miles short of the place and were still to take the small town of Ataquines. To the east of the area a woodland ran for about twenty miles. The division was worried what might be hiding in the trees and had asked the recon boys to check it out. Here though the road ran straight through dry open fields with little cover. Ahead, the village of Ramiro blocked the way forward. Sergeant Renwood ordered the M8 to stop and Charlie eased to a halt. A second M8 cruised up next to them quickly followed by Lieutenant Michealson in a jeep.

"You think the Jerries are home?" asked the young lieutenant.

Charlie didn't think their commander was a lot older than he was. Henry Michealson was a West point graduate with a New York accent.

He wasn't a bad commander but Charlie still thought he was a spoilt rich kid.

"Hard to tell, sir. There could be Germans hiding thirty feet from me and I might miss them. They're masters at camouflage."

"Intelligence says the 9th SS Herman Goering Division have units in the area," said the lieutenant.

"Well I can't see any of those SS bastards, sir," said the Sergeant.

"You stay here and cover us and I'll take Cortez and his M8 in closer. If there are any locals around he can speak to them and maybe we'll get a better handle on where the Germans are."

"Do you think that's wise, sir? I thought sneaking up on foot might be a better approach," said Sergeant Renwood.

Michaelson shook his head. "The Major wants us to hurry things up. He says the division needs to up its pace. That's the push from the top."

Charlie didn't like the sound of that. He knew that their army

commander, General Patton, was a firebrand who said speed saved

lives but that wasn't the case for the recon boys.

The jeep and the other M8 eased passed them and continued

up the road towards the village. The rocket came from thick scrub

fifty yards from the road. It hit the M8 in the side of the turret and

killed the gunner as well as wounding Sergeant Cortez. The radio

operator was slashed by hot metal but the driver was unaffected and

threw the armoured car into reverse. From a walled enclosure on the

other side of an intersection of two roads a MG 42 screamed out a

burst of fire at the lieutenant's jeep. The driver took two bullets in the

chest and the corporal sitting next to him shrieked as a ricochet from

the bonnet hit him just below the eye. The jeep veered off the road

before rolling in the ploughed field. The occupants, alive and dead

were tossed free and spun like rag dolls before hitting the brown

earth.

"Catinza, fire on the house. Keep the MG crew's heads down. Smokey, take the 50 cal and spray the scrub. Don't let that rocket fire again," yelled Sergeant Renwood.

Charlie saw Smokey, the radio operator, scramble passed him and cock the heavy machine gun before firing short bursts into the scrubland.

Charlie felt his bowels tighten. He hated this. Fear washed over him and he fought down the urge to put the M8 into reverse and speed from the fight. They were only two hundred yards from the scrub and theoretically in range of the German rocket launcher, especially the one on the two wheeled carriage. He knew the German MG rounds would bounce from the M8's armour but the small hole punched by a rocket launcher could spray him with hot iron which would melt his face. Charlie felt tears spring to his eyes. He wanted to scream at them to run but was frightened of being called a coward. Was dying horribly a bad thing to be so scared of? Didn't the Germans and his crew members understand how crazy this all was?

"Shit, shit, shit," said Renwood. "The lieutenant is still alive."

The damaged armoured car continued backwards until a second rocket hit it just above the rear wheel. The vehicle slowed and then rolled to a stop, smoke pouring from the engine. Men staggered from the M8 to be lashed with machine gun fire. Charlie heard the 37mm gun of his armoured car fire and the German MG42 abruptly stopped its chainsaw like scream. Looking through his viewing slit he saw it was too late for Cortez and his crew. None of them moved from where they had fallen onto the road.

The 50 calibre machine gun kept firing and no rockets came their way.

"Ease the car forward," said Renwood.

Charlie tried to put his foot on the accelerator but it was shaking so much he couldn't control it.

The M8 jerked forward a few paces and stalled.

"What the hell!" exclaimed Renwood. "Get your shit together Private Winklen, or get out of the driver's seat."

Charlie fought the urge to vomit and restarted the M8. He eased it towards the other smoking armoured car, just trying to concentrate on the act of driving. They reached the wounded lieutenant, and Sergeant Renwood jumped from the vehicle and scooped him up. He was a big man so throwing the officer over his shoulder and scrambling back into the M8 was a prodigious feat of strength.

"Oh no," said Catinza as Renwood laid the unconscious man down in the turret.

An Sd. Kfz. 231 German armoured car was nosing its way out of the small village. There was a low brick house with a surrounding wall blocking the ability of the two vehicles to shoot effectively at each other, but through gaps and holes the German armoured car could be plainly seen.

"When he clears the buildings shoot him," said the Sergeant. "The smoke from the burning M8 is giving us some cover and I don't think the Jerries have seen us yet."

The 231 cleared a low brick farm house and then spotted the M8 and accelerated. There was little angle on the shot Private Catinza needed to make and the 37mm shell hit the enemy vehicle on the driver's viewing port. The 231 rolled to a halt as German soldiers abandoned the armoured car. Private Smokey Gunroy fired at them with the heavy machine gun, hitting one of the enemy soldiers. Charlie was horrified as the man's head seemed to disappear. He was close enough to vaguely make out the details and he screamed as the distress of what he had witnessed overwhelmed him.

The rest of the Germans seemed to have disappeared and Sergeant Renwood gave the order for Charlie to take them back the way they had come. For a second he didn't respond.

"Wake up Winklen, it's time to go," repeated the big man.

Charlie eased the car into reverse and took the M8 back to the north. He drove off feeling some of the tension ease away. As far as he was concerned, the further from the front he could take them the better.

Captain Gyorgy Debrody eased his Fiat G55 into another slow circuit of the bombers he was shepherding towards the Baku oil refineries. Puma squadron had twenty four aircraft airborne and they had been joined by an Italian wing. The number three stormo was also equipped with the G55 and had been flown to Russia especially to escort these raids. All of the planes were carrying 100-litre drop tanks and were the only single-engined fighters in the Axis arsenal that could escort the bombers the 500 kilometres from Grozny to Baku and back again. The problem was that only a few of the aircraft were available. The Italian machines were a favour from Mussolini to Germany as it was.

Below them the JU290s, Heinkel 111s and JU88s droned southeast. It looked as though it was an all-out effort with just over one hundred of the four-engined machines and twice that number of the twin-engined bombers heading for the target. They were to attack the port itself as most of the oil was being moved by water to the Volga River now the Germans had reached the Caspian Sea and blocked the land route north. The individual

wellheads would be hard to hit from the air but transport and storage facilities were another matter.

The Flak started as the large formation of planes reached the neck of the peninsula on which the city sat. As it was daylight the aircraft were staying above the effective range of the 76mm Russian anti-aircraft guns, flying at twenty thousand feet. However, the 85mm guns could fire effectively to thirty-five thousand feet, so some anti-aircraft fire was going to cause damage. The He111s struggled at the higher altitude so they flew a little lower.

Black puffs appeared around the leading aircraft and it wasn't long before a Heinkel bomber fell away trailing smoke. Two other aircraft were hit and jettisoned their bombs before turning north for the safety of the German lines. Debrody knew they would be easy targets for Russian fighters. He felt for the crew that jumped from the burning plane. It was almost certain the German fliers would be captured and their treatment by the Russians would be brutal. One of the bigger Ju290s was hit in the outer port engine but the pilot shut it down and the big bomber continued. It was times like these that Debrody was glad he was a fighter pilot.

"Drop tanks," ordered Debrody.

They extra fuel tanks tumbled away but the Captain wasn't worried; they were almost dry anyway.

"Thunderbolts nine o'clock low," said his wingman.

Debrody glanced at the approaching Russian fighters. He had a lot of respect for these big American machines and was glad the Soviets didn't seem to have acquired too many of them. The enemy fighters were angling to come at the bombers from behind and Puma Squadron were in the perfect position to intercept them.

"Red Flight cover us, but watch your own tails too. It looks like out Italian friends won't be able to protect them."

Debrody noted a group of Yak 9s climbing towards the bombers. The Italians would find easy prey as the slim Russian fighter didn't perform well at these altitudes.

They dived after the Thunderbolts but the big planes moved away from them. Damm, but they were fast in a dive, thought Debrody. Soon the big Russian fighters were firing at a group of JU88s, chewing pieces off the German aircrafts' wings and engines. Two of the twin-engined planes spiralled away on fire, while one exploded in a flash of crimson and yellow. Debrody cursed and swore

he would avenge the German fliers. He followed the Russians through

the German formation and closed the gap as they started to climb.

The last machine in the Soviet formation seemed to lag a little behind

the others and he caught it as it curved gently to port. His 20mm

cannon and 15mm wing guns tore pieces from the Thunderbolt's

fuselage and engine, and there was a small explosion from just in

front of the enemy pilot's cockpit. Smoke streamed from the stricken

machine as it curved away, flipping over onto its back as it dived

towards the ground.

"There's a chute, skipper," said his wingman.

Debrody barely registered the comment as he chased after his next

victim.

"Break right Debrody!" shouted a voice and he did so

instinctively.

Tracers flashed passed his aircraft and another Thunderbolt appeared

in his rear mirror. The enemy had posted extra planes as top cover

and they now took a hand in the combat. He hauled the stick into his stomach and kicked the rudder, causing his aircraft to shoot upwards. His opponent was too close to react in time and shot by to his left.

Debrody lost track of the Russian and pulled his stick hard to the right. He didn't know that the Soviet pilot was flying inverted to his left and had chosen the exact same second to perform the same manoeuvre. He looked out of the top of his cockpit and saw the Russian not thirty yards from him. Both planes came together with the huge paddle shaped propeller of the Thunderbolt smashing into the top of the Fiat G55. The blade hit Debrody on the top of his head pushing it down into his chest cavity. He died instantly. A second later the Thunderbolt exploded and both planes disappeared in a ball of metal and flame.

v

Goering smiled as Kesselring and Werner Molders, the Inspector General of Fighters, entered. They were in the main dining room of the hunting hall in Bavaria and a fire had been lit to take the chill off the air, yet it made the room a little smoky as the chimney hadn't been cleaned properly.

"Not as thick as the smoke in Baku, eh?" Goering joked.

Kesselring nodded and a small grin of his own creased his face. He pinned the map of the Caucasus to a partition which was covered in red and blue lines, and put his briefcase on a large dining table. Goering sat in a comfortable chair and gestured for him to begin.

"The raids have been successful. The port of Baku was an excellent choice as a target. The only way the Soviets can move oil from the Southern Caucasus is by ship and we have closed off that option. No doubt they will endeavour to repair the facilities we have hit so it will be necessary to keep up the pressure. We have made an excellent start," said Kesselring.

"And the losses?" asked Goering.

"Six percent of the bomber force has been lost per mission, on average. If it wasn't for the Hungarians and Italian fighters it would have been a lot worse," said Kesselring.

"The Hungarians lost their top scoring ace in these battles my Führer," added Molders.

Goering frowned and then nodded. "I heard. He had just outscored the great Richtofen himself. We will honour him with the Knight's Cross."

"Anyway, there are not enough of these long range fighters to properly protect the bombers and the only reason they have been so successful is the Russians have few decent high altitude machines. Only the P47s they purchased from the Americans can match the Fiat G55s above five thousand metres. Luckily they have few of these aircraft. We want to purchase the Fiat G55 for our own use," said Kesselring.

"Is it as good a plane as they say?" asked Goering.

"It is a match for a Bf 109G, and handles better than our fighter. With two heavy machine guns in the wings and two above the nose, as well as the 20mm cannon shooting through the propeller hub, it has the firepower to knock any enemy fighter from the sky. Its greatest attribute is its range. With the drop tanks, it can fly out to eight hundred kilometres, fight, and then return," said Molders.

"Have you spoken to the Italians?" asked Goering.

"We have. A deal is on the table to swap one hundred FW190s for the same number of the Fiats," said Kesselring. "The problem is the Italian production levels are low. They lack a leader like Speer to pull their industry together."

"Albert is certainly worth his weight in gold," said Goering. "Leave it with me. I will ring Mussolini and see if we can create some sort of ongoing deal where we manage one of their factories, or set one up in Germany. It shouldn't be too hard as the Fiats use the same engine as the Messerschmitt. For now though I'll sign off on the swap. I'm guessing we will need the long range fighters sooner rather than later. Lucky the Americans don't have such a plane, eh? Otherwise they would be escorting the B17s into the heart of Germany."

"The Stormbird is almost ready, my Führer. When the jets take to the skies it won't matter if they do," said Molders.

Goering had a sudden thought. "None of this will affect Rommel's coming offensive in mid-October will it?"

"It isn't connected," said Kesselring. "The extra aircraft we have sent Spain will be unchanged."

"Good. With the panzers and other units I have sent him I expect to give the Americans a bloody nose," said Goering.

Chapter Two: October 1943

Twenty Tiger tanks sat hidden amongst the pines covered in white wash and grey paint. The new vehicles were drying after the camouflage had been applied the previous day. Older Tigers sat nearby, looking battered and worn by comparison. The 101st SS Heavy Panzer Battalion was taking a well-earned rest behind the front line. The 503rd regular army battalion of Tigers had been sent forward in their place and was counterattacking another Russian push. Hauptsturmführer Wolfgang Fischer heard that the Sixteenth Panzer Division had crossed the Don River and was driving towards Erzovka, to the north of Stalingrad. The 503rd was covering their flank as was the 1st SS regiment of panzer grenadiers. He could see what the high Command's plan was. The German Army was to cut the communications that ran along the Volga River. That giant waterway was a major communication route for the Russians and needed to be broken. It didn't particularly matter where. Some in his crew thought the army might be ordered to storm Stalingrad but Wolfgang didn't think so. If they were going to bounce the Soviets out of the city they would need to have done so swiftly. It was too late now.

The company had gathered around a bonfire in a glade in the woodlands. Nearby stood a small hut with a stove and an attached shed. The sky was grey and there was a soft breeze. It hadn't snowed yet but the surrounding roads were muddy. Here and there patches of green grass pushed through the soil, and the deciduous trees still held onto their red and golden leaves. Everyone knew the first snows were not far away and so the Tigers had been painted for winter.

Larisa stood in a shapeless grey coat with the forage cap pulled down over her ears. It was her birthday and the company was celebrating. Wolfgang shook his head and smiled. Here was a group of SS soldiers cheering a young Russian woman whose parents were communist officials. These same men fought her people every day and now resided deep within her country. It didn't matter that the Soviet Union had attacked them first. Germany was now poised to reach the mighty Volga River. If they advanced much further then technically they would be in Asia. War was surely the most bizarre undertaking.

She turned and caught his eye and smiled. He was spending every spare moment with Larisa these days. If the unit wasn't in action she ate and spoke with his crew every evening. When they were in battle Larisa assisted the medical detachment. He grinned back, drinking in her stunning green eyes and strong chin. Blond hair curled around the side of the cap and long fingers poked from the ends of ripped mittens. He had a solution for the poor state of her gloves and walked forward to join her. Everyone was cradling mugs of schnapps or vodka and the mood was jovial.

Wolfgang took the small package from behind his back and gave it to her.

"What is this?" Larisa asked.

"Just a little something for your birthday," Wolfgang answered.

He knew that wasn't strictly true. It had taken him months to organize these gloves and until three days ago he didn't know if he had pulled it off. First he had radioed a friend in Germany, against regulations, and asked him to deliver a message to his mother. Then he had to wait for the package to arrive. Larisa unwrapped the waxed brown paper and gasped with delight. Inside were fur lined leather gloves. She put them on and they fit perfectly.

"How did you get them?" she squealed.

"By breaking every regulation in the SS," he said.

"It will make my present look pretty weak," grumbled Otto.

Larisa leaned and kissed the balding man on the cheek. "I'll value all of your gifts."

"My mother found them," said Wolfgang.

"You told her about me?"

"When I get leave that's where I'll be taking you. My mother has a kind heart, and I'll work on my father. You will be safe there," said Wolfgang.

"First you need to get leave, sir," said Hans, the big gun loader for their Tiger.

"One thing at a time," said Wolfgang. "I hope when the mud season hits next April we will all get a break, but who knows? Maybe the war will be over by then."

A frown crossed Larisa's face and he wished he hadn't made the comment. Of course her loyalty would be divided on such an issue.

"Today though, we celebrate," he added hastily.

From somewhere Karl, their radio man, had found a dozen eggs, a bag of flour, and most impressively, a pitcher of cream. A candle was found and the company all sang 'Best of Luck on your Birthday' to Larisa. Someone then brought out a violin and started playing. Most of the songs were German folk songs but some were more recent tracks like 'Wir Machen Musik' and 'Sing Nachtigall, Sing'. Wolfgang was impressed by Otto's voice and soon most of the company had gone quiet and all listened to the driver of Tiger 305 and the lone violin player from the Second Company.

The light faded and the men continued drinking, but more slowly now. Wolfgang eventually found his eyes becoming heavy and drifted away from the hum of conversation and the lilt of the violin.

He made his way to a tent set up at the edge of the forest and washed in a basin of water. The tent flap opened and Larisa stepped inside. She smiled at him and he forgot his state of semi undress. Her coat came off and Wolfgang noted she wore nothing underneath it.

"I've wanted to do this for some time now. You have been so kind and my feelings have grown into something I'm just starting to understand," she said.

He crossed the room and pulled her to his chest feeling her warmth. She tilted his chin and looked into his eyes with a fierceness that almost frightened him. Then they were kissing and he knew he would protect this woman no matter what it cost him.

v

The FW190 was new and hummed with power. Oberleutnant Kurt Osser led his flight towards the B17 formation as it crossed Main at Karlstadt. American escorting fighters had turned back, or in some cases were driven off by Bf 109s as they crossed the Rhine. In many instances, all the attacks on the Thunderbolts and Lightnings were meant to do was make the enemy fighters drop their auxiliary fuel tanks early. Over three hundred B17s were making their way deep into the heart of Germany. They had never gone this far before. JG 26 had flown from bases near Frankfurt. The Gruppe had been transferred here in response to raids on cities along the Rhine by the big American bombers. Today nearly every fighter in Germany was attempting to intercept the enemy force.

As Kurt led his flight straight at the B17s he was aware of the rest of the squadron approaching behind him. Above and to nine o'clock he could see twin-engined fighters, which he believed were JU88Cs, approaching the enemy formation. These aircraft had been equipped with two extra 20mm guns in a pack under the belly of the plane.

"ME 410s climbing in from the west, skipper," said the pilot of Red Four.

The concentration of Luftwaffe planes was something Kurt had never seen and he felt a thrill at the thought of the power they would project on this day. He almost felt sorry for the American pilots.

Kurt's target grew in his gun sight as he got closer.

"Don't fire too soon," he warned his flight.

The tendency for fighter pilots was to depress the gun button before the enemy was in range. The closing speed of the Luftwaffe fighter and the American bomber was such that split second judgement was necessary. He had to get the timing right or his aircraft would plough into his enemy's cockpit. He waited until the bomber fitted between two lines he had drawn on his canopy. Then he held down the firing button for three seconds. His tracers tore metal from around the top gun turret and along the fuselage before ripping into the tail. Not a killing blow. He swore softly as he pulled gently back on the stick climbing slowly above the bombers. Two B17s were falling away in flames and another had smoke pouring from damaged engines. One FW190 was trailing white vapour which quickly darkened.

"Got to head for home, skipper. Oil pressure has fallen to nothing," said the pilot of Red Three.

Kurt acknowledged and ordered the Rotte leader's wingman to go with him.

"You are more important than the plane, Landers, so jump if it gets too hot," ordered Kurt. Hals Landers was a non-commissioned officer with three kills and had flown Stukas before transferring to fighters a year ago.

The JU88s attacked next and more bombers fell away, one of them disintegrating as its wing and tail burnt through. Kurt curved around the enemy formation, ready to make another run, when he noticed a ragged group of B17s out to the side of the main group. This bomber box had been hit hard already by heavy fighters and had lost their squadron leader. They were barely supporting each other with aircraft strung out in a line. Two of the B17s had smoking engines and one was missing a fair part of its tail.

"We will hit the group of bombers to the north of the main formation. It looks as though they are on their last legs. I'll lead from behind," said Kurt.

Ten FW190s swooped on the damaged B17s but flew into a storm of defensive fire. He heard one man scream and then glanced in his mirror. An Fw190 curled away burning. Another fighter was wrapped in smoke and soon the pilot jumped. Kurt couldn't see if the man's parachute opened. A damaged bomber grew slowly in front of him. The closing speed from behind on the big American planes was much slower, giving Kurt more time to aim. It also gave the US gunners the same luxury. He fired a burst which chewed up the tail gunner's position, before firing into the two port engines. Both came apart and started to burn. Then he was through the enemy formation and diving away. Kurt knew his squadron was low on ammunition and fuel so he took them away in a shallow dive. Behind him four more bombers dropped towards German soil. It was then he noted a single B17 flying below him.

"One more for the tally," he called and led three fighters towards the crippled machine.

"The rest of you go home and get the beers ready," he ordered confidently.

The four FW190s curved at the B17 from the starboard quarter and sprayed fire at the machine. These were deflection shots and good shooting meant the German pilots had to fire in front of the B17. The bomber's fuselage was hit in many places but none of the cannon shells or machine gun bullets did any fatal damage. A waist gunner on the bomber fired controlled short bursts back at the German fighters and one machine staggered as point five calibre bullets tore into the engine block. Hot oil sprayed on the cockpit and soon there was a fire. Then the German pilot was pulling back the canopy of his plane and leaping free. As he did more burning engine oil splashed his neck and ear causing painful burns.

"This one has teeth, sir," said Leutnant Hessler.

"One more run and he's history," said Kurt.

The remaining three planes curled around behind the B17 to attack it from the rear with Kurt leading the way. The Fw190 was now down to machine gun bullets, the 20mm guns having run dry. His rifle calibre bullets hit around the rear gunner's position but the American didn't panic. His bullets tore through Kurt's cockpit and shattered the instrument panel, sending glass flying into his face. If it wasn't for the googles he would have lost his sight. He eased the Fw190 away from the attack and asked his wingman for a report.

"He's still going, skipper. My last cannon shells took out his inner port engine but he still has two others. Klein's burst chewed up the area around the top gunner's turret, but his cannon was empty."

"Leave him. That American deserves to make it home. He almost destroyed two fighters. As it is I have a windy trip home. Kessler can check my machine for any other damage," asked Kurt.

His wingman flew around his machine and reported that the engine looked good, however there was damage to the wings. The flight back to an airfield was nerve wracking as strange noises came from the aircraft, though the engine appeared to be working normally. Kurt's face stung but at least it wasn't frozen as he had dived from the freezing air of four thousand metres down to half that. Hessler closed in next to him and radioed ahead as Kurt's radio suddenly stopped working. With the lack of communication Kurt felt cut off from the world. He concentrated on flying the aircraft and was soon over a bomber training airfield not far from Heidelberg.

Kurt eased the FW190 towards the runway and lowered the under carriage; at least, he tried to. He heard one wheel lock into place, but from his port wing there was no indication that the wheel had even lowered. He couldn't ask anyone to check as his radio was out but decided it wasn't worth the risk and retracted the starboard wheel. I'll have to put the plane down on her belly, he thought. Kurt took the plane around for another circuit and came back in slowly, aiming at the grassy verge next to the main stretch of concrete. Carefully he bled off speed until he was only a few metres above the ground, then he was on the dirt. Kurt flipped the switch for the engine and held tightly to the stick as the FW190 ploughed through the grass and earth. The propellers bent and the aircraft screamed in protest. There was a chance the plane could flip over but he had dropped his speed sufficiently to prevent that from happening. Slowly his plane slid to a halt and he quickly released his straps. Pulling back the shattered canopy he jumped to the ground as a fire truck and an ambulance raced towards him. Kurt fell to his knees before kissing the ground with relief.

v

The 11th Infantry Division was almost at full strength as was the neighbouring 30th Infantry Division. Paul had seen artillery shells being piled up and noted the delivery of a new type of tank to the 9th SS Panzer Division. He had asked around and been told the new vehicle was the Panzer Five, also known as the Panther. He didn't know of the tank's teething problems but rumour was that many of the problems had been sorted out due to the extra development time the army had allowed.

It was obvious to Paul that there was going to be some sort of attack, though the Wehrmacht went to great pains to hide its preparations. Everything was well camouflaged and increased German and Italian fighter numbers tried to keep snooping allied planes under pressure. Paul wasn't to know his division would be part of a diversionary attack on the Australian 9th Division, while the three panzer divisions and the one panzer grenadier division crashed into the Americans. The 22nd Airlanding Division and the German paratroopers would attack the British while the Spanish Blue corps assaulted the Canadians. The aim of the operation was to chop off

Clarke's extended thrust towards Madrid that had created a bulge from the allied lines.

The major town of Avila had been taken by the American 2nd Armoured Division which took it from the German Jäger Division a week ago. What the Americans didn't know is that Rommel had placed the lightly armed division there with the intention of having it forced back. He wanted Patton to overextend. The plan may have worked except for one problem. The Americans knew what the wily German General was up to. The British had cracked the code of the German Enigma machines and was reading Goering's mail. This was how the German battle fleet had been ambushed by American carriers and it was why currently, the U-boat refuelling submarines were being caught and destroyed.

Paul Backer and his friend Stefan were unaware of all of these facts as they sheltered in their foxhole outside Cordoba. The German Army still held the city, though it was only about ten kilometres from the front line. His battalion was going to hit the Australian bridgehead over the Guadalquivir river, just to the south of their position. Here the Allies only held a thin slither of ground on the northern side of the waterway but the Australians heavily supported their troops with artillery.

The sudden thunder of German guns startled Paul. He watched as shells rained down, churning up the dry Spanish soil. The Australian positions disappeared under a haze of smoke and dust before the German artillery moved on to its known enemy artillery concentrations. Overhead German and Italian fighter-bombers also attacked targets. Then Paul noted a different noise. British medium bombers appeared and flew towards the locations of the German batteries. Spitfires engaged FW190s and BF109s while new Australian Corsairs duelled with RE2005s. Paul was amazed at the number of aircraft he could see twisting and turning above him. He heard the sound of the bombs falling in the distance and felt the vibrations through the souls of his feet.

The company started to stir around him with men moving into nearby trenches. He and Stefan crawled to a slightly raised location under an earth covered tarpaulin to support the advance with his

sniper's rifle. Machine gun crews opened fire as men jumped from the

trenches and started to run forward. The Australians soon started

shooting at the approaching soldiers with Bren light machine guns

and rifles, and Paul even thought he heard an MG 42 shooting in their

direction. The company was halfway across the open ground when

Paul caught a sound like an approaching train.

"No, their artillery was supposed to have been knocked out,"

he said.

"The British bombers might have prevented the artillery from

doing the job," said Stefan.

The twenty five pound shells landed among the advancing men

throwing some into the air. Others completely disappeared as their

bodies were torn apart. Paul was horrified at the intensity of the

bombardment. He watched momentarily before Stefan pulled him

down into the fox hole. The screaming and the noise continued until

the barrage rolled over the top of them and into the buildings behind

them. Smaller explosions continued, though at a slower rate.

"The enemy are going to keep hitting our boys out there with mortars," said Stefan.

Paul peered over the lip of his hole and saw German soldiers pinned down. Some of the wounded crawled slowly back towards the trench. Many lay without moving.

"This is shit," said Paul.

Bullets still chewed up the ground near men who had taken shelter in shell holes or lay in shallow folds in the ground. Paul had found a measure of acceptance and peace in this company. The men had given him space but remained friendly. They had tolerated his strange ways and distant behaviour and now many of them were dead, or dying.

Before he realised what he was doing Paul had dropped his rifle and leapt from the foxhole. He crouched low and darted towards a crawling man sixty metres away. Paul could see the soldier was missing a hand and his legs were covered in blood. A bullet smacked into the dirt near him but he ignored it and pulled the man onto his back. With a grunt he started to drag his comrade back to the trench.

A burst of machine gun fire tore the earth up around him spraying small pebbles and soil. Paul pushed on and reached the trench in front of him, easing the man over the lip into the arms of a corps man with a red cross on his arm. He dropped over the sandbags that lined the top of the trench and crouched next to the man.

"I'll get one," said the young soldier.

"No, you have the equipment to treat him, at least initially. I will get them," said Paul.

He jumped out of the trench where a shell had collapsed part of the wall and sprinted to a man lying on his side. The soldier was facing away from him and when Paul rolled him over he could see the glassy stare of the dead. Shrapnel stuck from the soldier's skull just above the left eye. There was no time to mourn his comrade. Bullets were already smacking into the ground nearby. He ran bent over to man who was moaning and clawing at the ground in pain. Paul noted his wounds were in the back and arm as he reached him. Then he hoisted the soldier onto his back and carried him back to the trench.

The corpsman had bandaged the first man and Stefan joined him. Both took the second man and immediately started to work on him. Mortar shells started to fall with increasing frequency with some exploding only thirty metres away.

"That will do Paul," said Stefan firmly.

Paul shook his head. "This is for my old squad. Maybe I can make up for my fear, for killing them."

"We've spoken about that. It wasn't your fault."

"I've still got to live with it. Not a day goes by without me remembering that night. It just doesn't hurt as much now."

Then he was gone, back out into the field covered in bodies and blood.

Another man was screaming and clutching at his stump of an arm. The side of his face was bloody and he sat in shock near two dead men. Paul got to him and eased the soldier to his feet. At least he wouldn't have to carry this one. A mortar shell exploded nearby and shrapnel cut the air near Paul's ear. The man screamed again and clutched at his shoulder. Paul pushed him to the trench until his staggering comrade was pulled into shelter by Stefan. Another corpsman had joined the first and the original man he had brought in had been carried away to an aid station. Paul had no idea who had taken his wounded comrade away and didn't care.

Three more times he collected men from the field as mortar shells fell around him. He almost died when carrying the first of that trio back. The man was draped over his shoulders when a bullet hit the unfortunate soldier in the helmet. The projectile travelled through the metal and then the skull before continuing on to hit Paul in the back of the head. His helmet saved his life as the distorted bullet clipped the metal and ricocheted away. The force of the blow still sent Paul to his knees and his vision blurred. Blood and brains covered his neck and back. He wiped some of the mess away with a rag in his pocket which he usually used to clean his gun.

As Paul's senses returned he ran to another wounded man. The enemy seemed to stop shooting at him but mortar shells still fell uncomfortably close. And so he dragged more wounded men to safety. Every time he gave one to the corpsmen Stefan urged him to stop, but he just couldn't. He was now over one hundred and fifty metres from the trench and was running towards the young lieutenant who commanded the 1st platoon. The Australians still weren't shooting at him, which was a surprise but he didn't have time to wonder why. He was dragging the man back towards the trench when a mortar shell exploded behind him lifting Paul off his feet. The young officer took most of the blast but Paul didn't escape unscathed. Pain lanced through his arm and lower back. He somersaulted and landed hard on some broken equipment. Something snapped and Paul screamed.

The world went fuzzy and his vision went out of focus. He could see a man running towards him and wondered who it was. Then he recognized the skinny frame of Stefan.

"Bloody idiot," he muttered. "Poor fool will get himself killed."

Then there was another explosion and the world went dark.

The man sitting in front of him wore a slouch hat, yet he carried an MP40. Paul focused on the individual and decided he was definitely an Australian. He tried to move but a gentle hand pressed him down into his cot.

"You have been wounded badly Paul, so don't move."

Paul looked at the body that went with the gentle hand and noted a German nurse with a dimpled chin and red gold hair.

"We have been captured," she said flatly.

"How do you know my name?" he asked.

"Your Hundemarke told me," she said pointing at the metal disc hanging on a chain around his neck. The oval shaped piece of metal was still covered in blood and dirt but he could see where part of it had been wiped clean.

The nurse sat next to him. "My name is Inga Wagner. I was a nurse in Cordoba. The city was overrun and our army pushed back up the valley towards Madrid. I have been hearing tales of your bravery, Paul."

"From whom? Stefan? How is he?"

"Ah, your friend? The one who tried to rescue you. He lives, though we couldn't save his foot. The Australian doctor has worked miracles on both of you. It seems you have admirers who insisted that you receive priority."

A dark haired Australian sergeant who sat with the German gun spoke briefly to the nurse.

"He is asking if you need anything," said Inga.

Paul shook his head and the sergeant started to talk. As he did, a soldier with white blond hair and an officer joined him. Paul noted that the blond man carried a MG42 and he wondered if the entire Australian Army preferred German equipment.

"This man's name is Tom and he says you are the bravest soldier he has ever met. He should know as he wears his country's highest medal for courage. The Australian tells me they stopped shooting after you pulled in your third comrade. Unfortunately they couldn't get onto the mortar battery. Something about radio problems. Tom says that in his country looking after 'your mate', as he puts it, ranks above everything else."

Paul nodded at the tough looking soldier. He had heard the Australian 9th Division was one of the toughest divisions the German Army faced. Rommel himself had praised their qualities.

"Ask him why he uses German weapons?" said Paul.

Inga turned and the Australian shrugged and glanced down at the MP40 and then at the blond man's machine gun. Then he muttered a few words.

"Because they are good," answered Inga.

"Funny, some of our boys prize their submachine gun, the Owen I think they call it."

Inga translated and the three Australians chuckled. The officer then swung his gun around off his shoulder and Paul noted it was the reliable weapon he had just praised. One of his company had told him you could throw the Australian submachine gun in the mud and it would still work.

The Australian called Tom then reached into his pocket and pulled out a block of something.

"Real chocolate," said Inga. "God, it has been so long since I tasted the real thing."

The Australian stood and Paul noted how tall he was. He snapped off some of the block and gave it to Inga. Then he put the rest on Paul's blanket. He spoke to Inga again before leaving.

"Strange people," she muttered. "He says after the war is over and Germany is in ruins you should come to Australia. Ask for Tom Derrick in Adelaide and he'll get you set up." Then Inga snorted. "How can he think Germany will lose? Absurd!"

v

Carinhall rang out with the sound of yelling. Rommel stormed up and down the Persian carpet, gesticulating as he made his point.

"They knew we were coming and now I have the proof. German intelligence has been asleep at the wheel for most of the war and it has cost us many lives!"

"Calm down Herr Fieldmarshal!" snapped Goering. The big man looked drawn and was puffy around the eyes. Speer thought he had lost more weight and hoped he was staying away from the drugs.

Six men stood or sat in the drawing room of the opulent mansion. Speer had been invited because the Army of Spain needed to be reequipped after the recent disaster. Kaltenbrunner had come due to concerns over security. Kesselring arrived to represent the Luftwaffe and Walter Schellenberg was there as Head of Intelligence.

"We now have proof that that the Allies have been reading our mail," said Rommel forcefully. "An American brigadier general was captured in our failed attack and after an extensive subterfuge campaign, came to believe a major he was travelling with was planning an escape. Carefully confidence was built until the general revealed certain information. It seems this man was present in Patton's tent when material arrived from England that resulted in a flurry of orders. The American general stated that Patton said, 'the boys in London must be reading German mail'."

"This doesn't mean that they are," said Goering.

"Usually I wouldn't agree," said Schellenberg. "But certain pieces of evidence have come together that made me suspicious. The ambush of the carriers started me thinking, then there has been the sinking of a number of our Milch Cows in the Atlantic. These refuelling submarines have been caught on the surface often lately. I thought it was possibly bad luck, so I fed a number of parameters about air patrols, the size of the Atlantic, and the number of refuelling U-boats to the best mathematicians in Berlin. Now they didn't all come up with the same odds but the general message was identical. The chance of so many submarines being discover on the surface in recent months is extremely unlikely."

Rommel grunted, seemingly satisfied that he was being taken seriously.

"How is this possible?" asked Kesselring.

"I'm not sure yet but I have a strong hunch that the enemy has cracked the Enigma Machines," said Schellenberg. "Nothing else makes sense."

"I was told that was impossible!" exclaimed Goering.

"My predecessor thought so but I don't agree," said Schellenberg. "When we took England, documentation was found which indicated the British were attempting to break the Enigma code. We know the Poles did it, so we added more rotors to the machine and they couldn't read the messages any more. We found evidence in London that the Poles passed what they knew to the British. When we defeated them the Commonwealth didn't have the resources to pursue the project. Now Britain is free again, well, anything is possible."

"The information sent in those machines is garbled. They wouldn't understand it," said Goering.

Kesslering was beginning to understand the implications and he shook his head. "They would have specialized teams to interpret it, just as we have."

"Exactly, and we have reason to believe that is why the British almost defeated us when we invaded their country. They knew exactly where we were going to land and when," said Schellenberg. "When we arrived in London certain collaborators told us this. At the time not much was made of the tale as we were busy celebrating a hard fought victory."

"So what do we do?" asked Goering.

"Change the codes, add extra rotors. This will all take time and most orders will have to be sent by courier in the meantime," said Schellenberg.

Speer spoke for the first time. "I expect it will eat into precious resources."

Goering frowned. "It has to be done and I expect it will be a job for the experts. I don't think it will affect panzer production."

The leader of Germany turned to Rommel. "Can Madrid be held?"

"For now, yes. When I realised what was happening I ordered the Army of Spain to give ground. Units had taken an awful pounding but they weren't destroyed. The Tigers of the 504th hadn't been used in the initial attack and the enemy have no answer to the new

Panther tank as yet. We stopped the Americans at Las Rozas in the west and at Toledo in the south."

"That's very close to the capital," said Kesselring.

Rommel grimaced. "We had to give up much of the south of the country. The line runs south from Toledo to Linares and from there, east to Cartagena on the coast. Franco wasn't happy but what could we do? After the losses we took, we were lucky to stop the allied counteroffensive at all."

"At least things are going well in Russia," said Goering.

Kesselring looked at the ground before meeting his leader's eye. "Maybe not as well as we thought," he said.

Chapter Three: November 1943

The huge six-engined aircraft came in ponderously to land. Schutze Klaus Moller looked out of the small window of the ME363. He glanced around the cargo hold at the twelve other replacements and the sacks of flour and dried fruit. Klaus was relieved his plane wasn't loaded with fuel like the other three that had touched down before his huge machine. They also carried a smattering of replacements for the 3rd SS Panzer Division which was stranded on the coast of the Caspian Sea waiting for petrol. At the moment the formation was positioned at the mouth of the Terek River. The 5th SS were somewhere to the south near Grozny and the 13th Panzer Division was stuck somewhere out on Kalmyk Steppe to the north.

Klaus Moller had been a member of the SS for two years now and, after being trained, had spent most of his time as a guard at Dachau Concentration Camp. He knew it was important to watch and punish Germany's enemies but he wanted to fight. After repeated requests for a transfer to a fighting unit, Klaus now had his chance. He wondered if it was the training on the new Panzerschreck that had finally interested his commanding officer enough to recommend his transfer. Klaus was excited about his new unit. The 3rd SS Panzer Division had a reputation as an elite division now. He had been told the formation was absolutely ruthless against the enemy. He liked the sound of that. The Russians had stabbed his country in the back and deserved to be destroyed utterly. You couldn't trust a Slav and Klaus believed the leader of the SS Oberst-Gruppenführer Kaltunbruner was correct when he said that the east needed to be cleansed. At twenty years of age Klaus looked forward to the job of fulfilling this task. He wished the rest of Germany's leadership saw the issue in the same way, but Klaus supposed the importance of winning the war took precedence of the destruction of the Slavs and the stinking Jews.

The plane landed, throwing up a large dust cloud. The makeshift airfield was surrounded by tents and rough huts. At least twenty other transport aircraft lined the edge of the runway. He recognized Ju90s, Ju52s, the newer Ju252, and of course there were more ME 363s. Everywhere, fuel and ammunition was being unloaded, though there was also plenty of food. Klaus was pleased that the army wasn't letting them starve. Four fighters took off from

a parallel strip and flew north. The Luftwaffe patrolled the area with a

new Italian plane, a Fiat he had heard. It looked similar to the Bf109

and he couldn't understand why Germany was using foreign

machines.

A non-commissioned officer sat in an American jeep nearby

and gestured to him and the other replacements. Klaus and the

others picked up their packs and walked over.

The older man stood on the back seat. He had dark hair and a

scar on his chin. Klaus wondered where the American transport had

come from. He then noted some of the trucks loading the fuel were

Fords.

"Welcome to the Caucasus, children," said the man. "My

name is Obersturmführer Sauer, but you can call me God. I have been

sent to pick up you babies and bring you back to the bosom of our

company. The only problem is that there are thirteen of you and I

only have enough fuel for this tough piece of American shit. Just this

truck, and really, it's a tough little mother, as are all the Yank trucks we have taken from the Soviets, but that doesn't solve my problem, well your problem. So this what we will do. You may put your packs in with me and then you will have to walk. Keep your water and weapons and some of your ammunition. It is twelve kilometres to camp so we better start."

"Sir, they didn't give us any ammunition," said a wide faced teenager who couldn't have been more than eighteen."

The Obersturmführer rolled his eyes. "Of course they didn't. Well that won't do. Just because we hold the land doesn't mean it's safe. Come with me."

The older man took them to another non-commissioned officer who was talking to a truck driver. They exchanged a few words before Sauer took them to some crates.

"Fifty rounds for the rifle men. Four clips for anyone with an MP40 and one clip if you have somehow found yourself a pistol," said Sauer.

Nobody had, and most of the replacements carried rifles. Klaus spotted a long wooden box next to the ammunition and knew what it contained. He walked over to Obersturmführer Sauer.

"Sir, I know what's in that box and I'm trained on the weapon."

The older man looked him up and down and then strolled over to the box and studied the writing. "You know how to use these new rockets to kill tanks?"

"Yes sir," answered Klaus.

"What's your name, son?" asked the older man. Klaus gave it.

The non-commissioned officer glanced around. "Put it in the jeep but keep it quiet. Also, see if you can find any ammunition for it."

"I've already found a box, sir."

Sauer smiled and nodded. "Good work, son."

Klaus grabbed another recruit named Rainer Stein and both of them carried the box to the jeep and then took over the ammunition. Sauer pilled all of the men's packs on top of it and nodded at him. The jeep was heaped high with gear by the time they had finished and it crawled away from the airstrip slowly so it wouldn't over balance and tip the Obersturmführer off the top. As the line of soldiers trudged away from the airfield another four planes came into land. It looked as though the 3rd SS Division would soon have the fuel it needed to move.

V

The Messerschmitt 262 Stormbird was a thoroughbred. Kurt loved to fly the plane. He thought the jet might be tricky to handle but the controls proved light and easy. At high speeds the turning circle remained highly acceptable, though at lower speeds this was not the case. The leading edge slats that were used on the BF109 gave the wing of the Stormbird thirty five percent more lift than otherwise would have been the case. The engines however, were another matter. Some of the early versions of the aircraft had engines which had benefited from access to rare metals from South America. This was no longer the case and though some engines were still being produced with a stockpile of metals Speer had accumulated, other solutions to the elevated temperatures a jet engine endured had to be found. Kurt was told that the engine life was twenty hours and to treat the throttle very gently.

He and his wingman Stephan Hessler flew towards the JU86 training aircraft. They were practising attacks on enemy bombers and so far, there had been unexpected difficulties. The closing speed was such that there was only time for a three second burst with the low velocity 30mm guns. Three of four shells would be enough to bring down a B17 but the short amount of time barely gave a pilot time to aim. They had tried climbing into a bomber formation but Stephan had pointed out this would be a dangerous tactic if enemy fighters were around. Kurt wasn't sure if this was an issue as the Americans didn't have a plane that could stay with their bombers all the way to a target, yet he saw the good sense in planning for the eventuality.

Today they were going to try a rollercoaster approach. As they dived at a shallow angle towards the JU86s Kurt kept going down. When he was a kilometre and a half from the bombers he started to climb steeply. Speed bled away from the jet as the JU86 filled his gun sights. He held down the firing button and allowed the gun camera to whirl. Then he dived under the formation, allowing his jet to become faster until it was well in front of the German bomber.

"I think it will work, skipper. Still only allows us a brief squirt at the enemy, but it's better than before," radioed Hessler.

Kurt agreed. He turned the plane back towards the base and eased off the throttle a notch. The airfield was still thirty minutes away and the Stormbird only had a limited time in the air, such was the engine's fuel consumption. More ME262s shot passed for their turn with the tactic. His Gruppe now had fourteen of the jets and trained on them every day. Another shipment of planes was due today and that would bring their strength to twenty. As far as Kurt was concerned the sooner his unit converted and was used in action, the better.

The roar of the guns could be heard by the men of the Tiger battalion. Wolfgang had dreaded this day but intelligence had warned them the Russians were preparing an offensive. The 101st SS Heavy Panzer Battalion was based at the small town of Oblivskaya on the rail line that ran from Stalingrad to Rostov on Don. The front line was probably eighty kilometres away but the noise made by the Russian artillery could be clearly heard. His unit had thirty-two Tigers that would run but he knew if they drove under their own power all the way to the front, two-thirds of them would break down. Of course if the Soviets broke through then they wouldn't have to travel as far. A mixed blessing at best, he thought. Snow lay on the ground and frost had hardened the earth. At least there wouldn't be any problems with mud when the order to attack came.

Wolfgang knew the 1st SS Panzer Division was nearby on the other side of the Chir River. The 11th Panzer Division was somewhere further west and the 24th Panzer Division was stationed near Kalach only twenty-five kilometres away. The Hungarian 1st Panzer Division was even further west near Millerovo, but was supposed to be well rested from what he had heard. With these four divisions and two Tiger battalions, they would need to hold the enemy. He supposed the 16th Panzer and 14th Panzer could join them but those two divisions were at the tip of the advance just north of Stalingrad on the banks of the Volga. Infantry had closed in on the city's outskirts and reached the bend of the mighty river to the south of the city. Some units had fought their way into the built-up areas, but after taking heavy casualties had been told to stop. There was no need to take the city itself just yet.

Wolfgang wasn't sure what to do with Larisa. Their relationship had continued since her birthday and he wanted to ensure her safety. All of the battalion was bound to be ordered to face the enemy, including the medical platoon. She would be in grave danger and yet he couldn't think of an option where she would be safe. Leaving her with a rear unit where the men of the company didn't know her was also a great risk.

"I am coming with you," she said when he told her that it might be safer if she stayed with the SS unit guarding the supply dump. "I don't know those men or trust them. Besides the company will need me. I have learned a lot in my time with the medical platoon and would help treat the wounded, of both sides," Larisa said.

Wolfgang shook his head at her bravery and loved her all the more.

Soon after dawn's light crept into the sky the 101st SS Tiger Battalion received orders to travel north. The Russians had broken free and they were to meet the enemy armour and stop it. The rest of the division was to move on a parallel course, though the 3rd Battalion of the 2nd Panzer Grenadier Regiment was attached to their command to provide infantry support, as was one battery of Wespes from the 1st SS Artillery battalion. The self-propelled artillery would be able to keep pace with their advance and provide valuable backing.

The Tigers drove slowly for two hours along a well-made road north. Overhead in a partially cloudy sky Bf109s duelled with Yak and Airacobras. No Russian aircraft attacked them, and the only sign of the enemy they saw close at hand were the Soviet pilots who were captured. Four half-tracks drove ahead of the Tigers looking for any sign of the enemy, while a group of trucks and cars drove in the battalion's wake. The unit was lucky and only eight Tigers broke down on the journey, some throwing tracks, while others overheated. Orders then came through telling the unit to stop. The situation at the front was fluid and multiple breakthroughs had occurred.

Wolfgang returned to his crew as the short Russian day ended. The news was grim. Everywhere the northern front had been broken and columns of Russian tanks were driving south at speed. There was no doubt the Tigers would meet them on the following day. He sought out Larisa and told her the news. She seemed unworried.

"You know if the Soviets capture you, then your end will be swift," said Wolfgang. He handed her a pistol and she took it. "It's not for you to shoot your country men with; I just wouldn't want you to suffer," he said.

She kissed him on the forehead. "I understand. I must admit this is very confusing for me. I don't know which side I'm on anymore. I don't want you or the company to die and yet I want the Russian army to be victorious."

"You are still a patriot and I admire that. I hope that we win this fight and our two countries can end this madness."

She kissed him and held him close before returning to the medical platoon. That night he couldn't sleep and assisted with fixing one of the Tigers that had broken down. He snatched a little sleep after midnight and was awake before dawn.

They met the Soviet spearhead about forty kilometres south of the old front line, near a village called Pochta. Ahead of the Tiger battalion two small rivers came together. Small gullies and ravines cut the landscape leading up to a flat ridge which stood about five metres above the surrounding countryside. The slightly raised area of land kept the two rivers apart but the road went due north. It crossed the smaller of the two watercourses before traversing the low ridge. The river itself didn't pose much of an obstacle, being only a metre deep in places. The banks weren't too muddy in the colder weather and the bottom was firm according to the men who had reconnoitred the countryside in their half-tracks and kulbelwagens.

SS-Obersturmbannführer Heinz von Westernhagen called the company commanders together and explained the situation. "The Russians are charging south on the road with a force of about one hundred tanks, armoured cars and trucks. The bulk of the force is armour, though a few towed anti-tank guns were spotted. I had a quick word Hauptsturmführer Wittmann and we agree that we should split the force."

SS-Hauptsturmführer Rolf Möbius and Wolfgang exchanged a glance. Splitting your forces in the face of the enemy was never a good idea.

"I know what you are both thinking but hear me out. Wittmann and I will stop the Russians as they try to come down off the low ridge and cross the river. The 3rd Company will cross the river further to the west and then, using one of the gullies, approach the enemy unseen from their western flank. Hauptsturmführer Fischer will need to move quickly or his Tigers will be spotted from the high ground." The group started to break up when Westernhagen stopped them. "The recon boys spotted some of those Tiger killers among the enemy. We don't know if they are the newer ISU 152s or the older SU model. I expect it's the former as they are fast enough to keep up with the Russian advance while the ISU has thicker armour, but is much slower. Anyway, watch out for them and hit the Tiger killers first if you can."

Wolfgang ran to his panzer and quickly issued orders. Time was of the essence if this strategy was to work. His company had eight working Tigers while the rest of the battalion had twelve. The infantry deployed from their half-tracks while the Wespes took up a position five kilometres from the front line in a gully that ran east west. The 3rd company drove quickly for the Soviet flank before crossing the shallow river three kilometres from the blocking location of the rest of the battalion. Then Wolfgang led them east into a long gully which ran towards the northsouth road. He eased Tiger 305 to a halt and watched as the rest of his command closed in behind him. Wolfgang was nervous. The Tigers were well hidden here but they were still only eight hundred metres from the road along which the Russians were travelling. Now he waited for the sound of gun fire and soon he heard the flat crack of an 88mm cannon he was about to attack.

Minutes ticked by and Wolfgang started to worry. He wondered if the Soviets had changed direction yet they had half-tracks with powerful radios positioned to report such an occurrence. First, he heard the noisy engines of T34 tanks, then the sound of multiple heavy calibre guns firing and he sagged with relief.

"Tell the boys to start their engines," he told Karl.

The Tigers crawled along the shallow ravine slowly making their way towards the high ground where the enemy column had stalled. As they drove forward a T34 rounded the corner. It seemed the enemy had decided on a flanking move of their own.

"Target ahead," he screamed at Franz. The main gun fired and a round hole appeared in the middle of the enemy vehicle directly beneath the turret. Then there was an internal explosion which sent sheets of flames leaping from the T34's open hatch. A second tank appeared behind the burning T34 and fired but its shell broke up on the Tiger's frontal armour. Franz put an anti-tank round straight through the enemy driver's viewing port and the Russian tank started to burn.

"They have to know we are here now," muttered Wolfgang. He ordered his Tiger to nose passed the wrecked T34s, which they did with difficulty. Soon Kurt's head was above the level of the gully and looked at the chaos which surrounded him. He was driving out into the middle of the enemy formation where trucks and tanks charged in every direction. Burning KV1s sat about four hundred metres to the south and the enemy seemed to be gathering a little to the west of the main road, though this assembly of vehicles lacked any real cohesion.

It was still a concentration of striking power. Wolfgang ordered Otto to drive in that direction and told Franz to destroy the SU 152 which was side on to them. The main gun fired and he saw a hole appear in the side of the enemy machine just back from the join to the frontal armour plate. The heavy AT shell must have hit the gun breech inside the enemy tank because the big gun twisted savagely. Wolfgang didn't want to imagine what the large calibre shell would have done to the men inside the SU152. It would have either split into pieces of hot metal, or bounced around inside the main compartment smashing everything it touched.

The other Tigers emerged from the cutting behind him onto the flat area near the road, with guns blazing. The sudden emergence of the heavy panzers in the midst of the enemy force threw the Russians into chaos. A platoon of German infantry had accompanied the Tigers and they set themselves up on the lip of the gorge and started shooting at anything that moved. An MG 42 sprayed a group of Soviet soldiers who were trying to manoeuvre an anti-tank gun into position, killing the crew and setting a truck on fire.

Wolfgang ordered Franz to fire at a T34 which was charging towards them but a truck careered across their line of sight just as the Tiger fired. The shell hit the engine block in the side with such force that it tore from its mounting, ripping clear of the vehicle. The truck twisted sideways with the impact and tipped onto its side throwing the passenger and driver around the cab. Both crawled from the back of the cab through the rear tray and out onto the battlefield. They saw a Tiger bearing down on them and ran. The T34 was hit by the flying engine which bounced from the frontal plates of the armoured vehicle doing little damage. It veered around the wrecked truck but was struck by a rocket fired by the platoon's only Panzerschreck. The projectile hit just below the machine gunner's observation slit punching a small hole in the armour. A stream of liquid metal with an extremely hot temperature hit the man in the chest and neck killing him instantly. The T34 rolled on out of control as the rest of the crew opened its hatches and jumped clear. Eventually the tank stopped, to be captured almost intact after the battle.

An anti-tank shell hit Wolfgang's Tiger near the hull machine gun, breaking up on impact. He ducked inside the panzer and slammed the hatch shut. It was too dangerous to stay exposed though he preferred the clearer view it offered him of the battlefield. Franz was shooting at any Russian tank he could see while Karl blazed away with the hull machine gun. Wolfgang tried to see what was happening through the viewing periscopes but it was all smoke and confusion. He saw a T34 appear in front of them but before he could yell a warning, Franz had fired and blown its turret off. The other seven Tigers had fanned out among the Russian formation spraying death from their machine guns and blowing up any tank that passed in front of their guns.

It probably lasted less than ten minutes but by the time the action was over a Soviet tank brigade had been destroyed, but to the west another unit of Russian armour was advancing on the village of Pochta. From the raised ground it was easy to see the tanks and armour straggling into the village. It was only three kilometres away but Wolfgang knew his command needed to strike fast. They still had plenty of fuel but only had fifty percent of their ammunition. He radioed the situation to Obersturmbannführer Heinz von Westernhagen and told his commander he intended to attack the Russians. The battalion leader approved but asked he wait thirty minutes in order that both groups of Tigers would be in position to hit the Soviets at the same time. Wolfgang agreed reluctantly and used the time to share out the shells in Tiger 324 which had lost a track. It allowed Wolfgang to concentrate the heavy panzers and think of where best to hit the Russians. He decided to advance in a wedge shaped formation and aim at the northern part of the village. This would leave the rest of the battalion to hit the southern portion of the community and perhaps drive the disorganized enemy onto his guns.

When the half hour was up Wolfgang ordered the seven remaining Tigers to advance down the gentle slope towards Pochta until they were eight hundred metres from the river. On the other side of the waterway Russian tanks and anti-tank guns turned to face them. Wolfgang could see his plan wasn't going to work. The Soviets had clearly seen their approach and the rest of the Tigers were running late. There were a number of small hills, not really much more than ripples in the ground next to the river and he ordered his armour to use them as cover.

Wolfgang's Tiger sat in the open, shooting at T34s and anti-tank guns as they appeared between the wooden shacks of the village. 76mm shells bounced from the turret or broke up on the frontal armour of the Tiger. He thought the panzer would lose a track, or a lucky shot would damage the main gun, but this didn't happen. Franz quickly worked out that the wooden walls of the structures in the small town couldn't stop an AT round from the Tiger's 88mm gun, and he started to hit Russian armour that was trying to shelter behind the buildings.

A large SU152 tried to destroy the Tigers but the range was too great for their slow firing main guns. If they had been closer the massive shells of the assault guns could knock out the German heavy panzers but at seven hundred metres their accuracy was poor. The other issue was their rate of fire. Wolfgang's Tiger rattled to the sound of a near miss, as a one hundred and 52mm high explosive round sent a shower of earth and shrapnel clattering against their armour. The flash of the huge gun was easily distinguishable from that of the T34s and Wolfgang told Franz to switch targets.

"On it, skipper," said his gunner.

The anti-tank round of the Tiger tore through the Su152s frontal plates into the middle of the vehicle, causing a large internal explosion which ripped it apart.

Peering through one of the five slits in the cupola Wolfgang noted KV1s trying to flank his command to the south. This was dangerous as the 76mm guns this tank carried could penetrate the side armour of a Tiger, if they got close enough. It was then that Wittmann's company attacked. Panzer 205 roared out of the dust and destroyed a KV1 before rocking to a halt and firing into the milling Soviet tanks. The rest of Wittmann's Tigers joined him and soon the Russian tanks were fleeing. The other heavy panzers came into Pochta from the southwest overrunning an anti-tank battery and a group of infantry. The village had been briefly bombarded by the Wespe self-propelled artillery, throwing the enemy into confusion. The appearance of the Tigers out of the smoke and dust was the final straw and the Russians fled leaving many guns and trucks behind.

One of the outlying half-tracks attached to the 101st Tiger radioed in to warn of another column of Soviet armour and trucks approaching on the other side of low ridge. The German infantry still on the high ground confirmed the enemy's direction and Wolfgang cursed. He was low on ammunition and fuel and another one of the Tigers in his company had broken down. Bolshaya was a larger village than Pochta and nestled into the northern flank of one of the rivers that flowed to the east of the low ridge. It was four kilometres to the east of their present position but couldn't be seen because it was separated from them by the high ground they had previously captured.

The German infantry on the ridge was able to direct the Wespes to drop shells among the approaching Russians, just as they entered the large village. A thin line of German troops deployed before the Soviets being dropped off by half-tracks. Their job was only to slow the enemy, which they did with great bravery, shooting with Panzerschrecks and MG42s at the enemy in order to slow them down. The 101st SS Heavy Panzer Battalion was frantically loading more shells into their Tigers as the infantry bought them time. The fuel situation was poor but there was only a short interval to top up the tanks of a few of the giant panzers before driving towards the enemy. Tiger 305 didn't get any extra fuel but Wolfgang made sure they grabbed as many rounds for their main gun as possible. Even so, the ammunition racks in his heavy panzer were half empty.

The whole battalion, now down to twelve Tigers, drove straight up the side of the low ridge and then down the other slope towards Bolshaya. They stopped just under a kilometre from the village and waited until the Russians emerged from the buildings. A wave of T34s burst from the village, some having to recross the shallow river. There was no order to the attack, no formation, just a wild charge of every tank the Russians could throw at them. This included T70 light tanks and BA64 armoured cars. The Tigers stood calmly and picked their targets. As the enemy armour was coming straight at them it was difficult to miss. Tank after tank blew up or lurched to a halt spewing black oily smoke, and yet the Russians kept coming.

A T70 came apart directly in front of Wolfgang's Tiger when a high explosive round detonated on its frontal armour. Metal and fire marked the end of the Russian light tank and yet it rolled on, a shattered hull narrowly missing them. A BA64 somehow avoided all incoming fire and slammed into a Tiger at full speed. It bounced off the massive panzer and landed on its side. One of the crew members crawled from the wreck and down the slope, with a broken leg and a blood covered forehead. He was captured later by German infantry and treated by Larisa.

The T34s eventually melted back into the village where they attempted to dig in. The 101st Tiger Battalion didn't try to evict the Russians directly. They didn't have the fuel or the shells and the men were exhausted. Obersturmbannführer Heinz von Westernhagen managed to find a Luftwaffe command that was not engaged in other missions and directed it onto Bolshaya. Stukas screamed down from a partly cloudy sky to smash the village to matchwood. Bf 109s then sprayed the Soviets with machine gun and cannon fire. When another group of Wespes joined the four from the Tiger battalion they pounded what was left of the Russians in the village. The Soviets didn't withdraw until darkness covered their escape. SS infantry advanced into Bolshaya soon after midnight and declared the village empty. Fifty four destroyed enemy tanks were counted. A similar number of trucks sat damaged or destroyed, and another eight Russian guns were captured. Enemy dead lay everywhere.

With help from the Luftwaffe, the 101st SS Tiger Battalion had destroyed an entire Soviet Armoured Corps, and halted a dangerous thrust that would have cut off the German Sixth Army. Wolfgang didn't know this at the time as he was fast asleep wrapped in a thick blanket under his battle scarred Tiger.

Goering had flown to Manstein's headquarters in Rostov on Don. His JU90 had gone via Kiev and carried Field Marshal Keitel who had boarded his plane there and travelled with him. Now they sat with Field Marshal List, commander of the forces in the Caucasus.

General Paulus was not able to attend due to the crisis at the front.

The men sat around a large table in a room in the Nikolaevskiy Hotel, near the heart of the city. A large fire blazed in an open fireplace and outside SS men guarded every approach, while a portable Wuerzburg FuMG39 radar station watched for Soviet air activity. The sets were usually used for gun laying but the twenty-five-kilometre range would give the Germans enough warning to get the Führer into the deep cellars.

"Have we stopped them?" asked Goering.

Manstein shook his head. "On the northern flank the answer would be yes. The Tiger battalions did an amazing job of holding the Russian armour. The 1st SS, 11th Panzer Division and the 16th Panzer Division, as well as the Hungarian 1st Armoured Division have fought the Soviets to a standstill, but in the process taken very heavy casualties. The 24th Panzer Division was all that we had to hold the southern front, and its performance was mixed. As you know it was reequipping with the Skoda T25 Cheetah. One of the panzer regiments had its full complement of the new vehicles, the other had not and was using Marders as well as the Cheetahs as armour. Anyway, the 2nd Battalion got hit hard from the air on the first day of the break through and then crashed into a regiment of Soviet armour. It fled, and was later hit by a line of 88mm guns manned by Luftwaffe personnel. Seemed our boys thought the onrushing T25s were Russian tanks. They do look a bit like T34s so it was an understandable mistake. The 1st Battalion had a meeting engagement with two Soviet armoured regiments and the mutual destruction of the three formations resulted. To cut a long story short, the 24th slowed the enemy but was completely destroyed in the process."

"What are our options?" asked Goering.

"We hold the Don Bend but strong Russian units are advancing to the south of the river towards Rostov. The 14th Panzer Division is nipping at the flank of their advance but it is too weak after its race to the Volga. Infantry units hold the southern side of the great bend of the river but the countryside to the south of that is empty of our troops," said Manstein. "However, there is an opportunity here."

Field Marshal List stood at a nod from Manstein and walked to a map of the Caucasus pinned to the wall. He pointed to the Kalmyk Steppe and a line of lakes to the south of Stalingrad.

"These lakes are where the 24th was shattered and where the Russians broke through," he said. "We hold Kalach on the Don and the railway bridge there, but have been forced back from the Volga and Stalingrad. The Russians have reached the Mischkova River and retaken the small town of Aksoye. They are pushing towards Kotenikovo, which is an important railway station and crossroads. This is where my command comes in. The panzers of Army Group A have been idle in the Caucasus since mid-October. We didn't get over the mountains, though our bomber units have hammered Baku until it is rubble."

Goering interrupted. "Hopefully Russian fuel supplies will become a problem for them. I have had to order the bomber units north to help around Stalingrad."

List nodded and then continued. "We are actually using the JU290s to move fuel. The medium bombers are trying to slow the

Russian advance but we have tried to prioritize supplies to the army. As you know fuel, shells and food are hard to move around in Russia and the distances vast. The 5th SS Panzer Division has finally reached Savolnoya after a trek across the Kalmyk Steppe of over four hundred kilometres. Keeping them supplied has been a nightmare, but the Luftwaffe transport units have performed miracles. Now they don't have to provision the heavy bomber units it's a bit easier. The 13th Panzer was ordered to Mozdok where they bordered trains to Tikhorestsk, before changing to another line which allowed them to decamp at Proletarskaya. The 3rd SS Panzer is just north of Elista, one hundred kilometres south of the front. With these three units, we plan to hit the Soviets in the flank. The 13th Panzer is the blocking force and the SS will drive into the exposed left flank of the enemy. The 16th Panzer grenadier will join the SS forces and the 3rd Panzer will soon join the 13th Panzer. I'm confident that these forces will drive the enemy back and our army will soon sit once more on the banks of the Volga River."

Goering smiled. "Good."

V

The M8 armoured car sat hidden among the low scrub. Charlie sat next to the 37mm gun watching for movement in the nearby trees.

"Relax," said Catinza. "The sarge has checked the area on foot. There's no Jerries around."

They had come down out of the mountains and hills into the Guadarrama River Valley. The 4th US Armoured Division was now sitting only thirty miles from the centre of Madrid. Indeed, the outer suburbs of the city were in sight. The infantry had captured the town of El Alamo a week ago, after a set piece attack which had cost the US army a number of casualties. A Spanish Blue Division had defended every building and fighting had been

hand-to-hand at times. Charlie was glad that his recon unit hadn't been involved. M8 armoured cars weren't suited to urban fighting and so had been spared the ordeal. Now though, they were probing down towards the river.

The armoured car was nestled in a line of scrub just back from a road that ran east west towards the waterway. Just to the south of the road sat a farm surrounded by fields and olive groves. This is where Sergeant Fred Renwood had gone and waved an all clear from, then the big man had crept towards the trees that lined the river. The flood plain on the far bank was open ground and a low ridge climbed away, dominating the valley. Charlie glanced at the maps and knew the countryside to the south was more open. The US armour could cross the river to the south and advance east, before then swinging north. There was a smaller waterway that ran into the Guadarrama River from the east and the village of Batres which would block such a move, but the biggest problem would be getting across the water. The Guadarrama wasn't a big river but it was deep enough to need bridging equipment. There were probably spots where the river could be forded but at the moment, they didn't know where they were located.

"They haven't blown the bridge," said the sergeant when he returned.

"Is it mined?" asked Smokey Gunroy.

"Probably; I did see wires but I couldn't see the enemy. They must be there but are well hidden. I didn't want to take any more chances alone."

Charlie thought that was fair enough. He believed the sarge was mad for going by himself to start with.

"That bridge would be handy," said the sergeant stroking his chin.

"The river's not much more than a muddy trench here. Why can't the armour roll straight through it?" asked Charlie.

"It's deeper than it looks and a Sherman might get across, or it could easily get bogged. I'm going to radio the lieutenant and pass this up the chain."

Charlie cursed inwardly. He knew what would happen next and dreaded it.

When the orders came through they were worse than he had anticipated. The M8s and a group of half-tracks were going to force a crossing at high speed and grab a small bridgehead on the other side of the river. They would be supported by mortars and artillery and even a couple of Shermans were coming with them. Charlie wasn't sure if the inclusion of a couple of tanks made him feel better or worse. He worried about the ground on the far side of the river. There was plenty of cover on the slopes; a whole regiment could hide up there and you wouldn't see them.

Eight M8s gathered three miles back from the river behind a fold in the ground. Six half-tracks soon arrived carrying the better part of an infantry company. There was no sign of the Shermans. As they waited, artillery started to shoot over their heads at possible enemy positions on the far bank. Mortars soon joined the bombardment, such as it was. Charlie thought only a few shells were going over every ten seconds. He didn't think they were putting much effort into it. Eventually three tanks arrived, but by then the artillery had stopped firing. Lieutenant Michaelson ran to them and told them to mount up. The young officer had recovered quickly from his wounds and had insisted on returning to his unit as quickly as possible. Charlie thought he was crazy for doing so.

They were going to cross the bridge at speed and grab a farmhouse two hundred yards back from the river. The four M8s would lead the way, followed by the half-tracks and then the tanks, with another four armoured cars bringing up the rear. Charlie was glad his armoured car wasn't first. The lieutenant led the way.

The M8s accelerated quickly but were forced to slow when they realised they were leaving the Shermans behind. So much for speed, thought Charlie. They crossed the bridge without difficulty and were almost at the farmhouse when the leading M8 hit a mine. It slewed sideways coming to rest against a tree. Two men jumped clear of the smouldering wreck and hid behind a low rock wall. Then the last tank in the line exploded. It had just reached the middle of the bridge when a hidden PAK 40 anti-tank gun hit it where the turret joined the body of the tank. The tank crashed into the stone barrier on the side of the bridge and stopped, flames pouring from the hull, the turret having been blown into the water.

An ambush, and of course they had driven straight into it. Another AT round hit the next Sherman on the track ripping it clear and sending it curling and twisting away from the bogies. Its crew didn't wait around and abandoned the vehicle before another round smashed through the tank's frontal plates. At least two MG42s were firing, their tearing sound filling the air. American soldiers were jumping from half-tracks and running for cover but some were hit. A rocket sped out from the scrub and slammed into the side of the armoured car which was now just behind Charlie's. The vehicles had become bunched as they crossed the river and were now paying the price for sitting so close together. Charlie saw that they wanted to keep the force organized but perhaps it would have been better just to send a couple of M8s across first. Even if it meant not grabbing a bridgehead, it would have been better than this fiasco.

Without waiting for orders Charlie accelerated off the road and through the scrub. Ahead there was a dirt track so he took it. The M8 didn't like the rough so this was his best option. He didn't know it at the time but a half-track and a jeep followed him. The track took them around the back of the farmhouse and into a squad of Spanish soldiers. Above him the main gun barked and the fifty calibre machine gun fired. Hot metal casings rained down on him and he cursed as one burnt his cheek. Still, he kept the M8 charging forward. His sudden manoeuvre had taken the enemy by surprise and the small American group cut down the enemy squad and drove through the enemy ambush before following a dirt track south, away from the shooting.

"Stop, stop!" yelled the sergeant but Charlie kept going until a hand struck him on the top of his helmet. He eased the car to a halt and the half-track pulled up next to them. Another sergeant leaned out and called to Renwood. "What should we do? Our boys are being cut to pieces back there."

It was probably true but Charlie didn't care. The sound of firing from the north was intense and they had only fled about seven hundred yards. Trees lined both sides of the road but to the east, through the foliage, he could see open fields.

"We go back and hit the Spaniards from the flank. Our artillery won't be able to help our boys because both forces are so tangled. It was a close-range ambush, except for maybe the AT guns. I think we can turn out into that field, head north until we hit the trees again and then move forward slowly, with your guys on foot. How many you got?"

"With those in the jeep, twelve," said the other sergeant.

Renwood chewed on his lip. "It will have to do. We can't leave our boys there to get massacred."

It didn't take long to turn around and cross the field back into the scrub. Charlie wanted to scream at his leader. This was madness. There was a least a company of veteran Spanish soldiers in front of them. They eased forward into the wood line and came upon a squad of soldiers running to the west along a track, carrying what looked like a bazooka, only it was larger. Thompsons and Garands fired and the enemy fell and twitched. The other sergeant, a man Charlie found out later was called Harrison, picked up the rocket launcher and signalled his squad forward. The M8 drove slowly through the scrub and back onto the track. The rear of the farmhouse was now only eighty yards away from them. An enemy machine gun team was firing from a position to the armoured car's west and Renwood swivelled the turret and fired a canister round at the Spanish. The range was less than one hundred yards and the result was horrific. Hundreds of small pellets the size of a man's thumb shredded the machine gun crew. Charlie almost vomited at the sight. Then the enemy spotted them and a squad came running around the farmhouse. Sergeant Renwood fired at the Spanish troops with heavy machine gun and the American infantry squad threw grenades. A burst from an MP40 wounded one US soldier in retaliation, but all of the Spanish infantry were killed.

Someone was directing artillery at the PAK 40s on the far slope and the firing at the tanks on the road was dissipating. The Spanish still held fox holes near the road but the US infantry were hitting back. The sudden appearance of the small force in the enemy's flank had thrown them off balance. Then the bridge blew. Charlie didn't see it go but he heard the roar and knew what it was. No one had cut the wires as people had been concentrating on staying alive and fighting back. In the end, all of the Shermans had been destroyed and only Charlie's M8s had survived the river crossing; the other four never made it. In the end Lieutenant Michaelson led the survivors back across the river after the sun went down. The bridgehead had suffered ongoing mortar fire for the rest of the day after the

Spaniards had retreated, and two more men had been killed. Charlie was a little sad when they blew up the M8 but he was happy to be leaving. It had been a short sharp action but at least the Spaniards had taken casualties as well. Charlie didn't care. He just didn't see the point of it all.

Chapter Four: December 1943

The P51 Mustang had to be the best plane ever made, or so thought Lieutenant Henry Richardson. The 357th Fighter Group had only been reequipped with them a month ago, and was supposed to train with them for a lot longer before taking them into action. Yet the massacre of the bombers in deep penetration raids into Germany had shown the high command that an escort was desperately needed. The P51B was deemed the answer. It had the range to go all the way to Berlin and back.

The pilots of 357th squadron loved the new plane, saying it was a vast improvement over the old P39s. Sure there were still problems in terms of how the fuel load affected the plane's performance, but these had largely been resolved. Switching between tanks on long haul trips to Scotland and back had shown the best way of handling the issue. Henry wished for more firepower as well. Four point five machine guns in the wings were adequate, but only just. It was a far cry from the hitting power of a P39. But the plane could fly!

It was fast, stable, manoeuvrable, had a good rate of climb and high-altitude performance was outstanding, as the Luftwaffe had already found out.

Flights of the new P51 had fought FW190As (Shrikes) over France. The combat had occurred at 21,000 feet and three enemy planes had been shot down for no loss to the US Air Force. The Shrike seemed sluggish at this height and the Mustang ran rings around them. They were yet to face a Bf 109G in combat and the Messerschmitt was supposed to be better above 20,000 feet than its stable mate, the FW190.

Today they would find out. The entire group was escorting at least three hundred B17s and B24s into Germany. IG Farben had chemical factories there which the 8th Army Air Force wanted to destroy. The raid wasn't penetrating as deeply into Germany as some of the previous attacks but at least the P47 boys and the fighter groups using the P38 Lightning would be able to stay with the bombers all of the way. The 357th would meet the bombers just over the German border and take them the last eighty miles. This would be the most dangerous part of the trip and the Luftwaffe would attack with everything they had.

The squadron had flown over Belgium without incident. There had been a little flak but it had exploded well below their altitude and a little behind them. It was a routine flight. Now that was all about to change. They crossed the German border and spotted the bombers a little ahead of them. A squadron of P38s were just leaving but kept radio silence as they did. No point telling the Luftwaffe what was going on. The squadron then settled into doing slow circuits above the bomber formations.

Captain Calvert spotted the German planes first. "Twin-engined planes approaching from the north. My guess is they are JU88Cs," he radioed.

Henry swivelled his head and saw the aircraft flying towards the bombers. They were at a slightly lower altitude than his squadron but were otherwise flying straight at them.

Lieutenant Colonel Hubert Egnes radioed them, "Dollar, Roundtree, attack when ready. Stop those heavy fighters."

Captain Calvert led the group of P51s down in curving dives that would take them behind the attacking JU88s. Four of the enemy saw them and turned to face the attack while the rest of the Germans pushed on.

"Dollar, attack the aircraft tracking the bombers. We'll take these," said the Captain.

Harry felt sweat bead on his brow as he heard the order. The eight P51s he led would have to stop the enemy fighters. He ignored the Ju88s flying at them and curved under the Germans. He heard the chatter of guns and the steady thump of cannons behind him as his squadron engaged the enemy. Ahead, a twin engine aircraft grew in his N3 gun sights. At two hundred and fifty yards he settled the dot in the middle of his sights on the enemy machine and pressed the trigger. Nothing happened. Then he realised he hadn't flicked the gun switch. Harry quickly did so but by now the range was down to one hundred and fifty yards. The rear gunner was shooting at him and he could see lines on little yellow dots flying towards him.

He fired and watched as machine gun bullets tore into the JU 88C6. The glass disintegrated around the rear gunner position and then tracked forward over the cockpit. A stream of smoke suddenly poured from the port engine and the plane fell forward. He kept firing and bits of metal came flying from the main fuselage. Then the enemy machine was spinning away out of control. His wing man and another pilot fired at other aircraft and they were twisting and turning all over the sky. Harry felt a moment of confusion and then his intense training kicked in. He had over four hundred hours of flying time and it had all led up to this moment.

A Ju88 flashed passed to his right and he kicked the rudder and turned towards it. The enemy plane tried to turn away but Harry stayed with it easily. The rear gunner fired at him but the frantic twists and turns of his pilot were throwing off his aim. Harry stayed with the big German fighter as it tried to lose him. His first burst at one hundred yards went below the enemy aircraft but the next chewed into the starboard engine causing a small explosion. The JU88 tried to dive away and Harry followed, putting another burst into the same engine. However, he was going too fast and turned away in order not to fly in front of the enemy machine.

His wingman, Second Lieutenant Mac McConnell finished his work and announced the JU88's destruction. "The pilot's bailed, skipper. Guess we will have to share that one."

Harry grunted. Half a kill was better than nothing.

The JU88s didn't get near the bombers, and later on the 363rd Squadron ripped into a group of ME410s. Then a group of Bf109s and some sixty FW190s attacked and bombers started to fall. There just weren't enough P51s available yet to provide enough protection for so many B17s. Twisting and turning with his wingman, Harry managed to lock onto an unwary Messerschmitt and blow its wing off with a single long burst, but now he was almost out of ammunition. The bombers continued below him, losing more planes as flak exploded around them. Bombs fell towards the factory complex through a scattering of light cloud but Harry had no way of knowing if they had been successful.

The trip home was less eventful as the Luftwaffe seemed to have expended all its energy on the US bomber's approach. One group of BF109s did attack but the 364th chased them off. It seemed the Messerschmitt was not a match for the P51 when laden with cannons under each wing. Two fell to the guns of the Mustangs before the enemy dived away. Then P47s appeared. They took over escort duty for the remainder of the trip, for which Harry was extremely grateful. His bullet counter indicated he had only a handful of rounds left for each of his machine guns. As the 357th started to head home Harry looked at the bomber stream. He could see many of the big machines carried damage and were badly strung out. He wasn't to know it but German fighters would again attack the B17s as they crossed southern Holland, catching the P47s by surprise and destroying two struggling B17s. The FW190s wouldn't get away unscathed, as the 356th Fighter group sought revenge. Four enemy fighters were caught and destroyed and another two damaged.

Finally they had fuel again. The journey of the 3rd SS Panzer Division across the Kalmyk Steppe had been one of frustration and freezing cold. The two factors had been closely linked as snow storms and low cloud had often prevented the Luftwaffe transports from flying and delivering supplies by normal means. It was also difficult to get fuel due to the poor roads and long distances. Oberschutze Klaus Moller could see the JU252s flying away and watched the panzers and half-tracks being refuelled. What he didn't know was that the weather had played havoc with the German High Command's planned counterstrike against the Russians.

The 3rd and 13th Panzer Divisions had managed to block the Soviet advance down the southern side of the Don River, but damage to the rail network had meant the 3rd SS had to move north under its own power. Only now was it and the 5th SS Panzer Division ready to strike at the enemy's flank. Klaus didn't know any of this, though he heard that fighting around Kotelnikovo had been fierce but in the end the Soviets had taken the small town.

The 3rd SS were somewhere to the east of the battle zone in an area of white featureless steppe. There was the odd hillock and the ground was cut with plenty of gullies, but in the main, the horizons seemed endless. Klaus found it frightening and didn't know why anybody would want to live here. It was so very different to the hills and forests of Germany, yet the army said they needed to be here and would meet the Russians and destroy them in this flat expanse.

His patrol had come across a group of strange looking antelope the other day and shot two before the herd scattered. The meat was a little stringy but still a welcome change from the stale bread and mouldy cheese they had been eating. They had also captured the crew of a Russian light tank that had broken down. The two enemy soldiers were thin and dirty and didn't even seem to know where they were. Rottenführer Hugo Sommer had beaten the men for information, but it soon became obvious that they knew very little. Klaus held one of the Russians as Somme's fists had crunched into his stomach and jaw. The sound of ribs snapping had disturbed him at first but then he realised these animals had it coming. In the end they had stripped the Soviet soldiers and left them next to their wrecked tank. Sommer had taken a wrench to the vehicle's engine and checked that there was no clothing or tarps for the Russians to wrap themselves in. Then he had ordered the SS patrol away.

The Sd. Kfz.251 and the old British Bren carrier had driven off leaving the naked men standing in the snow. Klaus laughed about it with Hanno Schuster.

"If the stupid Russians had a radio they would have lived," said Sommer before spitting over the side of the half-track.

They prepared to attack northwest the following morning. The Panzer Fours of the 3rd Regiment led the way followed by the half-tracks of the 5th Panzer Grenadier Regiment. Klaus sat at the rear of a half-track with Rainer Stein and Vogt Adlar. The latter had found an FG 42 and was determined to use it despite the problem with its accuracy when firing automatic bursts.

"I plan to use it on single shot at long range and only switch to auto when those stinking Slavs are up close and personal," he said.

Klaus had his rifle but was hoping to get his hand on a Russian submachine gun as soon as possible. Everyone said the weapon was worth its weight in gold, though he found the idea disturbing. He kept asking how the Slavs could have made a better weapon than the Germans. His fellow soldiers just shrugged and told him to grab one as soon as he could.

It started to snow, but just lightly. Klaus was wearing a new M42 anorak and was fairly comfortable, despite the cold. Ahead, a small village appeared out of the gloom. Someone said it was called Pimeno-Cherni but it just looked like another Russian dog kennel to Klaus. These people seemed to live like animals in their mud and wood houses. A small -frozen creek materialized in front of the half-track but they drove straight through it. Then there was firing. Tracers zipped from around the buildings and windows, and rattled off the armour of their transportation. The MG42 mounted on the hull started to fire back in short controlled bursts. Somewhere a panzer fired. Klaus heard the flat crack of its 75mm gun.

"Time to get out," yelled Rottenführer Sommer.

Klaus followed Hanno and Rainer over the rear of the half-track with Adlar landing behind him. They set off in a hunched over jog to another group of men gathered around Obersturmführer Sauer. The tall man was pointing and yelling, and groups of men sprinted from him towards the village. When they reached the officer he glanced at Sommer and nodded.

"Alright Rottenführer, take your squad towards the small tractor workshop on the edge of the village. You are a little under strength so I'll give you an MG team and Sturmmann Braun's team. When you take the building push on around the western edge of the village until you hit the main road. The rest of the company is still on the other side of the river attacking into a small forest on the edge of the town. Part of the battalion is coming in from the east. Try not to shoot our own boys," said Sauer. "The panzers are skirting the place with the other battalion and pushing on. Only a single Zug is staying and they are to the east as well."

Sommer nodded and quickly checked his mixed squad; twelve men armed with an assortment of weapons. "Moller, get the Panzerschreck," Sommer ordered.

Klaus moaned, the anti-tank weapon was heavy but he jogged back to the half-track and picked it up. Hanno came with him and carried the ammunition for the weapon.

"Hope this beast is worth it," he said.

"If there is an enemy panzer it might be," replied Klaus.

Mortars were exploding on the edge of the village when they returned and Sommer used the bombardment as an opportunity to move the group towards an old brick church. There was little cover and the switch from high explosive shells to smoke from the mortars thickened the gloom. Tracers came out of the fog like little red bees and Klaus and his companions dropped down onto the snow. No one was hit and Sommer ordered them forward. Klaus felt fear but forced it down. He was finally fighting for the Fatherland. These Slav dogs would die for their attack on his homeland. Klaus crawled forward pushing the Panzerschreck along in front of him. The building became clearer and he could see dirty white walls and a sloped red tiled roof. Icicles hung from the eaves like clear javelins and large rectangular windows created dark patches from which tracers occasionally shot towards him.

The tearing snarl of the MG42 told him their machine gun crew was at work. Pieces of brick chipped and flew from around the windows and Klaus could see Rainer crawling forward. A stick grenade arced from his hand and flew into the building. There followed the dull crump of an explosion before Adlar and Hanno ran forward and threw more grenades. Then the squad was charging the building. Klaus left the rocket launcher and sprinted to the main door. Inside it was dark but he saw flashes as Rottenführer Sommer fired his MP40.

Three Russians were brought outside bleeding and stunned. One of them was younger than Klaus and another old enough to be his father. The third was so covered in blood it was difficult to make out his features.

"You wanted one of these?" asked Rainer. The man was handing him a papasha. The submachine gun had a round magazine and a scratched wooden stock. "I found plenty of ammo for it and it's always easy to get more," said the grinning trooper.

"Test fire it on these three," said Sommer gesturing at the captured Russians. "We can't spare anyone to take them back to the company. Anyway they are Slavs, so who cares."

"Really? I can shoot them?" asked Klaus. He felt excited at the prospect.

"Fire away," said Sommer.

Klaus grinned and cocked his new weapon. He pushed the Russians towards a wall and took a dozen steps back. When he raised the weapon and aimed it at the prisoners he saw the eyes of the oldest one go wide, while the younger one put his hands out in front of him and muttered something. The first burst sounded loud in Klaus' ears, almost surprising him. The oldest Russian was hit across the chest and slumped sideways. The wounded man fell groaning, while the youngest dropped to his knees with tears filling his eyes. Klaus took careful aim and fired a long burst ripping into the Russian soldier. Sommer nodded and shot the groaning man in the head with a pistol.

"You're a real killer," said the Rottenführer patting him on the shoulder.

Klaus had never felt prouder than at this moment.

"Right, we still have work to do," said Sommer, and he led the squad between the buildings towards the sound of firing.

The large hall was heated by two log fires, one at either end. Goering sat drinking real coffee with Speer and Kesselring around a small antique table that had been brought from Belgium.

"We stopped the Russian attack but failed to cut them off?" asked the head of the Luftwaffe.

Goering nodded. "It proved too difficult to get our forces in place. The weather, the Russians and the supply situation made it impossible to deliver a coordinated attack. The 5th SS and the 3rd SS eventually attacked the Russians in their southern flank but the 13th Panzer and the 3rd Panzer were too exhausted to support them. The enemy fell back Karpovka River. The Volga is out of reach for the moment but the oilfields are safe; those that we hold, and the Caucasus north of the mountains are ours."

"And we hold the Don bend?" asked Speer.

"We do. It seems everyone is now drawing breath. The Russians will keep the pressure on for now but intelligence reports indicate they are running short of fuel," said Goering. "However, the Americans are already trying to help their Russian allies in that regard. Tankers have been seen entering Vladivostok by the Japanese and others have made their way through the Arctic Circle to Murmansk."

"The Japanese will tell us but won't destroy them?" said Kesselring.

"They have their hands full with the Pacific War. They don't want a war with Russia as well," said Goering.

"It can't replace what they have lost," said Speer. "The reports I have commissioned show that maybe twenty-five to forty percent of the fuel they lost when we cut off the fuel producing areas, can be replaced by the Americans. The other issue is that the Russians are rebuilding the port facilities and oil storage tanks at Baku more quickly than we thought possible. With respect, Herr General, can the Luftwaffe stop them?"

Kesselring frowned. "It is difficult to do so in winter as the weather limits flying time. Also, supplying air bases so far from Germany is another problem. Yet with the easing of army operations, it is possible. We are readying the heavy bombers for another strike and now we have the long-range Fiat fighters to escort them. The engineers have even designed a slightly larger drop tank that further extends their range."

"What about our own oil?" asked Goering.

"It has increased by three percent and if we can get the Grozny fields operating again we could probably add another five to ten percent. The problem has been getting it back to Germany. I've got the rail link to the Maikop oil fields working but the line to Mozdok near Grozny is heavily damaged and will take a long time to repair. Also, the tracks are at capacity, some of them being only single lines. We need to increase how many trains they can take," said Speer.

"Use locals and prisoners if you have to. Just get those oil fields working," said Goering.

"I heard that the Americans and the Commonwealth are making another push," said Speer changing the subject.

"They are trying to keep the Russians in the war by supporting them in every way they can," said Goering. "We have been forced to send another infantry division from the northern Russian front to the Spain front, as well as two independent battalions of Nashorns. The Panzerjäger Abteilung 560 and 655 are already at Madrid. The 16th Estonian SS Infantry Division has taken their place in Russia and its sister division is almost ready to go as well."

"I sent another fighter Gruppe, JG4 to the area but as soon as they arrive the Americans will swamp the newcomers with attacks on their bases. However, I have a surprise ready to spring on the Allies. Twenty new Arado Ar 234 jet bombers are hidden at an airfield in Northern Spain and will strike soon," said Kesselring.

"Speaking of jets, how many of my Stormbirds are you making Herr Speer? They are about to go into combat and more will be needed," said Goering.

"There will be many, my Führer. The allied air force is about to get a nasty shock," answered Speer.

V

Sergeant Tom Derrick crawled forward over ground thinly dusted with snow. He didn't know it could get this cold in southern Europe but the locals said it would melt in a few days. Snowy followed, the MG42 cradled in his arms. To their left Freddy Peterson covered them with a Bren gun. The rest of the platoon waited back around the corner of a large brick house. The small gulley through which they were moving was surrounded by extensive olive stands of fully grown trees. The farm where the platoon had taken position was at the edge of the gully. A long driveway leading up to the house passed a concrete pond which was chipped and empty. Many of the surrounding olive trees were shattered by the recent bombardment and the scrub in the gully had been stripped of their leaves and smaller branches by the explosions of mortar rounds.

La Carolina was a small town on the main road to Madrid. There was nothing particularly special about it except that it stood in the path of the advance of the Australian 9th Division. It was also the last town in the valley. Ahead the Andalusia Mountains loomed. Tom wondered at the point of this attack. The Americans were much closer to Madrid in the north and even if they took the town, then the division would have a hard time forcing its way through the peaks and hills to the plains on the other side. He supposed it was about keeping the pressure on the Germans. The front was continuous after all. It ran along the mountains from here to the west before continuing to Cartagena in the east. Then it curved north in a slight bulge to Toledo, which was only forty miles from Madrid. After that the line ran north-northeast until it hit the Atlantic coast.

The gully was sloping upwards and slowly dissipating. He was still one hundred yards short of the main road and the cover was thin. There were the ubiquitous olive trees with their shattered trunks and twisted limbs offering some refuge, but when he reached the road there was nothing. To make matters worse two storey tenement houses sat back on the other side of the thoroughfare. The view from the side windows of these buildings was good which gave the German mountain division they were fighting excellent views of the surrounding fields. The only thought that consoled Tom was the rest of the battalion was approaching the town from the south and another attack was due to be launched from the southwest. His company was a diversion.

He looked at his watch and crouched low. Another bombardment was due and he didn't want to catch any stray shrapnel. The big shells from 155mm guns came screaming in right on time. They punched into buildings throwing debris and dust onto the streets. He knew the division had recently reequipped with the big American guns and this was the first time he had seen them in action. It was impressive. Walls fell away and fires started. The town had been hit before, but not like this. A barrage fell on the edge of town before switching to the south. Mortars joined in, though they did less damage.

Tom watched it all, looking for movement or any signs of the enemy. The Germans were too good for that and he saw nothing. Crawling back to his platoon he signalled them forward. Within moments the rest of the company was moving through the trees.

They didn't bunch up and the heavy weapons groups remained ready to provide covering fire. There was little noise and Tom smiled at the veterans of the 9th Division. These men all knew their job and wouldn't run from a fight. The problem was that the Germans were veterans as well.

A machine gun screamed from the upper window of an undamaged building and men groaned and fell. Lieutenant Harry Breman yelled an order and Bren guns smothered the Germans with fire. Another MG42 started firing but was quickly targeted with mortars. Soon the Australians had reached the road and were sprinting across into the rubble of the town. Rifle shots came from somewhere up ahead and an Australian soldier fell next to Tom. He dived through a doorway as another bullet buzzed passed his ear. He had been told the mountain divisions had less automatic weapons than regular German divisions but they made up for it with the accuracy of their snipers.

It was dark inside the house, the shadows competing with weak sunlight. From an upper floor he heard the crack of rifle and voices drifted up a set of stairs in front of him. Tom pulled a grenade from his belt and waited. He was aware he was alone and vulnerable. Outside he could hear firing and the rifle barked again from an upper window. There were more sounds from down-stairs and he heard boots thumping towards him. He threw the grenade and it bounced into the darkness. There was a flash and a high pitched scream.

Tom ran forward and peered down into what must have been some sort of cellar. There was little light so he fumbled for a torch. He turned it on and stared down at the bodies of the Spanish family. An older man lay on the stairs moaning softly. Below him, lying on the concrete floor, were the corpses of a young girl and a woman of perhaps thirty years old. Blood pooled around her. It was the eyes of the child which drew him. They were like glass and were open in shock and surprise. Tom ran down the steps and checked for a pulse. There wasn't one and Tom could see the damage to the little girl's body would have given her little chance of survival. He closed her eyes and saw the blood on his fingers. She couldn't have been more than six or seven years old. He went to the older man who had stopped moaning and died of shock. Tom's body shook with the thought of what he had done. A family killed because he had panicked.

Boots came running down from above him and Tom quickly returned up the stairs. He came out into the passageway to see a pair of German soldiers near the front door. It looked as though they were preparing to relocate. Tom raised his MP40 and aimed at the men, but then hesitated.

"Hande hoch," he said firmly. Tom didn't want to kill these Germans. They glanced at each other, both of them realising by the time they swung their rifles around they would be dead. The two men dropped their rifles and raised their hands carefully. Now what do I do, thought Tom? If he took these two soldiers out into the middle of a battle they might be shot out of hand and he didn't want that, not after what had just happened. He gestured for the Germans to follow him into a side room, which turned out to be a kitchen and pointed at the floor. They sat on a mat and he placed himself in a sturdy wooden chair.

"Looks like I'll sit this one out," he muttered.

He kept his machine pistol trained on the Germans and waited.

Chapter Five: January 1944

The jet climbed through the low clouds out into bright sunshine. Oberleutnant Kurt Osser eased the throttle forward on the turbine engines and led his section of three planes towards the approaching bombers. Behind these jets another nine followed. They turned southwest and headed towards the flight path of the incoming B17s. This was the third large-scale raid the Americans had launched since they started to escort their heavy bombers all the way to targets deep inside Germany. The P51 Mustangs which flew cover had been a nasty surprise. Many Luftwaffe pilots had lost their lives to the new fighter. Now it was going to be the Americans turn to get a shock.

JG 26 had been transferred to the Heilbronn airstrip two weeks ago, which had been upgraded and no longer had a grass runway. The choice was made due to the airfield's central location and the short range of the Stormbird. The Messerschmitt 262 Gruppe needed to be based at locations where they could cover central Germany as well as the route to Berlin. Kurt knew JG7 was based at

Hannover and the rest of JG26 was at Fulda, another upgraded airstrip. This way the jets covered most of the approaches to Middle Germany. More Stormbirds were being made operational, but it took time to convert from a single-engined prop driven fighter to a twin-engined jet. As it was, his Gruppe only had twenty-four operational aircraft. The other twelve were probably five minutes behind them and had been told to take a more southerly route to the bombers.

They continued to climb and soon the B17s appeared far to the southwest. Kurt wondered how they would go trying to bomb through the cloud today. The forecast had warned that it would break up as the day went on but the Americans would be bombing through fifty percent cloud cover at best. Maybe the enemy had received a different weather forecast. It didn't matter to Kurt. Above the cloud, visibility seemed unlimited.

The jets curved around behind the bombers just as the American fighters dived towards them. He smiled in his mask. They would never catch the Stormbird. He led the squadron in a shallow dive, dumping speed about two kilometres from the bombers as they had practised with a short climb. He looked at the dial and noted they were still moving at just under eight hundred kilometres an hour. He would only have three or four seconds to fire. They had tried this manoeuvre with the JU86s when rehearsing for this moment previously. The B17 moved faster than the old Luftwaffe bomber giving him a split second extra. He lined up on a B17 at the edge of the top bomber box and flipped the safety device to expose the top firing switch. With one switch you only fired two cannon at a time. Kurt had insisted that all four fire when he pushed the A button. The B button fired only the bottom pair of 30mm cannons.

His first burst was too soon and he stopped firing as he noticed the shells fall under the bomber. He counted, one, two, and fired again. This time he held the firing switch down until he eased the jet above the bomber. Kurt didn't see the results of his burst but the other jets reported his success. Only five shells hit the B17 but it was enough to bring it down. One hit behind the top gun turret, but failed to explode. It left a fist sized hole before deflecting downwards through the plane's belly, glancing off a bomb and then punching a out of the aircraft. The four shells that hit the starboard wing did the majority of the damage. One hit the inner engine and blew a massive chunk off it. Fire streamed from the damage and the pilot of the bomber immediately turned it off. The other two shells exploded against the inner starboard fuel tank starting a blaze that rapidly consumed the wing. The American fliers rapidly abandoned the aircraft, though only four made it out before the wing came off. The falling B17 eventually landed on a small stone bridge crossing a stream outside Schafhausen, blowing the structure to pieces but not injuring anyone except a few ducks in the water.

The squadron had only enough fuel for a single pass but it was enough to destroy three bombers and damage another three, none of which made it back to England. The Americans had been told the weather would clear once they reached the Rhine. It didn't and they were forced to drop their bombs through three quarter cloud cover. The chemical factories were only slightly damaged but in the end only forty two B17s were destroyed. There weren't enough jets as yet to make a dramatic impact. Huge air battles were fought with the P51s but enough Luftwaffe fighters broke through to the American bombers to make an impact. The American fighters only lost six of their number to the single-engined Luftwaffe planes, but JG7 had shot down eight of the nimble fighters after bouncing a group of Thunderbolts that was operating independently over the German border. The Luftwaffe lost forty-eight single-engined machines and three jets. More Stormbirds were desperately needed, yet it was a promising beginning.

"We need to decide what we will do in the east this year gentlemen, and to do so it is necessary to look at where we are," said Goering. "That is why I have asked you all here today to make your reports."

The leader of Germany sat in the main dining room of Carinhall with Kesselring, Speer and Field Marshal Keitel. All had brought folders and rolls of maps which lay across a large table. The wall was covered in charts and coffee had been served. All of the junior officers that had helped set up the room had been sent away and Goering now settled into a comfortable chair and waited. He gestured to Keitel who crossed to a large map of Russia hanging in the wall.

"As you can see the line has settled in the east, though strong Soviet attacks have continued they are only making localised gains." He stopped and pointed at the Don River. "This is where they continue to push but the 2nd SS Division has moved into the area, giving the 1st SS a much-needed rest. The 2nd SS Division has been reequipped with Panthers and has also swapped its PAK 40s for StuG3s. The high command is confident that with these reinforcements and the other divisions on hand, the line will hold. The Soviets are struggling to mount simultaneous attacks and intelligence believes fuel shortages are starting to affect them." Keitel paused to sip his coffee before continuing. "The line runs from the Caspian Sea, across the dry steppe to the Don River bend fifty kilometres from Stalingrad. It then follows the river to Vorenezh, which we still hold. From there we hold another thirty kilometres of the river-bank before the line heads almost straight to Kaluga. From there it runs with a few small curves to Rzhev. Nowhere are we closer than one hundred kilometres from Moscow. From here the front continues north to Tikhvin and then it curves to the southern shore of Lake Onega. North of the lake it heads to the Finnish border. Since Tikhvin fell the Soviets have tried to take it back twice. The northern front is quiet now but we cannot always count on that."

"How safe are the Caucasus?" asked Goering.

"For now they are secure," said Keitel. The steppe front south of the Don is unusual as it is not continuous. The 3rd SS and the 13th Panzer Division watch the area with a series of outposts. Behind them strong mobile forces are maintained. The country is so open here and the distances vast, so it seems like the best approach to take. To the south we hold one side of the mountains, except for the bridgehead near Sochi which we hold on the Black Sea, and the Russians hold the other side."

Goering turned to Kesselring. "Your raid on Baku yesterday, how did it go?"

"The cloud cover was fifty percent so it was less than satisfactory. The good news is we had few casualties and the long range Fiats we received from our Italian friends shot down over thirty enemy fighters. We will need to send the bombers in a few more times, but it's all up to the weather."

Goering nodded. "Sorry Field Marshal, continue."

Keitel turned back to the map. "So, we will need to decide what out next move is in the east, but before discussing that it is important to examine what is happening in Spain. The introduction of more Estonian, Latvian and Galician divisions to the Russian front has allowed us to send more German divisions south. Rommel has plans for them, which we will look at in a minute. The front has changed little since we spoke last, with the most pronounced change being just south of Madrid."

"Didn't the Australians take Santa Elena not long ago?" asked Goering.

"Yes," answered Keitel. "But now they are stuck against the mountains and the terrain has made their advance against our southern flank difficult. No, the problem is here at Aranjuez where the Spanish 30th Division gave way. The Americans have created a bulge in the line starting at El Alamo, heading out to Aranjuez and then following the valley south back to Toledo. This forty kilometre triangle pierces our lines, threatening Madrid from the south and our positions in the lower half of the country from the north."

"But Rommel has a plan," said Kesselring.

Keitel nodded. "The leader of our army in Spain wants to draw General Clarke forward. As you know Patton has been replaced for unknown reasons. He wants to give the illusion of falling back slowly from the bulge up the two valleys to the northeast and southeast. Rommel wants to pull more Americans into the triangle they have created. Then he will strike from the south, retaking Toledo and pushing north. A second thrust will come out of Madrid itself and head to Valmojado where the two forces will meet, cutting off five American divisions. The Army of Spain will turn west and push for Talavera."

"That town is over one hundred kilometres from the present front line," said Goering.

"If the Americans are smashed in the pocket we are aiming to make, then they will have nothing to stop us for some time," said Keitel.

"Their airpower will slow, if not halt our advance. Rommel is constantly complaining that his army can't move during the day without being hit from the sky," said Goering.

"He is unfair," growled Kesselring. "US airpower grows every day and ours cannot. We are stretched too thin, however we do what we can. In this case I plan a surge of fighters and jabos to the area. The army attack will coincide with bad weather. Unfortunately, that far south, storms and clouds only last for a few days. As soon as the skies clear the Luftwaffe will hit every British and American base we can. The Allies like to use the large strips so their forces are well protected. We are even transferring a small jet force to the area for the attack, though this is only temporary. The Stormbirds are needed over Germany to protect our industry." Here Kesselring stopped and nodded at Speer. "However, a unit from JG26 and the Ar 234s from KG76 will assist in the attack. The 262s will provide fighter cover for the jet bombers. We have managed to fit two 300 litre drop tanks to the Stormbird, increasing its range. It is hoped that this massed attack will take the Allies by surprise and buy Rommel at least another three or four days where he doesn't have to worry about the Americans blasting him from the air."

"So, this would give him a week to ten days with little interference from the allied air force?" asked Goering.

"We hope so," said Keitel.

"And they won't know we are coming this time?" said Goering.

"Not from the radio. All instructions are being delivered verbally and great pains are being taken to camouflage our efforts. Indeed the aim is to give the Americans the feeling we are weakening our forces. Our intelligence services have developed various schemes which are trying to give the impression we are sending forces to Russia, not bringing them from the east."

Goering snorted at that. He still hadn't forgiven the Abwehr for its incorrect assessments of Soviet strength and missing the attack on Spain in the first place.

"Are the Spanish in on this?" asked Goering.

"Only at the highest level. Franco is completely behind the operation and wants as much of his country as possible retaken," said Keitel.

"Good, and what can you add to this offensive?" asked Goering looking at Speer.

"Well, I'm actually here to give you my predictions on production for the rest of the year. On the Spanish question I can say that over one hundred Panthers and two hundred Skoda T25s have gone to reequip the panzer units that are either in Spain, or on their way. A number of the Leningrad T34s have also been given to the Spanish to use as well. This offensive won't fail because it is under equipped," said Speer.

Goering nodded. "Alright, tell us what you think this year's production will look like."

Speer opened a folder in front of him and scanned the numbers. He didn't really need to look as many of the figures were burned into his memory. "We are looking at producing four thousand StuG3s, five thousand Panzer Fours, two thousand Skoda T25s, two thousand T34s, eight thousand Panthers, and five hundred Tiger1s. Another five hundred Royal Tigers will start to reach units in June. I also expect five hundred Jagdpanzer to start rolling off production lines in March."

"That is an impressive increase. Do you think you can reach these targets and still make as many trucks as you want?" asked Goering.

"I am still aiming for Germany to make one hundred and fifty thousand trucks. Supply is a desperate issue in Russia, as is mobility. All the generals keep telling me this. Then there are the extra locomotives, of which we plan to construct four thousand. Our goal of making ten thousand armoured personnel carriers has been increased. We are using the chassis of T34s and redesigning them to carry troops or supplies. Reports of early models say that they can deal with the Russian mud better than anything we have. It also makes up somewhat for the loss of the British equipment."

"What of new models?" asked Keitel

"There is the previously mentioned Royal Tiger and the Jagdpanzer, then there is the Puma armoured car. The Hetzer is replacing the Marder and there are various Flakpanzers now becoming available. Oh, and the army will receive ten thousand medium artillery pieces and four thousand heavy pieces. Two thousand 88mm anti-tank guns and twelve thousand 75mm guns will be constructed. While over six thousand heavy anti-aircraft guns will be made as well as twenty thousand light pieces. Four thousand Nebelwerfer rocket artillery pieces will be sent to the front as well."

"And what can the Luftwaffe expect?" asked Kesselring.

"Sixteen thousand fighters, six thousand jets, six thousand ground attack planes which will be mainly FW190s, one thousand transport planes, four thousand trainers and three hundred heavy bombers."

"Those are impressive figures," said Goering.

"Production is almost in full swing but I warn you that without more oil I won't be able to squeeze much more out of the system," said Speer. "And it also depends on keeping the US Air Force out of Germany, though I have allowed for some losses due to bombing."

"The jets and the anti-aircraft guns should do that," said Kesselring.

"And we now have a means to strike back, or soon will have," said Goering.

Speer ground his teeth. The Rocket project was a waste of resources as far as he was concerned. At least he had been able to stop the Fi103 flying bomb development. He had used reports on their vulnerability during the launching phase to convince Goering that they were a waste of time. The long ramp that needed to be built to get them into the air could be spotted and destroyed by enemy fighter-bombers. He hadn't been able to stop the A4 rockets though as they were mobile and couldn't be shot down. The spin off guided anti-air rocket projects showed promise and if they could be made to work, it might be worth the expenditure. "The first A4 should be ready to fire at London in July," he said.

"Good, that is very good. I know you don't like them Speer but we need a way to strike back. It is very costly for the Luftwaffe to raid England these days and it's Moscow or New York I want to hit," said Goering.

"We can hit the Russian capital now," said Kesselring. "America is still too far away."

"Which brings us to the JU390," said Kesselring.

Speer nodded and tried to hide his feelings. This was another waste of resources he thought. "Twelve of the bombers will be ready in June, six reconnaissance machines in May and three long range transports to fly to Japanese held China are about to take to the air. I really don't think we will have more than twenty-five at one time without it impacting heavily on other areas," said Speer.

"Twelve is enough," said Goering.

Speer wondered what he meant by that. He knew work on the super bomb project had stalled, but wondered if there was something else going on he didn't know about.

"Then there is the navy," said Speer.

"Admiral Raeder is ill, but tell me the figures anyway," said Goering.

Speer had realised a while ago that the navy was out of favour. Its moment in the sun had come with the first carrier battle off Norway and the U boat successes in 1942 and early 1943. Since then the submarines had been defeated and the surface fleet damaged or destroyed. All the carriers were sunk and only one battleship and two battle cruisers were sea worthy. If they took on the British they would be sunk in short order. Though there was a promising new type of U boat that would be ready by the end of the year.

"We will make four destroyers and one hundred and fifty U boats this year. However, the type twenty-one submarine will come into service in December if we are lucky. This is a very advanced machine. There has been little in the way of air attacks on the construction facilities, so we are ahead of schedule," said Speer.

"That is hopeful," said Goering. "It would be nice if the navy contributed something to the war soon."

"What about Raeder's idea that he forms a couple of marine divisions?" asked Keitel.

"That is stupid!" said Goering. "If he has spare men then they can go to the army where they can be properly trained. I will speak to him on the matter. Maybe it's time we trim some fat from the navy. Now we need to finish, I have a meeting with the Japanese Ambassador."

"That won't be fun. Our allies are taking a bit of a pounding in the Pacific," said Kesselring.

"They have taken some hits, that is true," said Goering. "Yet we mustn't forget just how much of the enemy they divert from us. I'll do whatever I can to help them, within reason."

"It's sometimes strange to think of Panzer Fours in China and JU88s over Darwin," said Speer.

"They want to know how the anti-tank rockets work," said Goering. "I'm probably going to send them a batch on the first JU390 flight. They were also interested in the Fritz X but I told them that electronic countermeasures had degraded the weapon system's effectiveness."

"We find that they can still be useful when deployed in large numbers," said Kesselring.

Goering grunted. "That won't last. They'll jam them somehow. The radio signals will fail and then they'll just be expensive bombs. Well, that's it gentlemen."

With that the leader of Germany rose, straightened his jacket, and walked from the room.

v

The room was warm and he was clean and happy. Nestled into his side was Larisa, her hair spread across the pillow. He smiled and remembered the long train trip back from Russia. The 101st had handed their Tigers over to the new 508th Heavy Panzer Battalion and gone on trucks to Rostov. From there they had taken the train, first to Kiev, then to Berlin. He remembered their train being diverted into a siding for half a day, as first a locomotive pulling carriages carrying Panthers and replacement troops went east, and then another pulling oil tanks from Krasnodar went west. The battalion had cursed the cold that whistled through broken windows. They had cheered when they had started to move late in the day, away from the front.

In Berlin Wolfgang had received the Knight's Cross from Goering himself. The leader of Germany was of average height and had a solid build. He had heard that the Führer had lost weight after the attack by Russia in 1942 and worked hard to keep it off. There was a slightly perfumed smell to the man, though it wasn't an unpleasant odour. His smile seemed genuine and his handshake was strong, though the hands themselves were soft. Goering had been charming and cracked jokes with him and the other SS officers receiving medals. Most had been involved in the battle on the Don bend and helped stop the Soviet offensive.

Afterwards he spoke with the other officers and found them pleasant enough, except for a Sturmbannführer. This man had dark hair and a large nose. Fritz Beirmeier was another panzer officer but in listening to him, Wolfgang found him arrogant and reckless. His feeling about the Slavs and Jews were quickly made known to the rest of the group, though Wolfgang was disappointed when those around him seemed to nod in agreement. When Germans rattled off their belief in the superiority of their blood Wolfgang couldn't help but think of Larisa. He finished his glass of champagne, and smiled and nodded through the evening with the other high-ranking officers before escaping back to the flat where she waited for him.

Now they were at his family house in the village of Unterlub in Lower Saxony. The area was surrounded by forest, but not the type he was used to seeing in Russia. Maple, chestnut and alder trees were everywhere, though they were bare at this time of year. His mother was downstairs humming and he could smell bacon and eggs cooking. This simple joy almost brought tears to his eyes.

His father wasn't home, having been sent to Hamburg for treatment for stomach ulcers. Wolfgang's mother was the only one using the cottage at the moment, his older sister and her children being in Hannover. For this he was grateful. He wanted to introduce Larisa to his family slowly and not overwhelm her. His mother was a good place to start as she had a soft heart. Ursula was known to feed stray cats and put seeds out for the birds during winter. She had been hesitant around Larisa until they sat down for dinner last night. The Russian woman had tried to keep her emotions in check but when she was served fresh white bread with lamb stew her eyes had grown wide.

"I didn't realize there was such a wealth of food in the world," Larisa had said in German. "I know your rationing is tight but there is still so much more than in Russia."

"Is that why your people attacked us?" his mother asked. It was said in such a gentle tone it took a moment for the question to sink in and then Wolfgang gave his mother a withering stare and half stood.

Larisa had put a restraining hand on his arm and then looked the older woman in the eye.

"I was told that the Soviet Union attacked Germany in order to beat you to the punch. We were also told that it was necessary to free the workers of Europe. Looking around Germany I wonder why you would want to live like we were in Russia. I understand that I have been told many lies, yet I think both sides are guilty of that," said Larisa.

"That's the truth," mumbled Wolfgang sitting once more.

"Both countries have done terrible things Frau Fischer. What Germany is doing in Russia today is shocking, and yet were Russian troops any better in East Prussia? I believe the soldiers of my country behaved terribly."

"It is true Mother, SS units collect anyone deemed to be even slightly suspect and shoot them without trial. If Germans are attacked behind the lines, random hostages are taken and hung."

His mother went pale and her eyes round.

"Your mother doesn't need to hear that, Wolfy," said Larisa. She then turned back to the older woman. "All I'm trying to say is the war is terrible and people we know die randomly. It all seems very unfair at times."

"Larisa's parents were killed in Smolensk by SS troopers," said Wolfgang.

Without thinking Ursula's hand shot out and caressed the young woman's arm.

"You poor thing," she whispered.

Larisa wiped away a tear and took the other woman's hand in her own.

"Your son saved me. He cared for me and never made any advances. Wolfy was, no is, an honourable man and the rest of his crew have followed his example. I fell in love with his strength and caring nature. This has not been easy for me as I was brought up to think of all Germans as my enemy. Your people killed my parents. Yet I have come to see you can't define a people by the actions of a few. Germans have been fed the myth of the filth of my blood, that I'm less of a human. Hopefully, someday, as a people you will see that as a lie."

"I've never believed it," said Ursula. "Too many of our neighbours were Jews and they were good people. I hated it when Wolfgang spurted Nazi nonsense, yet his father encouraged it so I stayed quiet. Now the Jews are all gone off to labour camps. It's not right."

"You will not hear me saying anything about the purity of German blood anymore," said Wolfgang.

His mother tuned to him. "Your father may be a problem." She sat back and had a good look at Larisa. "However Larisa exhibits certain attributes which may sway him."

"What do you mean?" asked Wolfgang.

"Hals is a sucker for a pretty face and this young lady who sits in front of me is close to one of the most attractive women I have ever seen. A little flattery and he will melt. I know your father and trust me, such a tactic will not fail."

Larisa smiled from ear to ear and then ate her food with a dedication Wolfgang could only admire.

It was a strange type of war on the Kalmyk Steppes. Klaus huddled in the trench with Hanno and Adlar. Rainer and Walter were out in the listening post and the rest of the company was probably

asleep. It was dark and a chill wind hissed across the snow. The

countryside around them was flat and bare. The Fort, as they were

calling it, was set on a small rise in the land. The ground then fell away

to an eroded gully that would run with spring melt when the weather

warmed. Beyond that was another low rise, and passed that, the

Russians.

The fort had been hastily constructed. Trenches had been

blasted using hand grenades and barbed wire brought in from the

Don Front. Wood was in short supply so the roofs to most of the

dugouts were canvas. Mines had been flown in on an old JU52, along

with food and ammunition. There was no airstrip but the land was flat

and the company marked out an area clear of potholes and rocks.

Klaus thought the hardest work was excavating the earthen walls to

protect the half-tracks and the kubelwagens. Two of the new T34

turretless vehicles had been delivered though Klaus didn't like them.

They were noisy, crude Russian constructions and he preferred the

German machines. Rottenführer Hugo Sommer had told him that the

Cockroach, as they were calling the new machine, was fast, well

145

protected and could cross ground that the German transport would become stuck in. "Those wide tracks are a blessing, boy," he had said.

Klaus didn't care. Like everything the Slavs made, the Cockroach was simple and rough, just like the people who made them.

The company was to stay here for a week before being rotated out and re-joining the main reaction group. The rest of the division was split into Kampfgruppen ready to throw back any Russian thrust in the area. To warn the rest of the division, a line of forts had been created to signal that any large attack was on its way. These small fire bases also sent out patrols to search the steppe for Soviet activity. The enemy had chosen the same approach and a routine of ambushes and raids was developing between the two sides. It was the same to the southeast where the 13th Panzer Division held the line. Romanian cavalry also patrolled the area along the coast of the Caspian Sea. There, among the swamps and sand dunes near the mouth of the Volga River they fought Russians on horseback.

The listening post rang in. Klaus felt for the two men huddled in a hidden fox hole almost five hundred metres from the forward trenches of the fort. They had to crawl along a narrow tunnel in the ground covered by a blankets and tarpaulins cut into strips and covered with earth. These hidden positions were very vulnerable but essential if early warning was to be given of Soviet sneak attacks. Klaus picked up the receiver.

"We have movement in front of us. At least one hundred Russians are crawling your way," said Rainer. "We are coming back in along the tunnel. Warn the company."

Klaus had been cold and sleepy but now adrenalin kicked in and he felt himself come alive.

"Rainer says the Slavs are on their way. Company strength raid he thinks," he said.

"Fire a flare and I'll get the Obersturmführer," said Hanno.

Klaus grabbed the bulky pistol and pushed the flare into the tube before pointing it at the sky and firing. A white globe arched up into the sky before bursting and falling as a bright light slowly towards the ground. Klaus shaded his eyes and looked towards the gully to see it was alive with figures. There was a roar and the Russians rose from the ground as one and charged. He snatched up his rifle and started to fire as the enemy was too far away to accurately use his submachine gun. Further along the trench a machine gun screamed into action. Mortar shells started to drop inside the fort and Klaus saw another wave of Russians appear from a fold in the ground to the east. He realised that this attack was larger than the usual raid. Then he heard the sound of tanks approaching. They were still a long way off, as the enemy couldn't have brought them too far forward without them being seen or heard, but they were moving quickly.

A man was blown into the air as the Soviets ran into the minefield. Klaus was glad they had taken the time to bury the devices in the snow. The problem was that they had so few of them. It didn't seem to slow the Russians' charge and more soldiers were killed as fire and steel erupted under their feet. The Rottenführer and Obersturmführer Sauer joined him in the trench looking dishevelled and bleary eyed. Both carried MP40s but Sommer had thought to snatch up a bag of grenades. Another group of Soviet soldiers joined the charge and Sauer's eyes widened.

"This attack is at least a battalion in strength. Schuster, get back to the radio shack and tell the division what's happening, then bring back the Panzerschreck," ordered the officer.

Hanno disappeared along the communication's trench at a jog.

Machine guns and rifles were joined by bursts from submachine guns as the Russians reached the wire. There were only two thin strands to slow them and these were swiftly cut.

"I told the boss we needed more," said Sauer as he fired a burst at the man with the wire cutters. The Russian was hit across the chest and collapsed sideways where he was hung up on an uncut strand. His companions ran through the gap he had created, throwing grenades as they came.

Klaus ducked as one of the projectiles burst just back from the lip of the trench, showering him with dirt. Rainer appeared out of the darkness with Walter carrying the FG42. He set it up on a sand bag and opened fire while his companion handed him the twenty round magazines. In front, the Russian soldiers fell like wheat before the sickle. At the other end of the line Soviets hit the trenches and became involved in vicious hand-to-hand fighting. Explosions rocked the night, and men screamed and died.

Hanno came running along the communication trench puffing and sweating. He stopped in front of Klaus gulping in air. "Heavy bastard this thing," he panted.

There was an explosion further along the trench and Walter screamed. Rainer fell backwards into the trench unconscious and his companion was looking at where his arm used to be. Klaus looked at the man horrified. Walter was missing half of his face and blood was squirting from a tear in his neck. He fell to the ground trying to put his hand over the wound but dark liquid kept pouring between his fingers.

"He has had it," said Rottenführer Sommer. "Grab the Panzerschreck and get ready, Moller!"

The T34s were sitting one hundred metres from the trench line, spraying it with machine gun and cannon fire. There were two of them and they both seemed to have a more hexagonal turret. Klaus guessed they were a newer model. He moved to a position closer to the nearest tank and away from some of the fiercest fighting, and pulled the protective mask over his head. He had seen some of the newer Panzerschrecks with the blast shield, but the version he had was an older model and to stop himself receiving any burns he needed to wear the mask. He was supposed to wear a poncho as well but had no idea where it was and hoped his thick clothing would be protection enough.

The T34 was now less than eighty metres away and had stopped moving. Klaus took careful aim and slowly pulled back the large trigger. The tube jerked on his shoulder and he was enveloped in a cloud of gas. The rocket hissed forward and struck the enemy tank on the turret where it skidded off and flew into the sky. Klaus cursed and dropped into the trench as the turret on the T34 turned in his direction. Machine gun bullets tore up the top of the trench as he scrambled to a new position fifty metres further on. Hanno caught up to him there and reloaded the Panzerschreck. Klaus stood and took careful aim at the hull. The second rocket hit just below the machine gunner's position where it exploded. The tank hatches flew open and men exited the vehicle quickly before fire burst from the openings. Only three men made it clear.

The second tank fired its main gun at a sandbagged machine gun post, as Russian infantry threw grenades. Klaus jogged with Hanno to where dead Russians lay heaped on the top of the trench. He pushed the leg of one of the Soviet soldiers out of the way and took aim at the side of the oncoming T34. The range was over one hundred metres, but the tank was clearly silhouetted against the skyline by the glare of burning huts and the illumination provided by the steady rain of parachute flares. He fired and the rocket smashed into the side of the turret where there was a bright flash. An internal detonation, followed by an intense fire rocked the T34. The Russians near the burning vehicle started to fall back.

Klaus dropped back into the trench and let out a long breath. He placed the 'Stove Pipe' against the side of the trench and picked up his Papasha submachine gun and grinned at Hanno. Both of them stood and jogged a few metres along the trench. Then a grenade fell behind them.

Hanno yelled for them to drop as earth showered over them. Two more explosions followed and Klaus felt something hot lance into his calf. His friend was pulling him up and dragged him another dozen paces before three more grenades filled the area behind them with flame and iron. If they hadn't moved both of them would have died. The gentle curve of the trench had meant they were around a slight corner away from the detonations. Russians sprang into the trench behind them and Hanno fired his rifle from the hip, hitting one of the men in the chest. Klaus then opened up with his submachine gun. He saw his bullets chew into both Russians. Exit wounds burst from their backs spraying the trench walls with blood. A Soviet soldier jumped from above them, bringing a spade down on Hanno's helmeted head. There was a loud clang and his friend dropped to his knees. The Russian turned, swinging the trenching tool at Klaus. He brought up the submachine gun by instinct and the spade struck it on the magazine before glancing away. The force of the blow pulled the weapon from his hand and Klaus staggered back a step. The Russian swung again but missed, hitting the trench wall instead. Klaus sprang forward and grabbed the spade and both men started wrestling. He

153

could see the man's eyes were the same blue as his own. The soldier

was young, probably the same age as Klaus. The Soviet brought his

knee up, hitting him between his legs. It was a glancing blow but still

enough to send Klaus to his knees. The Russian raised the spade

above his head and then there were two shots. The man fell forward

onto Klaus' shoulder before falling face first into the dirt at the

bottom of the trench. Behind him Hanno stood holding a smoking

M1911 pistol. He had taken the weapon off a dead Soviet officer only

two weeks earlier and liked the accuracy of the American gun.

Klaus just stared at his friend and tried to ignore the pain

between his legs.

"You're welcome," said Hanno.

The Russian attack ebbed away from the trenches before

fading back into the darkness. The night was lit by the single burning

T34 and the crackle of flames, and the moaning of wounded soldiers

overrode the sound of the wind. Klaus started to feel the cold again,

marvelling at how it had seemed to disappear when he was in

combat. Hanno was walking around shooting wounded Russians when the Rottenführer stopped him.

"Just leave them to freeze, they'll all be dead in the morning," he said.

Klaus felt exhausted and wanted to sleep but the Obersturmführer wanted the wire restrung. Personally he thought it was a waste of time as the Russians had taken such a beating it was unlikely that they would return tonight. Hundreds of them lay dead or wounded before the trenches.

"Eight dead, twelve wounded, four of them seriously, sir," Hugo Sommer reported to the commanding officer.

Sauer wiped his brow and nodded. "It could have been worse. I was just on the radio and heard that the Russians attacked three more posts like ours. The second company just held on and the third company hasn't answered. A group has been sent to see what happened to them."

"Do they think this is the start of a Russian push, sir?" asked Sommer.

"No, the enemy just appears to have used infantry and a few tanks. They are just messing with us."

"Well we made them pay here, sir."

"We did, but the Russians seem to have a bottomless supply of men. We kill them and more just appear."

Klaus heard this and realised that Hitler's warnings about the Slavs were true; they bred like rats. He sighed when he thought of the great man's death. Goering seemed a little soft on Germany's racial enemies. He understood that the Baltic States had traces of German blood, but he had heard of Ukrainian divisions forming and that just didn't feel right. In the end it didn't matter, he would keep killing Russians until there weren't any left.

Chapter Six: February 1944

The weather had turned, with sleet coming down across the fields at an angle. This is when Charlie most wished the M8 had a roof. The canvas they had tied in position over the top of the open turret just didn't do the job. It was cold but he supposed he was mostly dry. The 25th Cavalry Reconnaissance Squadron was slightly back from the front line where the 4th Armoured pushed forward against weakening resistance. They were just outside the town of Titulcia. Here the river valley split with the Jarma river continuing towards Madrid, and the smaller Tujna flowing onto it from the east. They were less than a mile from the town where the infantry was trying to push out the Spanish paramilitary. These half-trained boys were brave but poorly equipped. They would soon have to retreat.

Charlie watched the rain and smiled thinking about his medal. He couldn't believe that the army thought he had acted heroically at the ambush back in December. He had been recommended for the Bronze Star, as had the sarge. His quick thinking had been brought about by naked fear, yet it had led to a positive result. Renwood was the one who deserved a medal. He had turned them around and led the counterattack. Maybe the army was desperate for heroes.

A and B troop had gathered in a small group of trees by the river. The rain eased slightly. Then the bombardment started. Shells started to come down on the forward units and a mortar battery, which was dug in only two hundred yards away. Men jumped from their vehicles into foxholes that were knee deep in water. Charlie was lucky as Sergeant Renwood had insisted they drive the M8 over the top of their hole. He found Catinza and Smokey Gunroy already in there and had to squeeze in next to them.

"Where's the sarge?" he yelled over the noise.

The two men shrugged and covered their ears. Shells came closer and they heard shrapnel pinging from the side of the M8. After five minutes the barrage moved on.

Charlie lifted his head and listened. There were screams coming from the mortar position which made him appreciate that the armoured cars hadn't been the target.

"What's going on?" asked Catinza. "I thought the Jerries were on the run."

Smokey had no idea but when he heard the rumble of tank engines he pulled himself from his hole and headed out into the light rain. The sound of fighting in Titulcia suddenly grew louder and to the east of the town a line of strange tanks could be seen advancing. A dripping Sargeant Renwood appeared next to him and stared at the scene with his Westinghouse binoculars.

"T34s, I heard the Germans were using them; the Italians as well. These ones have German markings," said the big man. "Our pop guns will be useless against them."

"What's going on, sarge?" asked Charlie.

"Some sort of counterattack I guess. We'll get on the radio and whistle up the 37th and their Shermans."

The M8s were started and Lieutenant Michaelson soon sent a message over the radio. "We have to pull back. The armour is locked in combat with German StuGs. The attack is wide spread and we are on our own."

They pulled out and fell back passed the mortar platoon. The men here were loading wounded onto jeeps and getting ready to leave when more German artillery came down. Charlie was driving over the sodden field when a jeep carrying four men and a wounded man on a stretcher, disintegrated in front of him.

"Get us out of here," yelled Renwood, and Charlie put his foot down before turning onto a dirt road that ran next to the river. They accelerated away from the carnage driving quickly towards the southwest.

v

Two days later the unit was travelling with armour and motorised infantry in the small railway town of Algodor. They had fallen back over forty miles and all was chaos. Units of the 4th Armoured were mixed in with units of the 34th Infantry Division and even some soldiers from the 9th Infantry Division were present. Charlie and his squadron had six M8s, nine jeeps and four half-tracks in their little group. They had also picked up two M7 Priest self-propelled artillery pieces on the retreat from Titulcia. From what

Charlie could work out, the Germans had used the severe weather to mount an offensive which aimed to cut off the American forces advancing to the south of Madrid. Scuttlebutt had the Germans at Yuncos to the north, though some soldiers said they had reached as far as Bargas, only five miles from Toledo. The southern attack, which mainly seemed to be comprised of SS troops was definitely at Nambroca and were pushing north. There were Germans just outside Villasequilla and the 25th Panzer Grenadier Division, which had hit them originally was moving west down the valley towards the small village of Villemejor. Four US divisions were being squeezed into a triangle which was probably twenty five miles along each front. The Big Red One US Infantry Division was holding somewhere to the north.

Charlie was unaware that Clarke had already put together a force to rescue the situation. The General had been caught out by the German attack but had responded with his usual energy. The 3rd Armoured Division had been pulled from the line north of Madrid and had moved quickly to Lominchar on the German's flank and was about to attack while the 2nd Armoured had been rushed from reserve and had advanced to the Guadarrama river just to the west of the main enemy thrust. Clarke was gathering other units to pressure the German flank but the problem was the southern thrust. Here the Germans were using the 9th SS, 21st Panzer and the 1st SS Panzer Divisions as well as a Tiger battalion and a mountain division to attack. The Northern thrust was an all Wehrmacht affair with the 23rd and 2nd Panzer Divisions as well as the 89th and 11th Infantry Divisions attacking. The Germans were guarding their flank with the 90th Panzer Grenadier Division reinforced with the 655th Heavy Anti-tank Battalion and its Hornets.

It was misty and light rain continued to fall on and off, yet Charlie had heard the weather would clear tomorrow. By God he hoped it would. They really needed the air force to help them. He sat under the overhang of a veranda and across the road he could see the wreckage of a train at the railway station. The wagons were overturned and the locomotive was twisted on its side. General Wood appeared, walking from a large house and he turned to talk to a major. Then he looked at the line of vehicles that made up Charlie's little group. He gestured at Lieutenant Michaelson and the man trotted over and saluted.

"Son, are your boys up for a fight?" asked the older man. The General had a reputation of leading from the front and was known for arguing with Patton. He would pace back and forth while fighting with his army commander, and so had earned the nick-name Tiger Jack.

"Of course, sir!" answered Michaelson.

Charlie didn't like the sound of this.

"I have a dozen Shermans, some M10s and two companies of infantry and we are going to Villasequilla to stop the Nazis. We have to give them a bloody nose or they'll cut the valley in two and trap our boys, who are further up the valley to the east."

"My command is itching for a fight," said Michaelson.

Just shut up lieutenant, thought Charlie.

"Good, wait here and make sure you have all the ammo and fuel you need. I'm trying to gather another unit to come as well, but it's a mess right now," said the general.

They sat near their vehicles for over an hour before a column of Shermans appeared from the east. Other units filtered in and Charlie noted the general had found a battery of three inch guns from somewhere. The mixed unit headed the ten miles to Villasequilla in the early afternoon. It should have been a half hour journey but the road was clogged with fleeing Americans. Jeeps and trucks were mixed up with half-tracks and even the odd tank. The general managed to sweep up four of these into his command. He berated men who continued to run and even threatened to shoot a captain, who broke down in tears. In disgust he waved the man away and ordered his mixed unit southeast.

Charlie heard the fleeing soldiers speak of flamethrowers and indestructible tanks with cannons like telegraph poles. They said the SS had swept all before it and their armour blew Shermans apart at over a mile's range. Nebelwerfers had pounded dug in infantry and the American artillery had been caught in the initial bombardment and heavily damaged. The retreating soldiers complained of ammunition shortages, lack of support, and said they were running out of fuel. The abandoned trucks and half-tracks by the side of the road suggested there was at least some truth in the last rumour.

The journey took close to two hours. A pair of jeeps raced down the road. Then an officer jumped out and ran to the general who spoke briefly to the man. Apparently the Americans still held the town but the Germans were trying to flank them from the northeast. Not far from the column's position was a grain silo and a small hill. The ground dipped away gently to the east and it was very open with only a few olive groves breaking up the landscape, as well as the odd farmhouse. General Wood ordered four armoured cars onto the hill with the rest screening the country to their left. The infantry went into town to reinforce the troops there and the Priest self-propelled artillery went with them. The armour gathered behind the grain silo and the low hills. Charlie drove his M8 onto the forward slope feeling terribly exposed. There wasn't a scrap of cover but at least the misty rain limited visibility to just under a mile.

They hadn't been on the hill long and had only just managed to drag a light coloured tarpaulin over the M8 when Sergeant

Renwood swore. He was peering through the mist when three powerful looking armoured cars drove forward. They had eight wheels and were camouflaged in white paint with brown splotches.

"What are they?" asked Smokey.

"New Puma armoured cars. The have a powerful 50mm gun that will go through our plate like it was paper," said Renwood.

"That's a cheery thought," said Catinza.

"Shut up and get the gun ready," said Renwood. "Our gun can still make holes in them if we let them get to within five hundred yards."

Charlie heard the conversation with a sense of impending dread. These were SS armoured cars. The 1st SS was supposed to be attacking Villasequilla. The best of the German Reich was coming their way. He glanced up and saw Renwood speaking into the radio. More armoured cars were moving east around the hill. It was hard to pick out the sound of the engines due to the continuing battle which was only a mile away.

"Five hundred yards, Sarge," said Catinza.

"Fire when ready," said Renwood.

The gun cracked and the shell kicked up a puff of dust next to the German Puma. The German commander was standing in the turret and immediately spotted their location. His vehicle instantly accelerated but suddenly veered sideways as a large tyre on the left hand side twisted and came apart. Lieutenant Michaelson had fired and his gunner was more accurate than Catinza. The Puma twisted, sliding on the loose earth. It almost tipped over but then came to a halt side on to the position of Charlie's M8. The crew hastily abandoned their armoured car and scrambled into a nearby ditch.

The other two Pumas opened fire and Sergeant Matherson's M8 was hit. It was further down the slope, and for some reason the crew hadn't tried to camouflage their armoured car. Charlie saw the 50 mm shell rip into the front of the open topped turret and then punch a hole through the back of the plate armour. Then the M8 was burning. None of the crew got out.

"Oh my god," said Charlie.

Catinza's next shot punched into the closest Puma dead centre, just below the driver's viewing port. Smoke began to billow from the hatches almost immediately. Two coughing Germans emerged from the vehicle and staggered away.

"Finish them with the MG," ordered Renwood. Before Catinza could fire Charlie slammed the M8 into reverse and gunned it up the gentle slope, throwing clods of dirt from the tyres.

"What the hell?" yelled the sergeant.

Then Lieutenant Michaelson's M8 blew up in a flash of fire and metal.

"Tanks," screamed Charlie.

Emerging from the mist, which was now thinning, were monsters the like Charlie had never seen. He had spotted the huge bulk of the first Tiger as it moved quickly over the Spanish countryside and hadn't waited for orders. One of the enormous tanks had stopped and fired a high explosive shell which had destroyed his commanders M8. Now six more had come thundering out of the haze.

They were so much bigger than any US tank he had ever seen with guns that stuck out in front of the vehicle like small pine trees. Charlie swerved the M8 and an explosion rocked the armoured car. Dirt and shrapnel bounced from the steel and Charlie heard red hot metal whizzing through the air. The Tigers were firing at them. He changed direction again and another shell exploded to their left. The M8 rocked as the pressure of the blast pushed at it. Again metal screeched off their armour. Charlie often felt fear but this was something else. He felt his bladder go and warm liquid ran down his legs into his boots.

Then they were over the hill.

Sergeant Renwood was on the radio to General Wood's command group warning them of what was coming and Charlie saw the Shermans take position. A Group seemed to be driving east and he thought maybe they were running until the Sergeant spoke.

"General's trying to flank the Nazis; hope it works."

The three-inch guns were being readied by their crews near the wheat silo and jeeps were driving into cover when the first Tiger came over the hill. It stopped eight hundred yards away and was struck

almost immediately by six anti-tank rounds. Charlie was amazed as all

of them broke up in the Tiger's frontal armour. He had parked the M8

behind a silo and watched the encounter with the rest of his crew

from the edge of the structure. Charlie felt like he was a macabre

spectator at a very dangerous sporting event. Fifty yards away an

M10 tank destroy fired and another round stuck the Tiger, this one

tearing the track loose, sending it curling away from the vehicle like

an enraged python and forcing the monster to stop. Usually when this

happened a crew would abandon their tank. These men did no such

thing; instead they shot back. The first round from the Tiger's gun hit

a Sherman on the road, ripping its turret off in a shower of sparks.

The driver and the radio operator crawled from the smoking hull and

limped across the road to the silo.

Then the other Tigers started to appear. One was hit in the

belly as it crested the hill. The lucky shot punched into the crew

compartment, killing the driver and wounding the loader. A small fire

started and the commander quickly abandoned the vehicle with another man. Then there was an internal explosion that caused a sheet of flame to roar from the open hatches on the turret.

But the Tigers hit back. In no time six Shermans were burning or missing their turrets. The M10s were targeted by H.E. rounds as were the three-inch guns. Charlie looked around and saw carnage. The gun crews were torn apart by the force of the 88mm shells and the surviving tank crews had horrible burns. Some staggered around in shock and soon the medics were overwhelmed. Charlie soon found himself helping carry a stretcher back to a jeep. The man who lay on it was covered in blood and was missing his right hand. Nearby, another anti-tank gun disappeared in a large explosion and men screamed. Charlie hunched his shoulders and placed the stretcher across the back of the jeep. Soon the vehicle was driving away back to the north where a field hospital had been established just outside Algodor. Charlie wished he was going with them.

When he returned to the M8 he saw two Tigers had been knocked out. Sergeant Renwood pointed to the east. "The Shermans that took a flanking position have been firing into the weaker armour on the Germans' side."

As Charlie watched he saw the Germans slowly reverse back up the slope and onto the other side of the hill. Four of the huge tanks remained on the slope in front of him, two of them belching smoke.

"We stopped them," he muttered.

"Yeh, but the cost was high," said Renwood. "Only one three-inch gun remains and we lost nine Shermans and all four of the M10s. Of our troop, only we remain." the sergeant glanced down at Charlie's crutch. "Why don't you go and get changed. I think we've got a short respite."

He felt ashamed and nodded.

Renwood must have seen the expression because he shook his head. "Nothing to be ashamed of. Matter of fact you did a good job today. If you hadn't taken off when you did, we would be up on that hill like the lieutenant. Your sharp eyes saved our lives."

Yes, but for how long, thought Charlie.

V

The jet wallowed in the air under the weight of the drop tanks, yet Oberleutnant Kurt Osser recognized they were a necessary evil. If they were to cover the bombers as they headed south, then they needed the extra range to stay with them. They were actually covering a staffel of JU88cs that was going to hit the US fighter base at Salamanca. They tried to cruise at a lower speed than normal through the predawn light. He had ten Stormbirds and all of them had been extensively briefed about today's attack.

Yesterday at about noon the weather had started to break up. From what Kurt could gather Rommel's attack had gone well, but the jaws of the trap had yet to snap shut on the Americans. By the end of the previous day the allied air force had been able to mount a number of attacks on the advancing Germans. Clarke had sent two divisions against the attack which had pushed south for Toledo. Vicious fighting had stopped the Wehrmacht's thrust at Yuncler and Yunclillos, though a thrust across country by Major von Luck's 125th Panzer Grenadier Regiment had taken Magan. Only a ten-kilometre gap existed between the two German thrusts and a lot depended on whether the SS could take Toledo. If it fell then the southern thrust could push north and the Americans would be trapped. For that to happen the Luftwaffe needed to neutralise the allied air force, at least for two or three days.

At Spanish airbases and some even in France, German planes had taken off before dawn and headed for the enemy airstrips. Kurt wasn't to know that many groups had lost their way but pilot training was still good in the Luftwaffe and many units had been directed by specially assigned pathfinder aircraft. The anti-aircraft batteries had been warned not to shoot down their own side but some mistakes were still made. Kurt heard that six FW190As had been destroyed flying near Madrid by a unit of 37mm guns which hadn't received the order to be extremely careful on this particular morning.

As it was his unit flew south until eight P38 Lightning were spotted. The sun had crept above the horizon, but not by much. The American fighters dived in from slightly above Kurt's formation. He gave orders and his staffel released their drop tanks. Then they slowly eased the throttles forward. The Stormbirds started to pick up speed and Kurt led them straight at the Americans. Within a few seconds the two formations were on top of each other, the P38s firing first. The closing speed was so fast that neither side scored any hits, however a novice American pilot made an error of judgement and held his line for too long. His plane collided with a jet with such force that both planes disappeared in a massive explosion.

Kurt turned his plane in the vertical, using its speed to loop over the top and come around for another attack. The lines of the jet were very clean so high-speed turns didn't bleed away the plane's velocity with the same quickness that occurred for prop driven machines. The trick was not to engage in low-speed turning competitions with the enemy. He came out of his loop to find the sky full of planes heading in different directions.

"You still with me Hessler?" he called into the radio.

"Always, sir," came the answer.

The jet came around behind a P38 which was by itself. He dived in behind it and fired a short burst. The slow thump, thump of the

30mm cannons filled his ears and he watched as two shells tore off the Lightning's port wing. He curved around in a long loop and looked for the JU88s. Kurt spotted them below and noticed two P38s heading in their direction. He led his wingman in a dive after them and caught the enemy machines just as they opened fire. The gunner on the last JU88 was firing back but his brave defence couldn't save his plane. The concentrated firepower of the Lightning tore into the fuselage of the Luftwaffe machine and it fell from the formation pouring smoke and flames. Kurt fired at the American, hoping to gain some measure of revenge, but the range was too great. His wingman was in a better position and he shot down the other American with two bursts.

They climbed above the JU88 formation and turned again looking for enemy machines. The Americans had gone and Kurt guided the Stormbirds back to him, though in the end he only managed to gather six machines. One had been shot down, two were damaged and flying home, and a third was lost and Kurt told the pilot to fly north until he picked up a landmark. He glanced at his fuel gauge and saw they still had enough to get to the target with the heavy fighter-bombers.

When the allied air base came into view he could see enemy machines lining up to become airborne. Realising there was no time to waste, he led his jets into a dive. They needed to disrupt the take-off of the American fighters and allow the Ju88s time to attack. His squadron had the faster aircraft so he came in quickly.

It was a ragged attack but it had the desired effect. His jet was moving at over eight hundred and seventy kilometres per hour when it opened fire. The 30mm cannons mounted in the nose of his plane weren't really meant for strafing but the enemy fighters were lined up like ducks on a shooting range. The American planes were big P47s and they were loaded with bombs for today's attacks on German targets. His shells tore apart the first one in the row waiting to become airborne and the machine exploded as full fuel tanks were pierced and the bombs beneath went off. The other six jets all created similar results and the line of P47s was halted by wrecked aircraft and burning fuel. Then the Ju88s arrived. First they dropped their bombs on the lines of P47s and then they strafed the dispersal areas with machine guns and 20mm cannons. Kurt could only marvel at the number of explosions. As he climbed away he hoped the other attacks had been as successful as their own.

The result of the Luftwaffe surprise attack that February day were mixed. Some allied bases were devastated and others were barely touched. It all depended on when the German fighter-bombers reached their target, or if they even got there at all. In some cases, groups of fighters from both sides met and huge dog fights ensued in which heavy losses occurred. In the end, the Allies lost over three hundred and fifty aircraft on the ground and another thirty-two in the air. The Luftwaffe lost two hundred and twenty-five planes and another forty-four came back with varying states of battle damage. The operation was a partial success as the allied air forces were unable to significantly impact the ground operations that day. The next day the Luftwaffe tried to throw a protective net above the battlefield with varying degrees of success. Both sides lost another fifty machines and many American fighter-bomber attacks were turned back. Attempts by allied B25 Mitchell medium bombers to attack German positions were prevented by a low-level attack on their airfield by Ar 234 jet bombers. These aircraft dropped canister bombs which ripped open the American machines as they readied themselves for take-off. Other B25s from different airstrips continued their raid on the SS, attacking Toledo but their numbers were halved. Then they met a determined attack by Re 2005s flown by Spanish pilots. This further disrupted the American raid.

Yet as the week dragged on, the Luftwaffe found it difficult to maintain the high level of sorties. There were just too many allied aircraft. Even with Italian and Spanish help the Luftwaffe was ground down, but they had bought the Wehrmacht the time it needed. The trap snapped shut at Bargas the day after the surprise attack.

Spain was supposed to be sunny and up until today it hadn't been. That had all changed with the dawn light. Wolfgang had heard that the American air force would greet this day with swarms of jabos, yet the sky remained surprising clear. His Tiger was idling just outside Toledo. They had crossed the pontoon bridge during the night, the structure straining under the weight of the heavy panzer. The Americans were still holding out in the large town so it had been decided to bypass the built up area to the east. There were minor roads that ran around the edge of Toledo and so all the SS needed to do was to clear enough rubble on the outskirts to make using these roads safe. The 101st SS Heavy Panzer Battalion had been ordered to support the infantry in their efforts to clear the area of Americans.

It had been a sudden shift for his unit from their rest in Germany to go to Spain, but the 1st SS had been pulled from Russia and reequipped to help Rommel's offensive against the Americans. His battalion had received new Tiger tanks and half-tracks as well as four anti-aircraft panzers.

It had been hard saying goodbye to Larisa but his mother promised she would take good care of her. His father had been very disapproving of his future wife to start with, but his mother had been correct about the older man's susceptibility to Larisa's beauty. He chuckled at the thought. Were all men so shallow? His sister had been the problem. Years of indoctrination at Hitler youth camps had left her with an ingrained hatred of Slavs and Jews. In the end his father had made it clear Larisa was welcome in his house and his sister had been forced to swallow her pride.

Shaking himself, Wolfgang cleared his head. He looked at the building in front of him through powerful Doppelfernrohr 6x30 glasses. Fighting with Tigers in built up areas was a nightmare. The large gun and size of the vehicle made the panzer difficult to manoeuvre among the buildings, and the Americans had bazookas. These smaller versions of the Panzerschreck couldn't penetrate the frontal armour of a Tiger but were still dangerous from the rear or sides. At least they would have plenty of infantry support. Wolfgang was determined he would only use the Tiger to blast American strong points. He wasn't going anywhere in that town until the streets had been swept clear by the infantry first.

The battalion had taken a number of losses to get where it was. The fight outside Villasequilla had been a tough one and he had been forced to abandon his panzer after the Americans had blown off the track. At first, he had stayed with the machine and they had destroyed three enemy tanks, taking their tally to one hundred enemy panzers. When they returned the following day the Americans were gone, though they had blown up his stranded Tiger before leaving. The 1ˢᵗ SS had then crossed the Rio, leaving most of the fighting around Toledo to the 9ᵗʰ SS. Now they were going to skirt the river and the city, and eventually drive on Bargas twelve kilometres to the north. There they hoped to link up with units of the 21ˢᵗ Panzer Division who were pushing across from Magan.

Overhead aircraft appeared and as soon as they did, aerial combat ensued. Wolfgang could see the twisting vapour trails far above him. He had no way of knowing Italian Fiat 2005s were duelling with American P47s and holding their own. Further north BF 109s were bounced by P38s, losing four planes in quick succession. None of that mattered to Wolfgang as long as the planes stayed up there and none of them came towards his Tiger.

Soon an Obersturmführer was guiding them forward. Wolfgang led his panzer and Oberscharführer Peter Kisters' Tiger 312 up a slope and into town. He had taken over Tiger 311, though Untersturmführer Alfred Gunther hadn't been very pleased when told to leave his vehicle. SS troopers from the 1st Regiment trotted along in front of them as the ground levelled out. Ahead, a block of flats dominated a small market square.

The Obersturmführer climbed onto the turret and came next to Wolfgang. "There is an American platoon holed up in that building with some heavy machine guns. We need you to blast them out."

Wolfgang nodded and gave Franz the order. He warned the SS soldiers near the Tiger to get clear and then the gun roared. The building in front of them collapsed after four shells, and the SS soldiers rushed forward. A machine gun opened up on the troopers from a smaller building and two men fell. Wolfgang told Franz of the new target and soon it had been destroyed, or the MG team had relocated. The SS soldiers stormed the wrecked flats and secured the area before leading the pair of Tigers slowly forward. Wolfgang looked at the wreckage and was glad he hadn't been forced to fire on the Santa Iglesia Cathedral or the Palacio de Galiana. He had heard that the old city had been extensively damaged with the narrow streets and thick-walled buildings of the area proving very difficult to take. Out here in the northeastern suburbs the going was a little easier. The city had taken some damage in 1936 when the Nationalists had raised the siege of the Alcázar. The damage to the historic city this time was much worse. They cleared another street when a rocket streaked towards Tiger 311. It exploded on the front just next to the driver's slit but didn't penetrate. The SS soldiers located the position where the bazooka had been fired from and hosed the spot with bullets from an MG42. Franz then hit the small garden where the rocket had streaked from with a high explosive shell. A radio message came through.

Wolfgang was relieved that the remains of his company had been told to withdraw. The edge of the town was now in German hands. The 2nd SS Panzer Grenadier Regiment had found a road leading from Azucaica going north to Bargas, and Kampfgruppe Peiper had made its way around the edge of the town towards Olias del Ray. There was resistance to the 2nd Regiment's move but the SS troopers were accompanied by forty Panthers and twelve Hummel self-propelled artillery pieces that blasted the Americans from their path. The high ground to the northeast of Toledo had also been captured, helping make it possible to bypass the town's centre. The two arms of Rommel's offensive were soon to join.

It had been something akin to his worst nightmare. Private Charlie Winklen had seen men blown up and burnt, had seen friends killed horribly and had witnessed a US army wrecked. Yet somehow General Wood had pulled together twenty Shermans and thirty other assorted armoured vehicles to make the breakout attempt. There seemed to be every sort of transportation available to the US army at present. The artillery were somewhere behind them firing off the last of their ammunition before they would join the rear-guard, as the long column of vehicles tried to break through the German lines.

Between Olias del Ray and Cabanas de la Sangra there was a wide plain held by a thin smattering of German infantry. The American column had to push through ten miles of enemy-held country until they reached the line of low hills south of Yunclillos. Every inch of that country was visible to surrounding batteries of German artillery. The biggest threat was from Magdan where the 21st

Panzer Division held the village. Here the Germans occupied villages that were only four miles apart. Then there was more difficult country in front of them. Small fire bases of German troops had been set up along the line of retreat, which the Americans would have to overwhelm.

Trucks stopped and had their petrol syphoned before being either abandoned or destroyed. Fuel was in short supply, as was ammunition and food. Medicine had almost run out and there was no morphine to ease the pain of the wounded. Charlie had managed to fill the petrol tank of their M8 and his crew had still found themselves attached to an escort group which accompanied General Wood everywhere. Three jeeps, a pair of half-tracks filled with exhausted infantry and two battered Shermans were all that remained of their little group, but these men had tried to help the General enforce his will. Now they were held up before a small farmhouse equal distance between the German held town and a village which had been fortified by the enemy.

"The General says we have to clear those Germans," said Sergeant Renwood.

"It's a lot of open country and they are bound to call in artillery support," said Private Catinza.

"Nevertheless it has to be done," repeated Renwood. It will soon be nightfall and we need to be passed Magan by then. We have to keep this mob moving or the column will fall apart. As it is we are very exposed and have been since leaving Mocejon. Only the artillery has kept the Nazis off our backs and they will soon run out of shells."

"Why don't they help us Sarge?" asked Smokey Gunroy.

"Because, as I just said, they are doing another job," snarled Renwood.

Charlie was surprised by the sergeant's response, as he was usually very level headed. He supposed they were all tired. Who was he kidding; they were hungry, exhausted and strung out. Charlie had managed to snatch maybe four hours broken sleep in the last three days. It was to be expected then that the Sarge would flare up when asked stupid questions.

The general charged over to them and yelled that they move forward. The Shermans drove towards the house and started firing and the Germans replied. A Pak 40 fired and one of the tanks erupted in flames. Renwood opened up with the fifty calibre machine gun and mortar shells exploded around the enemy trenches. American soldiers rushed forward and soon the German position was overrun. As Charlie breathed a sigh of relief he heard a sound like an approaching express train. What he wasn't to know was that the Hummels, that had travelled to Olias del Ray with the 2nd SS Panzer Regiment, had received firing coordinates from the commanding officer in the farmhouse just before he was knocked out by a flying piece of masonry.

As 150mm howitzer shells started landing around the head of the column, trucks and men were thrown into the air. Charlie saw General Wood dash to a radio and then the remnants of four US division, or at least those the General had managed to gather, moved forward. The M8 bumped over the muddy field as the shells blew olive trees to splinters around them. Charlie caught a glimpse of the General's jeep and wondered how they weren't hit. Then as they approached a small dirt road that ran east west across their path the firing slackened. It was getting dark and possibly the enemy artillery had lost track of them, however it was more likely that the Hummels were short on ammunition. The night closed in on the column and it split in two, one group losing contact with the leading elements. At the same time, the 34th US Infantry Division was trying to escape around the northern side of Magan, distracting the enemy.

All through the night the column broke up as it crashed into groups of Germans in the dark. Four enemy armoured cars were destroyed in one brief but violent encounter. Three American soldiers were killed at the same time and a half-track lost. The general urged his shrinking group to continue until they could hear the sound of fighting to the west.

"Those are our boys," he told the soldiers as he drove passed in his jeep. "That's the direction we need to go."

They didn't know it, but after a night of fighting and driving, the remaining troops under General Wood had almost reached the Guadarrama River. They were only a mile short of their own troops when they crashed into the T25 Skoda Cheetahs of the 23rd Panzer Division. These tanks were facing west but had turned their engines off and so heard the approach of the Sherman tanks and M3 half-tracks. There was only a single company of enemy tanks but it was enough to create havoc.

The night had been chaos for the Germans as it was for the Americans, with units running through their thinly held lines and other US divisions attacking from the west. The panzers fired parachute flares and then hesitated, unsure if the approaching column was friend or foe. The Americans didn't wait but they could barely see their targets. Charlie's M8 was up front and saw a Cheetah fire hitting an M3 half-track, which exploded in a rain of metal and body parts. Catinza fired and then cursed as his 37mm shells bounced from the T25s sloped armour. One of the enemy tanks fired three shells in quick succession and Charlie wondered how the Germans loaded their 75mm gun so quickly. Three armour piercing shells hit a Sherman on the front, punching holes into the interior of the tank. It burst into flames with a roar and lit up the surrounding plains. This panzer had been equipped with one of the new self-loading guns that used compressed air to clean the barrel. The gun was still in the development phase and often didn't work after a few shots, which is exactly what happened to this panzer. Another Cheetah fired three more shells which hit a half-track in the side. All of them were anti-tank rounds and punched three fist sized holes through the vehicle's thin armour. One man inside the M3 was cut in half but the other soldiers all lived and the half-track continued operating.

General Wood's jeep drove rapidly passed Charlie's vision slip and then rocked to a halt near the offending T25. The general jumped from the back of the vehicle with a bazooka and took aim at the German tank from only fifty yards. There was a flash and the rocket streaked into the side of the Cheetah, exploding with a thump. The crew of the panzer promptly abandoned their vehicle and ran off into the darkness with General Wood firing at them with his pistol. Suddenly the jeep was raked by machine gun fire and the driver was hit. A second man, probably a young officer, tried to pull the dead man off the steering wheel and the general ran to help him. A T25 drove out of the gloom and fired a round from it 75mm gun. This panzer wasn't using the new gun system and its high explosive round hit the side of the jeep just above the front tyre. The explosion tore the vehicle apart and General Wood was thrown backwards onto the ground.

A Sherman fired from the darkness and the T25 was hit in the gap between the turret and the hull. It smashed into the tank causing a fire that trapped the Germans and left them screaming. The sound was horrible but part of Charlie enjoyed it. These men had killed the general and their end was a type of revenge. The Americans recovered General Wood's body, lying it across the rear deck of the M8 and then drove for the river. Not far away the attacking US 3rd Armoured Division had created a number of penetrations in the German's line through which most of the survivors of the 4th Division were able to escape.

v

"It was a great victory," said Goering holding up his glass of champagne.

"Many Americans escaped," said Rommel.

Goering pursed his lips. "Don't kill the moment, Herr Field Marshal. This is the first time we have defeated the Amis so let's enjoy the moment."

Rommel's face remained impassive but he sipped his drink.

"Thirty-five thousand prisoners are not to be sneezed at. Not much by the standards of the Russian front, but we know the war in the south is a different kettle of fish," said Goering.

"Forty thousand escaped," said Rommel.

"We took five hundred working trucks, two hundred half-tracks and the same amount of jeeps. We captured fifty tanks and one hundred guns. Stop being so hard on yourself, Herr Field Marshal. We have rocked the Allies. There are rumours that the Americans are not very happy about the lack of British assistance during the Battle of Toledo. Montgomery didn't get his armour to attack until the fourth day of our offensive, and then it made little progress due to the terrain he chose to move through."

"General Clarke reacted quickly and nearly stopped the two arms of the pincers from meeting. His counterattacks were well placed and caused many casualties. My follow-up offensive towards Torrijos has made very little ground and the SS thrust towards Talavera was halted after an advance of ten kilometres," said Rommel.

"Madrid is safe, for now, and Franco is happy for once. I need the line to hold in Spain while I tackle Russia. If we take Moscow this summer, maybe the Russians will sue for a favourable peace. Then we can finish the Allies in the west," said Goering.

"Reinforce me and I'll drive the Americans back to the sea now," said Rommel.

Goering sighed and shock his head. "The effort it took for the Luftwaffe to buy you three days almost free of interference from the enemy air force exhausted them. We still have too few jets and the enemy probes German air space nearly every day. They rarely attack passed the line from Bremen to Frankfurt, but now the British are starting to come at us at night. They use B24 Liberators and are said to be developing their own heavy bombers. The British are still playing catch up due to our occupation of their country, but soon their factories will be making a very important contribution to the allied war effort. This fight is on many fronts and it is for Germany's very existence. I cannot take the Allies on until I have enough jets to challenge their air superiority over the battlefront. It is hard enough keeping them from German skies."

Rommel stopped and thought for a while. "I guess you will be taking divisions off me then?"

"The SS are all going east. Russia is a holy crusade for them. That is one reason why I have allowed their expansion. Spain will get more infantry to replace them and independent StuG or other Panzerjäger units. The 21st Panzer Division, the 2nd Panzer Division and the 25th Panzer Grenadier Division will stay. I'm also going to build a reserve in Germany around the 23rd Panzer Division, the 22nd Air Landing Division and the 1st Fallschirmjäger Division. The new German Youth SS Division will soon be ready as well. I think we need to guard against other surprises."

Rommel nodded. He could use those four divisions but could see the sense in what his leader was saying. Allied strength was growing and even though they had just given the Americans a bloody

nose, they would be back stronger and more experienced.

Chapter Seven: March 1944

The weather in Germany was improving so at least the bombers would have a better chance of hitting their targets, thought Lieutenant Henry Richardson. He had four swastikas painted beneath his cockpit and was hungry for a fifth that would make him an ace. Yet he was also worried. Bomber losses had been very high, hell, the number of P51s not getting back to England was a concern. The 357th Fighter Group had been bounced twice by jets the preceding week, losing four of their number each time. The 262s would swoop in and fire and then dive away at such high speed that there was no chance of catching them.

Today they were escorting the heavy bombers to Hannover. The rubber factories of Continental AG were the target. The Luftwaffe was likely to show up in force today. There wouldn't just be 262s; plenty of Bf109s and FW190s would also make an appearance. The Germans were now using the former aircraft to attack the bombers and the latter to help hold off the fighters. Bf109s now had MW50 water injection and superchargers. Some still had the extra cannons under the wings, but those that hunted the Mustangs didn't, and they were dangerous opponents. The jets of course, just seemed to attack whatever they felt like.

The 362nd Squadron was sweeping ahead of the bombers when single-engined fighters were spotted off to their left.

"Look like 109s, skipper," said Second Lieutenant Mac McConnell.

"They are trying to out climb us, go with them," ordered Captain Calvert.

That's going to be a tall order, thought Henry. The Bf109 could just about out climb any fighter in the air, except the jet. Still, up they went, following the enemy fighters higher. In the end, the two groups came straight at each other at an altitude of thirty-five-thousand feet. They flashed through each other, with some falling in flames. Both the Bf109 and the P51B were lightly armed compared to other fighters, so a few planes dived away scared instead of on fire.

Henry found himself chasing a 109 which had become separated from his wingman. In a dogfight like this encounter, you needed to stay with your partner. He tried to get into the aircraft's blind spot but the German pilot didn't fly straight for long. The plane started to turn and then he spotted Henry coming in from behind. The Bf109 tightened the corner and he tried to follow the enemy fighter. The g-force started to build and Henry fought against the urge to black out. The edge of his vision became blurry but somehow he managed to get the Bf109 in his sights. He fired his four heavy machine guns and saw pieces fly from the enemy fighter's tail. The German machine seemed to sway in the air. He lined up for the final burst when Mac McConnell yelled a warning. "Two fighters on your six, skipper, break to port."

Henry didn't hesitate. He knew his wingman wouldn't yell the warning unless the enemy planes were right on him.

He swung the P51 around and felt the g-force again. Somewhere behind him traces flashed. McConnell yelled in triumph and a burning 109 spun away. Then his wingman screamed and Henry managed to catch sight of a P51 losing its wing over to his left.

Swivelling his head he looked for the attacking fighter and spotted it

behind him. Lines of yellow flashed passed his wing and he saw a

couple of holes appear. He changed direction and pulled the nose up

but the German stayed with him. Henry tried to dive away but the

Bf109 was right there. Every trick he tried, the enemy pilot seemed to

anticipate. In desperation, with the 109 closing in, Henry pulled the

stick back into his stomach. Then he counted to two and pushed the

stick forward and turned hard. The P51 had been in a dive, with the

enemy pilot probably no more than two hundred yards behind him.

His plane shot towards the heavens and he hoped the wings would

stay on. It took the German by surprise and the enemy machine shot

by underneath him. Henry didn't chase the enemy hotshot pilot and

counted himself lucky to be alive.

He then spotted a Bf109 diving away from the combat and

decided to follow it. The enemy machine slowly lost altitude and

Henry followed carefully. At ten thousand feet he slipped in behind

the enemy machine and opened fire. The Bf109 lost part of it wing

and pieces flew from the fuselage, yet it wasn't a killer blow. The pilot put his plane into a steep dive and Henry followed. He knew the P51 could out dive the 109. They reached a shallow valley and the German started to fly even lower but he had run out of space. There was nowhere to go. Henry fired again and saw hits on the engine. A fire started and then suddenly the German opened his cockpit and jumped. Henry watched horrified as the man hit the ground and bounced. He had never actually seen his enemy die before and this felt personal. The Bf109 flew ahead for another half a mile before smashing into a barn where it blew up. Henry climbed away shaken by what he had witnessed, praying that it would never happen to him.

The jet staffel was in perfect position to hit the bombers from behind. Oberleuntnant Kurt Osser had a sore head as he had been up late the previous night celebrating his one hundredth kill. It was quite an achievement as most of them had been scored in the west against well trained pilots. He loved flying the Stormbird and felt as though nothing could touch him. Of course, he guarded himself against hubris. Some of his comrades had fallen. They were still vulnerable to the enemy, especially when an engine flamed out.

The Americans had also tried to fly patrols over some of the jet airfields, but that was difficult to do from bases in England and made the P51s targets for light Flak as well as single-engined German fighters which would pounce on them from above. It seemed as though the enemy were still trying to find a solution to the jet menace, as they were calling it. The Americans' problems were growing as the number of German fighter units which had converted to the Stormbird grew. ZG26 had recently changed over to the jets from their old ME410s. Kurt wasn't sure if the heavy fighter units should get the jets before the regular fighter groups, but could see the sense as these pilots were used to operating twin-engined machines. All of JG26 had now made the change, as well as all of JG7. Kurt guessed probably three hundred jets were airworthy over German skies. Of course only a third of those would be in position to intercept the incoming raid.

Tracers flashed from the gunners of the B17 making Kurt want to hunch in his seat. Logically he knew his plane was difficult to hit because it was moving so fast; difficult, but not impossible. He concentrated on the target, knowing he had a very brief window in which to fire. As the bomber filled his sights he pushed the trigger with his thumb using all four cannons. At least six shells slammed into the starboard wing, causing it to fall apart. The B17 started to flip over and then it went into a spin as the entire wing came off. Kurt flashed passed the formation of bombers, gaining height as he did. He had a brief feeling of sympathy for the Americans in the plane but then reminded himself of what they had come to do. These men were dropping bombs on the people of Germany. Sure, they tried to hit the factories making weapons of war but often their bombs fell on the houses and schools of his people. He decided those airmen deserved their fate.

Looking back, he noted that a number of B17s had been hit by his squadron's attack. It was hard to tell how many, as at least one of the big bombers had exploded. He thought he could see a jet falling in flames as well, but it was difficult to tell.

"Break Brutus One, break," yelled Leutnant Kessler, his wingman.

Recognizing his call sign, Kurt pulled his Stormbird into a hard-left hand turn. A burst of heavy machine gun bullets hit part of his wing and the engine flamed out. He shut down the engine and dropped the plane into a steep dive. Somewhere he thought he heard the heavy thump of a cannon. Then a P51 flashed by, followed by a jet. Kessler was trying to clear his tail.

Kurt felt his plane shudder and knew he had been hit badly. The P51 must have built up speed in a dive and caught him while he was having a look back at the bombers. It was a rookie mistake and he cursed himself. The Stormbird could still get caught and any hit to an engine placed the pilot in extreme danger. The ME262 didn't fly well on one engine and the drop-in speed allowed them to be caught by just about any allied fighter. Kurt had to decide what to do. He hadn't been hit himself but landing the plane was going to be difficult. He kept a careful eye out for any more enemy fighters but the sky seemed empty. The vibrations continued to grow and he wondered if the wing would hold.

At three thousand metres the whole plane started to shudder. Kurt realised he might not have much time so he opened the cockpit and was hit by the force of a cold wind. After undoing his straps and tipping the aircraft over he fell out of the cockpit and into the frigid air. He tried to remember what the instructions for bailing out were and thought he needed to count to five. He did so and then pulled on his rip cord. With a feeling of great relief Kurt felt the jerk as his parachute opened. He drifted with the wind towards a small village and wondered at the peace he felt as he hung suspended beneath the white canopy. Below and slightly north was a small village. People were pointing at him and he waved at them. Then the villagers turned and ran. A burning B17 tumbled from the sky. It was a mass of flames and missing most of its tail. Kurt heard the sound of its one remaining engine and saw the cannon hole near the cockpit. Then it slammed into the middle of the village and exploded. The heavy bomber still had a full load of bombs on board and the affect was devastating. Buildings collapsed and debris filled the air. Kurt was buffeted in his parachute but was far enough away to remain unhurt. When the dust started to clear he could see at least half of the village had been flattened. Then he heard the screaming and the wails of anguish.

He landed heavily at least five hundred metres from the village. He tucked himself into a ball but still managed to give himself a bloody nose. After collapsing his parachute he released the buckles and ran to help. There were burning buildings along the edge of the village square and at least four structures had collapsed, half burying a statue of a figure on a horse. Some old knight or baron from the area he supposed. Bloody figures lay on the cobblestones and a woman sat alone against a tree. Kurt went to her to see if he could help, but noticed the glazed eyes. She was dead and so was the young boy that was tangled in the bushes next to her.

There was yelling nearby as an elderly man clawed at collapsed masonry. Kurt ran to his side. The man looked at him in shock as he approached.

"I'm a Luftwaffe pilot," he said.

The man didn't acknowledge the comment but instead pointed at the rubble. "My wife and her whole family were in there," he said.

Kurt looked at the destruction and grimaced. There was little chance that anybody in this house had survived, yet he had to try. With an effort he lifted a broken beam and tossed it aside.

Kurt worked in the village until night fell. The German Feuerwehr were late in coming due to the damage on Hannover, but local farmers and other villagers arrived and helped dig for survivors, of which there was only one. A young girl had been playing in the basement with her pet dog when the house had fallen down around her. Both were pulled from the wreckage after a local German Shepard had started sniffing and digging in the rubble. The feeling of euphoria which swamped Kurt as the girl was lifted free almost overwhelmed him and he was forced to sit.

"Are you alright, Herr Oberleutnant," asked a polite voice.

Kurt looked up and saw an older man in a uniform looking at him. He was obviously a member of the Ordnungspolizei. The man's clothes were smudged and dirty and there was soot on his hands.

"One of the rescuers told me you are a fighter pilot and you were shot down near here," the man continued. "A jet pilot?"

"How did you know that?" Kurt asked a little harshly. He hadn't told anybody that information.

The policeman held up a hand. "Deduction. Two of the wonder weapons crashed in the forest near here so I thought it logical."

Kurt nodded and then shrugged. Of course the man had worked it out; that was his job after all. Anyway, it didn't matter.

"I'm with JG26 flying the new Stormbird," Kurt said tiredly.

"Does your unit know where you are?"

"No, I've been a little busy here."

"I'll inform them and then we better see what we can do in the way of getting you back to them. We need you heroes in the sky."

"If I was a hero then this wouldn't have happened," said Kurt.

The old policeman shook his head. "This was a tragic accident. The fact you boys are up there protecting us is what gives Germany hope. Now, I'll organize some food for you and a drink, but first I need to make a phone call to your unit."

Kurt gave him the phone number of his base and then the man saluted and walked quickly away. By midnight he was back with his staffel.

v

He now hated partisans more than he hated Jews. Klaus and his company had driven into the small town of Kransy to discover the administrative personnel all dead. Two men had been captured and gutted whilst alive g and that had driven Hauptscharführer Hanson into a rage. Local men and women who were hiding in their cellars were dragged out onto the street and shot out of hand. Then the officers regrouped and started to question some of the Russian townsfolk. They knew very little and most said they had hidden when the partisans rode into Krasny. That these men were mounted was

209

one interesting piece of information. It made them mobile, but also easier to track. The other fact they obtained was that the partisans had come from the north. Then the Hauptscharführer ordered the flame throwers to burn Krasny to the ground. The inhabitants moaned and screamed at the destruction until Rottenführer Hugo Sommer told his squad to shoot some of them. Klaus took careful aim and shot an old man in the chest, then as the Russians scattered he put a bullet in the head of some fleeing grandma.

Some of the men had grabbed a young woman and were starting to rip her clothes away. Klaus was disgusted by this and went to the officers.

"Sir, there are strict laws in Germany about not mating with the Untermensch. What some of the boys intend to do with that woman is wrong. It stains them."

Sommer was standing nearby and snorted. "We aren't in Germany Moller."

Hauptscharführer Hansen looked him up and down. "You are the man who destroyed the two Russian panzers back in the Caucasus aren't you?"

"Yes sir," answered Klaus.

The officer thought for a moment. "You are correct. The men won't like you for this but I commend you for your adherence to Nazi values." Hansen turned to the Rottenführer. "Stop them, and shoot the woman."

Sommer shrugged and strode over to the group drawing his Luger pistol. The Russian woman was half-naked by now and tears streaked her face. He cursed and yelled until the men were off her. Then he stopped and turned.

"You do it Moller."

Klaus looked at the tear stained woman who was trying to gather up her clothes. She was skinny but part of him felt a primal urge. He could see why the men wanted her. He forced the feeling away. She was a dirty Slav tempting his comrades.

"Turn away," he said in poor Russian.

The woman stopped and looked at him. She saw the pistol in his hands and started blabbering words he couldn't understand. The woman lowered her top allowing him to see her milky white breast and then she crawled towards him and pawed at his crutch. He heard the laughter of the other men. He felt something growing between his legs.

"Changed your mind have you Moller?" yelled Sommer.

Rage overtook him and Klaus kicked the woman hard. She grunted and fell forward on her face. He then pointed the Luger at her head and squeezed the trigger. He fired two shots at close range and she twitched, then didn't move. He walked over to where a Russian man knelt in the mud crying over the body of a child. He shot the grieving father and then went looking for other victims.

That night some of the men avoided him but Hanno sat with him.

"I understand what you did today Klaus but you must understand we are young and need release occasionally," said his friend.

"They are rats," said Klaus. "We don't mate with vermin."

"Maybe, but they look a lot like people and out here we need to make do. The boys just wanted me to say they don't want you going into one of the whore houses in Smolensk and shooting all the girls," said Hanno.

"I'm not stupid. I won't do that," said Klaus.

"On the upside you have a new name. The squad is calling you 'Killer.' You're really one of us now."

Klaus smiled at that. It felt good to be an accepted part of the 3rd SS. He was now truly a Crusader for the Reich.

"These raids, are they severely damaging our capacity to produce weapons of war?" Goering asked.

Speer was sitting with the leader of Germany on the balcony of his hunting hall in Bavaria, enjoying the late March sunshine.

"A little, my Führer. The Americans do not dare go as far as Berlin, or passed the Elbe. Also, the south is untouched. I have moved some industry east but this has caused some dislocation to industry, and has created a few bottlenecks. We are working through these issues," said Speer.

'Well, for the limited success the Amis have enjoyed, they have certainly payed a price. Eighty bombers were shot down on the last raid out of perhaps five hundred that attacked."

"We lost a similar number ourselves didn't we?"

"Yes, but I didn't add the escorts that were downed. At least thirty-five of those P51s were downed. More jets are coming. I'm starting to think we could win the air war over Germany!" said Goering.

"The loss of experienced pilots is becoming an issue I believe. Herr Kesselring was just telling me the other day that the supply of pilots is running low."

"Smiling Albert has been unusually pessimistic of late. I have told him that we should retrain some of the bomber pilots. He said they still needed them for the bombing of the Baku oil fields but later he admitted to me he probably could spare some. I could tell he wasn't happy though," said Goering.

"Do we need to expand the pilot training program?" asked Speer.

"It has already been done. The problem is that it takes so long to train a pilot. We are now sending the less experienced ones to the quieter areas of Russia and transferring the Luftwaffe Experten back to Germany. This has helped a little though it breaks unit cohesion." Goering shrugged. "It has to be done."

"Have you read the reports on the new Tiger?" asked Speer, changing subjects.

"Yes, I've decided we need a couple of front line soldiers, probably one experienced crew to give the engineers some advice," said Goering. "These teething problems need to be sorted. I want these panzers ready for the summer offensive on Moscow."

"The engines aren't powerful enough to carry the extra weight," said Speer.

Goering sighed. "You told me there is no alternative. We don't have time to create a new engine from scratch so the Panther's one will have to do. Trim a little weight from the Tiger, but don't compromise its armour protection."

"If we could just trim the armour a little, by say five or ten millimetres in a few areas then it would help," said Speer.

Goering nodded slowly, "Alright, but none from the front and I want to approve each cut before it happens. Also, keep working on the HL234 engine. The fuel injection will really help give the panzer more power. And keep working on the Jagdpanther."

Speer nodded. The conversion of the Panther into a tank destroyer was an easier project by far than the creation of a new heavy panzer.

"Now, how are the latest jet designs coming along?" asked Goering. "I hear the HE162 is progressing nicely."

"We have switched to making it out of metal and that has solved the glue issues with the wooden wings however the BMW003 engines still flame out far too easily. Instability issues have been addressed with a new wing tip and the armament had to be changed to 20mm cannons. We are looking at changing to the Jumo 004 engine. It is heavier than the BMW, but more powerful. The metal structure makes the plane stronger and able to handle them," said Speer.

"I thought the whole point of the project was to avoid using scarce resources?"

"Iron is still available in decent quantities, and you said to move development along. It is still a lot cheaper than the Stormbird, and it will do the job as a fighter interceptor. We are working on one final issue which is the fuel tanks. The Swallow, as they are calling the new plane, can only stay aloft for thirty minutes."

"Drop tanks?"

"Maybe, but the whole point is to try and keep the aircraft light. Anyway, we will keep working on it," said Speer.

Goering nodded and pointed at a sheet of paper. "The new Ukrainian Divisions are after more equipment."

"Of course they are," muttered Speer. "This is not the single SS division?"

"No, it's the four regular army divisions I have allowed."

"I thought they were going to arm them from captured Russian stocks." said Speer

"They have tried to, but are short on motor transport.'

"Send them the trucks captured in Spain?"

"Good idea, but I also want to sweeten the deal. This idea to set up a buffer state in the western Ukraine as well as the semi autonomy I have given Galcia and the Baltic States was opposed by Kaltunbruner and others, but we need the troops."

"The head of the SS was happy to accept the extra men into his divisions!"

"True," said Goering. "But there were even rumblings in the army when I said there would be a regular army from the Ukraine."

"Understandable, Herr Hitler had the area marked as Lebensraum," said Speer.

"Well that all changed when Russia attacked. Our casualties have been huge. We need extra men. Combing out the navy provided us a mere fifty thousand, a third of which volunteered for the SS. Anyway, can you provide them with some decent anti-tank weapons?"

"Rocket launchers?"

"Something with more range?"

"I'll find them some PAK 40s," said Speer with a sigh. "On another front, speaking of manpower shortages, I need more workers."

"What about the Russian prisoners?"

"Half of them died from neglect before I got hold of them."

"Poles, Jews?"

"I have managed to get as many Poles as I can and it is a constant battle with Kaltenbruner for me to keep the Jews I have in the labour camps. He would kill them all if he could."

"I have given him orders on that front. None are to be harmed."

"I believe we have a partisan problem in the east, beyond the borders of Belarus and the other buffer states. Why can't we grab some of the villagers in that area? If the terrorists have no support then it will be harder for them to operate."

Goering stroked his chin. "Put them on trains coming back from the front. Hmm, sounds feasible. I'll look into it."

Chapter Eight: April 1944

The US 4th Armoured Division had been moved back to Portugal, what was left of them. In the end, eight thousand of the eleven thousand men in the unit escaped the German trap. The same couldn't be said of the other divisions. The 34th Infantry Division lost more than half its strength and the 9th and 36th Divisions were almost completely destroyed. If it hadn't been for General Wood, Charlie wasn't sure how many men in the 4th would have escaped. It made him angry that the General hadn't made it. His hatred was mainly directed at the Germans but a little of it fell on the high command that had let them become surrounded in the first place.

It was not going to take as long as Charlie thought to rebuild the division. Replacements were flowing quickly across the Atlantic as well as equipment. Major General Hugh Gaffey had been transferred in from the 2nd Armoured to take command of their unit. Training to mould the new with the old was already taking place around Lisbon, with units learning how to coordinate the different areas of the division. Charlie just did what he was told and drove their new M8 in the exercises without complaining. But for the first time some part of him wanted to get back into action. He wanted to pay the Germans back for the mauling of his division.

"You're getting your own car." said Sergeant Renwood early in April. It was a beautiful day and Charlie was checking the engine on their armoured car. Charlie was dirty and not wearing a shirt.

"What?" he responded.

"Someone decided the way you handled yourself during the breakout warranted a reward," said Renwood. "They are promoting you to sergeant, and me to staff sergeant, so I'll still out rank you."

Charlie was stunned. He never expected to climb the ladder of rank while in the army. Part of him wondered if he was up to the responsibility.

"The good news is more pay, the bad news is you'll get a bunch of wet behind the ears pukes that you'll have to knock into line as a new crew."

Charlie could see some advantages to that. A group of veterans would have left him feeling intimidated. He decided to embrace the opportunity. Maybe, with a crew of his own, he could kill more Nazis.

"When do I meet them, and when do I get the car?" he asked.

Renwood looked at him carefully for a moment. "Good, good," he murmured. "Your new crew is driving an M8 out here to the camp later today. They are all at the docks together."

Charlie thought for a second. "Could I get a lift in and bring them out here Sarge?"

Renwood smiled. "I think that could be arranged. You better clean up and stitch these on first." He handed Charlie a set of stripes.

The jeep dropped him outside the busy docks in Lisbon after about an hour's drive. Charlie had to ask a number of military policemen questions before he eventually found his crew filling a shiny M8 with fuel. He approached the three men feeling very self-conscious. All of the men standing around the armoured car looked like kids. They lacked the slightly worn and jaded look veterans had.

"Alright, I'm Charlie Winklen and I'm to command you sorry lot until we get blown to hell, or the war is over." He had rehearsed this line in his head on the drive in and decided it struck the right note. Sergeant Renwood had advised him to go hard with his crew to start with. "Don't smile at them for a month," he had said. Being a hard arse didn't come naturally for Charlie but his older brother Tim had always said to fake it to you make it. That attitude had got his brother into pilot school and then into the cockpit of a B17. Tim had been shot down by a jet two weeks ago, and Charlie only found out when his division had camped outside Lisbon. It was unknown whether he was alive or dead but it was just another reason to want to kill Germans.

The men looked at him. "An introduction and your rolls are in order, or do I need to send you back to the States for more training? Have I been given a group of mute monkeys?" Charlie yelled at them. Actually, the shouting was starting to feel good.

"No sir, I mean yes sir," said the men.

A big man with red hair and a flat face stepped forward and stood at attention. His uniform was as clean and as sharp as he was.

"Private First Class Maclukscey, sir. Gunner, sir," said the man.

The two smaller men glanced at each other, then one shrugged and stood next to the red head.

"Private Patterson sir, driver."

This one was almost too small for his uniform. His hair was cut very short like he was a marine and his teeth were sharp and neat.

"I was the driver on my old car, Patterson, so you have a lot to live up to," said Charlie.

The man seemed to shrink even further with this comment. The next man was only slightly taller than the driver but was as wide as a barn door.

"Private Occelshaw," said this man in a deep voice. "Radio operator and spare driver."

Charlie looked them over thinking how fresh and keen they seemed. "Are we ready to roll? I want us to get back to the unit as

225

soon as possible. The 4th Armoured has a lot of work to do before we will be ready to kill more Nazis."

Another stinking Russian village was burning, thought Klaus. He held his submachine gun at the ready. He wanted to gun down the group in front of him but the orders were to let them gather a little food and some clothes and then truck them to the railway station. They would have to hose out the back of the vehicle later. These people stunk. Of course Klaus and his companions weren't exactly fresh themselves. Only the old and young could stay, said the orders. Anyone else who could work was going west.

The old men and women stood to one side trying to comfort crying children. A few dead lay where Hanno had shot them when people had refused to be separated from their children. More like grubby little rats. Klaus watched the young and the old with his finger on the trigger. The orders said to torch the village except for the two biggest dwellings. That was soft! Burn them all and let the bandits try and care for those left behind. Klaus didn't care if every last one of these Russians died. Actually, he hoped they would when the seasons changed again. Those left would find it hard to feed themselves. They had no heavy equipment, and no young bodies to plough or plant the fields. The horses had all been taken and all that was left were picks, shovels and the seed needed to go in the ground. Klaus wanted to take that too.

"Orders, Killer," said Sommer. "We aren't to take anything that slows us down."

"Why don't we destroy it then?" asked Klaus.

Sommer laughed, "You'd kill every last one of them, wouldn't you!"

"I thought that was why we were here," grumbled Klaus.

"We are in Russia because they attacked us. Our fearless leader had decided Poland was enough extra living space for Germans. Personally, having been through a couple of winters here I don't know why any right thinking German would want to live in Russia," said Hanno walking up to them.

"It was Herr Hitler's dream," said Klaus.

"Well, he is dead and times change," said Sommer. "Me, I follow orders and don't worry about the current philosophy of our glorious leaders."

"Goering is a great man, but sometimes I wonder if Herr Hitler would have led us east to destroy the Slavs before they attacked us," said Klaus.

"Well, that's the thing about time, we'll never know," said Hanno.

Behind them there was a commotion as a young man and woman broke from the line while they weren't being watched. They ran straight to a pair of crying children and an older woman. They scooped up the boy and the girl and held them close.

"How touching, the rats have feelings," said Klaus.

"Hanno, you speak the language. See if you can calm them down without killing anyone. Bottom line is the adults go west. Orders are they want the able bodied, alive," said Sommer.

Hanno frowned and looked at the ground. "My brother's got kids that age."

Sommer nodded. "I know it's tough sometimes. Our job goes beyond that of being a soldier. I wish it didn't, but it is what it is."

"They are rats sir, I'll handle it if you like," said Klaus.

"Stop trying to be such a hard arse and lighten up," Sommer snapped. "Hanno, I'll leave it with you."

The exchange left Klaus confused. These men were hard as steel, he knew that. They'd hung families, burned villages and even killed children when they'd got in the way. Now his friend Hanno was quietly talking to a Russian family about going west. He watched in amazement as the two children were allowed to board the trucks with the other adults. Hanno had even written them a note which Rottenführer Sommer had signed. He shook his head trying to understand why this particular incident had touched these two SS men. He thought the adults should have been executed. They had to teach these people to fear German might. This random act of kindness could undermine their position in Russia. Klaus supposed the mitigating factor is that the people who had witnessed his comrades'

weakness were all heading to Germany to work for the Reich.

The Royal Tiger was a monster and Wolfgang thought it would

never work. It was his job to advise the engineers about what they

needed to do to get the new tank battle ready by July. At this point in

time he believed the task impossible. His crew tested the mammoth

panzer two days ago and it had broken down in the drive from the

workshop to the testing grounds. They left the first panzer and

walked back to the workshop to get a second vehicle. That one

wouldn't even start, so they tried a third one which did make it to the

firing range. Here, Wolfgang had seen the devastating fire power of

the L71 88mm gun. The accuracy was amazing and the hitting power

beyond anything he had ever experienced. He knew that the Hornet

tank destroyer had the same gun, but he had never seen that vehicle

in action. He had also heard the powerful tank destroyer was very

vulnerable. With an open top and a high profile it was difficult to hide

and easy for artillery to destroy. The Tiger 2 would be hard to hide as well but the thick armour was the engineer's attempt to make the vehicle almost impenetrable.

Wolfgang thought the weight of the panzer was part of the problem. It was much heavier than the Tiger 1 yet it had the same engine. He decided to try and reduce the armour on certain parts of the vehicle to get the weight down in any way he could. On the drive back to the workshed the engine overheated and a small fire started. They jumped out of the panzer and put out the flames with a fire extinguisher. Wolfgang stood next to the Tiger shaking his head.

Later, they checked on what had caused the fire and found leaking seals had been the problem. The engineers informed them that sometimes they split, and poured oil onto the hot engine. Wolfgang insisted that they were strengthened and not to deliver to units in the field until the issue was resolved.

The suspension was another issue. He argued with the engineers about the need to strengthen the steering gear but they pointed out to him it would increase the panzer's weight. So he pushed for changes and modifications, many that were not in line with the designers' brief. He also pointed out that any unit that contained Tigers needed a mine clearing detachment and a bridging unit. He wrote reports with the help of his crew and found his driver Otto Lange made many sensible suggestions. He knew half of the ideas he put forward wouldn't be followed but used his status of one of Germany's leading panzer aces to make sure he was listened to.

It had been his commander's idea that he undertake the role of liaison officer with the Panzerkommision, to help develop the heavy panzer. The request had come from the High Command to supply a team to help with the Tiger's development. The only suggestion Wolfgang made was that his crew go with him. Michael Wittman had been the other option. As another highly decorated panzer ace himself, the leader of the second company would have been a logical choice. In the end it had come down to drawing a card from a deck. The highest card was to go. Wolfgang had drawn a seven of clubs and resigned himself to staying with the battalion but then Wittman had pulled a three of hearts from the deck. The young officer had smiled and shrugged.

"Say hello to Larisa form me," Wittman had quipped before he walked back to his Tiger.

The days away from the test facility at Kummersdorf had made the time apart from his unit all worthwhile. He managed to catch a ride back to his family home either on a truck or he caught the train and then got a lift back to Unterlub. The first time Wolfgang made the journey he found his mother and Larisa in the backyard turning over the warming soil in order to plant it out with summer vegetables. His father was in the workshop sharpening axes and saws to prune the small orchard. Wolfgang had watched for a minute enjoying the scene of the two most important women in his life working in the garden together. When he had announced his arrival Larisa had squealed and thrown herself into his arms. His mother had waited with a smile, stretching her face before making her way across the ploughed earth to him.

Wolfgang's father had been more restrained, as was the German way, but he could tell the old man was pleased his son was home. Without going into detail he explained what he was doing away from the front.

"So do you think this position could be permanent?" asked Larisa hopefully.

"I don't think so," answered Wolfgang as they sat around the kitchen table. "Once they think the new panzer is ready I'll probably be sent back to my unit. I don't think I've made many friends while I have been at the proving grounds. Most of the engineers would be glad to see the back of me."

His father shook his head. "They should be glad of your expert advice, but I know how it is. Some people don't like to be told their precious idea or creation has flaws."

"How long do you think you will have?" asked his mother.

Wolfgang shrugged. "There's no way of knowing. Until they deem the panzer ready and I think that time is a while off."

His mother and Larisa exchanged a meaningful glance and his father smiled.

"Why? What's going on?" Wolfgang asked.

Larisa looked extremely nervous as she approached him and kept glancing at Ursula. His mother gave the younger woman a reassuring look.

"Wolfy, this was not something we ever discussed or planned but we should have. I mean we took enough chances," said Larisa.

He felt a moment of panic, not knowing what was going on. He assumed an illness or maybe an issue with the authorities.

"If some public official is causing problems they better back off or I'll bring in some of my SS contacts," he growled.

"No, no it's nothing like that," said Larisa. She took his hands in her own and stared into his eyes. "Wolfy, we are going to have a child. You are going to be a father." Then she laughed. "I'm going to be a mother."

He was stunned. A feeling of overwhelming joy swept over him that was so intense that he sat back down on the wooden chair. "A father," he muttered.

"Are you alright with the idea?" asked Larisa tentatively.

Wolfgang turned and then jumped up and kissed Larisa on the mouth. "This is the best news!" he exclaimed. "We will be a family. This is amazing, wait until I tell my crew! Larisa, marry me!" he blurted.

The young woman yelled. "Yes, yes, yes."

His mother started to cry and hugged the young couple, and even his father had to wipe a tear from his eye. Wolfgang would never forget that feeling. It was a euphoria that he would only experience when he heard of the birth of the twins. Later, she warned Wolfgang there was a family history of non-identical twins in her family and he should be prepared for this.

He immediately started making plans. Wolfgang wanted them to have their own house but not far from his parents. His father and mother were to play an important role in his family. He also decided he needed to prepare his new family in case the war went badly. Wolfgang changed some of his saved pay into gold and hid it in the garden where only Larisa and his parents knew its location. His father didn't approve, pointing out that his son's actions showed a lack of faith in Germany's final victory. Ursula cut her husband down quickly, pointing out they had lost the last war and there were no guarantees this one would be any different. She pointed to the sky while making her point, as they had all heard the drone of heavy bombers flying to Berlin the previous day. Yes, the radio had announced that the raid had been a disaster for the USA with many planes having been shot down but the fact was, they seemed to keep coming.

Wolfgang had tried to explain the odds Germany was facing. "Father, when we accepted the surrender of the Americans at Toledo we were stunned at the amount of equipment they had. When Germans go anywhere we pile troops onto panzers or put six men in a kubelwagen, but the Amis never have their troops ride around on tanks and usually only have three or four men in a jeep. Their food, clothing, medical facilities, everything was in quantities we couldn't believe. The Russians just keep coming. We destroy one army or a couple of hundred panzers, but before we know it there is another army. If it was just one side or the other I would be confident of us winning, but against two such opponents I just don't know."

"Are you saying the war is lost?" his father snarled.

"No, we could still win or possibly force a draw. If we can hold out and equip those in the east who want their independence, then there is a chance. Our weapons are superior and man for man a German is a better soldier that most of the enemy troops I have faced. There are elite forces or certain groups that are a match but these forces are not enough to make the difference. Also, the US troops learn. They are adaptable and given time I fear how good they may become."

"We have the super weapons!" his father said.

"I have friends in the Luftwaffe and they say the jet has given them a strong advantage, which is just as well, because they believe US airmen are better trained and highly aggressive. If we didn't have the jets, these pilots believe the Amis would have already won the war in the air."

"So we have a chance?" his mother said plaintively.

"Yes," said Wolfgang with more confidence than he felt. Deep down he thought it wasn't much of a chance.

Another raid like this and the Mighty Eighth would be finished.

Lieutenant Richardson was deeply disturbed. He had seen B17 after

B17 fall from the sky as they tried to hit targets in Berlin. Somehow

the Eighth Army Air Force had scraped together six hundred bombers

for the attack if you included the B24 Liberators. They were now

crossing the Dutch coast and the attacks seemed to have ended.

Henry was not sure if he had enough fuel to make it home as he had

done so much fighting. He knew his guns were empty and that the

damage to his tail was making it difficult to fly his P51 straight. But

this wasn't what troubled him the most.

The ME262s had been up in numbers and had torn through

their formation after dropping from some high cloud, destroying two

Mustangs with their first pass. They had chased the jets and been out

of position when the heavily armed ME410s arrived. Of course, his

commander hadn't been a fool. At least some of the group had

maintained their position with the bombers and he had been one of

those pilots. Henry had barrelled in on the twin-engined heavy fighters and shared in the destruction of at least one. At least eight of them had been close enough to unleash their barrage of rockets, then they had moved in to fire 20 and 30mm cannons at the B17s. Four bombers went down in that attack.

The FW190s had arrived, escorted by Bf109s. A huge dogfight developed but again enough German fighters broke through to damage or destroy more heavy bombers. He had managed to blow the wing off a Messerschmitt and as the light fighter had spun away Henry saw that the pilot had somehow managed to get out and parachute to safety. This made him feel relieved. He didn't want to kill people, though he knew it was part of the job. If he could destroy the machine and leave a man alive, so much the better. It had been kill number eight and a half, by the way the US Army Air Force counted aerial victories. The incident was in stark contrast to what happened later.

Twenty jets had used the confusion of the American fighters to charge into the bombers and attack without fear of any interception by the P51s. Stopping the jets reaching the B17s was difficult but not impossible. If the American fighters were in the right position with plenty of height they could dive on the ME262s and force them to flee. This time there was no chance of that. At least five bombers went down immediately, with others to follow later from battle damage. One jet staggered away with an engine out of commission due to the return fire of the gunners on the heavy bombers. As Henry watched, two P51s chased the damaged 262 and shot it down. The German managed to bail out and was drifting towards the earth when another American fighter dropped out of formation and opened fire. Henry watched horrified as bullets shredded the luckless pilot's parachute and he plummeted towards the ground.

After surviving another two combats in which more planes from both sides were destroyed, Henry finally had time to reflect on the act of that American pilot. He had seen the plane's markings and had a good idea of the fighter group and the squadron. The question was whether he wanted to do anything about what he had seen. Part of him understood the anger, the need for revenge on the German airmen who were destroying so many bombers. He had also heard the argument that every enemy pilot who lived would soon be back in a fighter killing more Americans. Part of him was worried what would happen to captured US airmen and fighter pilots who now bailed out over enemy territory. What would their reception be on the ground if it was known that Americans were killing Germans while hanging in parachutes? Also this is not what he believed in, this was not how his side fought. Henry knew war could be a dirty business but this was going too far. He had heard that in Russia terrible atrocities were committed by both sides but this rarely happened between the Germans and the US forces. There was the odd instance when the SS had killed prisoners well after the fighting had stopped but he had met American soldiers who admitted killing captured soldiers when it was inconvenient to keep them alive. Somehow this was so much more personal.

v

"The raids have stopped!" exclaimed Goering.

"For now," said Kesselring. "Their attempt to hit Berlin was a disaster for the Americans. One hundred and twelve bombers were shot down, well over the ten percent rate that some analysts believe

is acceptable. Then there were also thirty-eight escort fighters shot

and destroyed. Our losses weren't light but are recoverable. We lost

twelve jets, thirty-two FW190s, eighteen heavy fighters of various

types, and twenty-six Bf109s. Half of the pilots from those aircraft

lived and will be back in the air very soon."

"A great day," said Goering. The two men sat in the Mercedes

as it cruised north towards Carinhall. Behind and in front of them

were armoured cars, as well as trucks filled with SS troops.

"We need to be careful though, my Führer. The Allies will be

back and they will adapt," said Kesselring.

"Is there any sign of them getting their own jets? I mean, how

else could they defeat the Stormbird? The Arado 232 is flying over

Britain taking photos with impunity. We have even raided Portsmouth

with the Blitz Bomber and the British have been powerless to stop it.

We need more jet bombers," said Goering.

"Speer is working on it. All I'm saying is don't strip Germany of too many fighter groups just because the Amis seem to have given up for now."

Goering fingered the eagle head on the top of his oaken cane and considered. "I will be careful, though I want some of the jets for the attack on Moscow. Also, we need to develop a way for the Blitz Bomber to hit ships. Sooner or later the Americans and their allies will land somewhere and we need a way to hit back."

Kesselring nodded. "We are working on it. Torpedoes aren't the answer and the guided bombs are no longer effective due to radio jamming. Our Pacific allies have reported a method used by the Americans against them that has created some interest. It is called skip bombing and it is something we are looking into."

"Keep me informed," said Goering.

Chapter Nine: May 1944

His hands were shaking and he couldn't sleep without fear. Tom Derrick remove he image of the dead child from of his mind. He had tried to tell himself it had been an accident, that these type of mistakes happened all the time in war, but the self-talk didn't stop the nightmares. So, he was using the tried-and-true way followed by most Australian males when in an emotional crisis; he drank. At the moment it was a bottle of cider, but he had also developed quite a taste for sangria. He had been told the drink got its name from the colour of blood and to him, in his bath of self-pity, that seemed appropriate.

The 9th Australian Mechanised Division as it was now called, had been withdrawn to Gibraltar. Nearby, the New Zealand 2nd Mechanised was also resting and reequipping. Both divisions had spent March and April grinding into the German lines. They were trying to help recapture what had been lost in February when the Americans had been surrounded and its army had broken out to the west at great cost. The American push on Madrid seemed to be coming from directly to the east of the capital city. Even though the countryside near Mentrida was hilly, it was still close to Madrid and the assault centred on the use of artillery and airpower to grind a way forward. It was slow but effective.

Patton and a number of American formations had disappeared. The scuttlebutt was that the Americans were rebuilding formations and perhaps creating a new army for the American general. Others thought he had been sacked for allowing the Germans to surround his formations. Harry Breman, Tom's officer, had said this was unlikely. Intelligence had missed the gathering of Rommel's forces. General Clarke though had responded quickly and with energy. Sure, the armchair warriors would second guess some of his decisions in years to come. Another general might not have gathered the forces needed quickly enough to punch through to the trapped army and allow a lot of US soldiers to escape. Harry believed the offensive had changed the Americans' attitude to the war. Their approach to the war seemed to be harder now, more professional and determined.

Tom agreed. There was one thing he had noticed about the men and women of the USA; they didn't like to be beaten.

As for Tom, he sipped his drink and enjoyed the night air. It was warmer now and sometimes it even reminded him a little of home. The dry air and the smells were similar, but without the tang of eucalyptus. And the sounds were different. The insects and birds of Australia have their own special symphony that is impossible to explain to an outsider. It's more than the warble of a magpie or the harsh shriek of a cockatoo, it's a combination that says, 'this is the Australian bush'. He missed that sometimes with a longing that made him ache. Growling at his own foolishness, he took a large mouthful of cider.

Snowy and Stan found him outside the inn an hour later. Tom was well into his cups by then but still had an awareness of what was going on around him.

"Harry thought we might find you here," said Snowy.

"Well, he was right," muttered Tom.

"Thought we would share a few with you," said Stan.

247

Tom waved at the surrounding chairs and called for the barkeeper. An older man with olive skin and grey hair appeared. He kept his face neutral and went to get more cider.

"The trouble with the Spaniards," said Snowy, "is you never know whose side they are on. Were they a Franco supporter, or maybe they wanted the Republicans to win back in their little civil war?"

"Or perhaps they just want to be left alone to bring up a family and run a business," said Tom. "Isn't that what normal people want?"

Stan shook his head. "I don't know. We ain't normal people any more. Four years of war has gotta change a man."

Tom looked at his friend in surprise. "You are right. This mess," he waved his hands around. "Has scarred us."

"We'll go home, change into civis, watch the football and go to the races," said Snowy.

"Do you think we'll shake it off that easily!" exclaimed Tom. "We've done things, I've done things..." he trailed away.

Stan and Snowy exchanged uncomfortable glances. They knew about the death of the child and its mother, and thought it was bad luck. As for supporting their mate through his trauma, they had no idea of what to say or do. The raw emotion left them uncomfortable.

"On another front," said Snowy. "I found out that German who you so admired is here in the local hospital. Seems the story of him pulling his mates in when under fire has done the rounds. Now he is more popular than a lucky punter shouting beers at the pub."

"Paul Becker is here?" said Tom.

"Yes, in the Gib hospital. His mate Stefan developed an infection in his leg and while the new wonder drugs were fixing him, they let the Jerries stay together. Normally of course, they wouldn't do any favours for a captured soldier, but this one is different."

"That he was," said Tom.

v

The Australian who sat before him was a shadow of the man Paul had met more than a season ago. He was still tall and lean with hard muscles but his face was haggard. Stefan sat with them in his wheel chair out in the sun, on the south facing veranda. Both of them looked at the Australian sergeant in surprise. They knew that this man had won the Victoria Cross, the Commonwealth's highest award for bravery, akin to the German Knight's Cross. Yet when the Australian picked up his cup of tea, his hands shook.

"We are pleased to see you are alive and unwounded," said Stefan in heavily accented English. Paul's friend was to be the translator as he spoke three languages.

"Are you?" said Tom.

Paul spoke through his friend. "Of course. We don't really want anyone to die."

"My friend here doesn't like shooting people. You have heard the story of how he always tried to wound his targets?"

"Yes I did, and I wondered why? I'm sure it wasn't part of your training," said Tom.

"No, the German army frowned on such weakness," said Paul through Stefan. "But the unit understood and even supported my actions.'

"Why? I mean, I know my mates would stand by me, but they would need a reason."

Paul wondered later why he told the Australian his story. The tale of that horrible night in Russia where he had survived the trench raid only by killing everybody, even his own squad still haunted him, yet he had come to terms with his actions. The story seemed to spark something in the sergeant and his eyes filled with tears.

"Is that why you risked your life to drag your mates in?" asked the Australian.

Paul had thought about that. He wasn't completely sure why he had continued to pull the wounded back to the trench as shells and bullets rained about him.

"I think it was because they had accepted me, despite my strange behaviour. It was also a form of redemption."

When the sergeant heard that last word his eyes went round. He stared with frightening intensity at Paul.

"How do I find redemption?"

Paul could feel this man's pain and he wanted to help him. He didn't know if whatever was chewing at the Australian's soul would leave him but he decided to give him hope.

"You are in a war, sergeant. I'm sure an opportunity will present itself."

v

It was so stupid. They wouldn't let them marry because Larisa was a Slav. Race laws even stipulated that he shouldn't even share a bed with her. Yet, in Russia the Ukrainians fought in the SS. Soldiers visited Russian brothels that had been set up by the army and Slavs worked side by side on farms throughout Germany. SS Obersturmbannführer Heinz von Westernhagen had given him the bad news when he visited the battalion's temporary quarters outside Berlin at Zossen. The nearby panzer school provided a training ground where they could practise with the new Royal Tigers. These were still only prototypes but many of the improvements Wolfgang and his crew had suggested had already been incorporated into the heavy panzer.

He had tried to contact the various departments involved with marriage both in and out of the SS, and had hit a brick wall. In the end, Westernhagen had been forced to warn him to stop pushing. Various SS departments were making unwanted enquiries about Larisa and it was only Wolfgang's status as a panzer ace that had forced them to back off. It made him ball his fists in frustration. Larisa had told him not to worry and to stop making a fuss. She pointed out that in the Soviet Union if you pushed the State, it pushed back. Wolfgang could see in this regard, their two countries weren't that different. If anything, Germany was a little softer in this area. He started to become resigned to the fact his children would be born out of wedlock.

Wolfgang's father wasn't happy about it either but understood the government's position. This had led him into a massive argument with the older man. His father believed it was important not to dilute

German blood, though he could make an exception for Larisa as she was obviously different. Wolfgang saw her face twist at this statement and he had exploded. He told his father everything that was happening in the east and the hypocrisy of Nazi policy. His father responded by pointing out he was an SS officer and was supposed to be the upholder of these policies. Wolfgang responded with the fact that a third of the SS would soon be comprised of foreign troops. In the end, his mother Ursula stepped in to calm the situation. Yet Wolfgang had not forgiven the old man.

Truth was that he wasn't sure what he was fighting for anymore. Russia had attacked, this was true, but they had been punished and thrown out of Europe. Why couldn't both sides negotiate some sort of peace settlement? Then there were the Allies who were obviously still angry at Germany's initial aggression back in 1939. Yet the Fatherland had deserved the right to re-establish its old borders hadn't it? The Jews had brought his country down and had conspired with the communist, or that was what he was told. Larisa had informed him the Jews were often persecuted in Russia before the war. None of it made sense. He fought for his unit and to protect his country; that much remained unchanged, but he was starting to doubt he could believe anything else he had been told.

And he had to put his feelings behind him. Wolfgang could see his heavy panzer battalion and the 1st SS Panzer Division were being prepared for battle. He noted the 9th SS had been moved into Eastern Germany as well. A summer offensive was on the cards and he guessed it was in Russia. The Americans had been hit hard and logic dictated that the next large scale attack would be on a different front. Maybe that was what he could fight for. If the Soviet Union was knocked out of the war then the Allies would be forced to sue for peace. It was something to hold on to.

v

The twelve ME262s cruised at a height of five kilometres over the German Dutch border. The US bombers had not come back in force since the Berlin raid but they still probed the defences of the Reich. B26 Marauders were below the formation of jets escorted by P47s. The Thunderbolts had seen Kurt and his Stormbirds, and were climbing desperately. The Americans had learned that the best way to stop jets attacking was to dive on them as they dumped speed for the final run in to attack the bombers. This tactic need precise timing. These P47s were too low as the 262s had a higher service ceiling and had climbed above the escorting fighters. Kurt still meant to dump speed on his final approach to the bombers and this would leave him vulnerable for thirty to forty seconds, but he was not going to slow the plane as much as he usually did. The Marauder was probably one of the fastest of the American medium bombers and this would reduce the closing speed.

"More fighters, these are P51s," said Hessler over the radio.

The Allies were smothering these shallow penetration attacks with escorts and it could make it hard to get through, but Kurt was determined.

"Push on, Red and Blue flight," he ordered. "Green flight try and scatter those Mustangs."

The Schwarm turned slightly towards the P51s while Kurt kept the rest of the jets heading towards the bombers. The formation made the short dive and climb manoeuvre to lose some speed and then lined up on the medium bombers. They hadn't lost enough speed and many bursts from the jets were quick and inaccurate. Even Kurt only managed to hit the outer wing of his target. Hessler's cannon shells tore the wing from a B26 and then his wingman narrowly avoided a collision as he pressed home his attack to the very last second. Other bombers were wounded but none fell from the sky. Kurt thought of taking his formation around again but knew they were low on fuel.

A Stormbird suddenly blew up. Four P47s were coming down at a very steep angle firing their machine guns at his formation. Immediately, he ordered the jets to put their noses down. He could see traces flashing passed as the 262 pulled away but the P47s fired even as the range increased. Young Eindermann screamed as heavy machine gun bullets shattered his canopy. The pilot had only been with them a week, having come fresh from training school. The young man started bellow as flames enveloped the cockpit. Kurt yelled for him to jump, to abandon the aircraft, but there was an explosion and then silence.

They left the American fighters behind. Kurt was cursing his lack of vigilance. He should have scanned the sky more thoroughly. The scattered high cloud made it easy to miss small enemy formations, yet at the altitude at which the jets had approached, he should have spotted the small group of P47s. What he didn't know was that his attack had drawn the full wrath of the fighter screen his way. When fourteen Bf109Gs turned up five minutes later they found the way to the bombers open. These aircraft had been configured to duel with P51s and so had no wing armament. The centre line 20mm cannon and the twin heavy machine guns could still bring down a B26, but only if they spent some time pouring bursts into the American bombers. This exposed them to the return fire of the rear gunners. The B26s formation had been disrupted by the jet attack so the overlapping fields of fire weren't as affective as they usually were and the 109 pilots were very determined.

Gunners and the lightly armed fighters fought a running battle for ten minutes until the P47s began to return. Two 109s fell to the return fire and another two were damaged, with one of these being caught and destroyed by an American fighter pilot. Four bombers were destroyed and another five damaged to varying degrees. Though this type of combat was rare, small actions took place between German and American aircraft all along the line of the northern Rhine, yet little impact was made on the war industry of the Reich.

Soon after they landed back at their base, Kurt's commanding officer met him. Orders had come through and JG26 were going east. KG27, now equipped with Ar 234 Blitz bombers were coming with them.

v

"Are we going to be ready in time?" asked Goering.

Keitel stood and walked to the large map of the Moscow area pegged to the

corkboard in the command carriage. The train was cruising along through the German night towards Berlin. Overhead, a squadron of night fighters kept watch on the leader of Germany.

"We believe so. The Russians have recovered slowly since the fighting around Stalingrad and the Don. We have continued to hit their oil facilities and so their production has slowed. The Americans have sent them tankers but it has only replaced thirty percent of their losses. Extensive examination from the air has led us to believe that the Soviet Union has only managed to reach sixty percent of their early war capacity to produce oil. Of course if the Americans are sending the stuff, it means that they aren't sending other items, we hope."

Goering snorted at that last comment. He had no doubt that Soviet oil production had been hit hard and that had knock-on effects, but he was learning not to underestimate the Americans' ability to supply Germany's enemies.

"We have gathered the best divisions Germany has and will attack from the area just east of Tula and the environs of Rzhev. Both of these armies are to converge just behind Moscow," said Field Marshal Keitel. "The southern flank is nearly an all SS affair with the 1st, 2nd, 3rd, 5th, 9th, and the 12th Charlemagne French Panzer

Grenadier attacking. The 101st SS Heavy Panzer Battalion with their new Royal Tigers, supported by the Walloon SS Brigade will go with them. Covering the flank of this force is the 16th, 12th and 11th Panzer Divisions. In the north, the Grossdeutschland Panzer Division, the 1st, 5th, 13th, 16th, 19th, 20th and the 501st Heavy Panzer Battalions will attack, as well as the 29th Panzer Grenadier. Over one thousand planes including forty jet fighters and thirty jet bombers will support the attack. My Führer, we haven't gathered a force like this in some time. It is also supported by many reinforced infantry divisions."

"We now have what, twenty-eight panzer divisions, counting the SS ones?" said Goering.

"That is correct. The army has twenty-three, with there no longer being a 17th or 18th Division. The SS have five with one forming, and the German Youth Division is due to become operational in July. The army is forming two more. The 16th Panzer Grenadier is to become the 116th Panzer Division and the Panzer Lehr is almost ready for action. After this we are just going to concentrate on keeping these formations as close as we can to full strength."

"I understand," said Goering. "No use creating new formations if the old ones are just shadows. I agree with the army on this. So our operational reserve will consist of these divisions only?"

"No, there are also two paratrooper divisions and the 22nd Air Landing Division. This last formation is now equipped with StuG3s," said Keitel.

"The Allies are up to something. It doesn't leave us much up our sleeve. As it is we have stripped the Spanish front down to just two panzer divisions. Fourteen of our twenty-eight panzer divisions are committed to this attack on Moscow."

"To succeed we need to use a strong force. Except for local attacks the Eastern Front has been quiet for months. The Soviets are gathering their strength too. They know we are coming."

"They will probably try and distract us by making attacks elsewhere on the front, like towards the oil fields in the Caucasus," said Goering.

"The 1st and the 24th Panzer Divisions are covering that area and the 2nd and the 7th covering the Don Bend. The 8th is in local reserve near Rostov on Don and the Hungarians 1st Panzer Division is based near Kursk. The Romanian armoured division is at Grozny. We have forces poised to respond to Russian threats in the south. In the north there is only the 6th and 4th Panzer Divisions but we have a Tiger battalion and the 29th Panzer Grenadier Division in the area as extra support."

"So it all depends on the Allies and what they do," mused Goering.

"The Italians have been rebuilding as have the French. These forces can provide some help in the south. The French now have one of their own panzer divisions totally equipped with T34s and their air force has over one hundred Bf109s. The Italians have three fully functioning panzer divisions that now use the P40, a tank almost equivalent to our Panzer Four, or their own T34s. They have even delivered ten of the new P43s with the

90mm gun for combat testing to the 131st Centauro Division. Our allies will have to take up some of the slack in the south. The Italian air force is not without strength and it has used the second half of

1943 to reequip and retrain. The only army that is struggling is the Spanish. They have four combat-worthy divisions at most and no armour to speak of. Their air force is a shell and their navy has been sunk."

"The Italians won't send any army units to Spain. I have asked and received a firm no," said Goering. "Neither will the French."

"That might not be a bad thing, my Führer. If there are allied forces landing in either country then they will have to respond. All we can do is give them some back up," said Keitel.

"Let's hope that is enough," said Goering.

Chapter Ten: June 1944

The extra work on the runway had barely made it suitable for the jet. Two had been damaged already due to landing mishaps and Kurt wasn't satisfied with the metal mesh which lay over the top of the earth. Every time it rained mud seeped through the gaps, making the airstrip impossible to use, yet when the sun dried it out the resulting dust was just as bad. They found that the best way to solve the problem was for the fire engines to lightly spray the area with water before every takeoff. His commander, Major Emil Lang, had warned the experts in Germany that the jets needed hardened runways but it had been decided that mesh was enough. It wasn't.

Still, his flight of four aircraft was aloft and hunting. They had just dropped their drop tanks and were looking for customers. So far trade had been slow but then Hessler called over the radio. "Bandits nine o'clock low. Look like Il2s. Maybe twelve of them."

His wingman had spotted the Russian attack bombers through scattered low cloud. They were above and behind them but there had to be an escort. Sure enough a squadron of LA5Ns were off to the right at a higher altitude. They were in the right position to prevent an attack by prop driven fighters, but not to stop jets. Kurt gave the order and the ME262s dived behind the Sturmorviks. The Russians saw them and tightened formation, just as they would normally do when under attack. Heavy 12.5mm machine guns started to fire so Kurt took his plane under the IL2s to attack from below. This manoeuvre also allowed the Stormbirds to lose some speed.

Kurt's target loomed up quickly as he started his approach on the enemy. He knew the Russian fighters were still far away, trying to close the gap to his jets, but they had little hope. He selected only two of his cannons to fire and then opened up. At least four shells hit the Sturmovik in the belly. Despite the thick armour that encased the Russian plane it was no match for the heavy cannon and Kurt's target disintegrated. His squadron ripped through the Russian formation, dropping four aircraft. Kurt used the 262s speed to go around for another attack. The pursuing Russian fighters tried to chase them but the jets lost little forward momentum in the high-speed turn, such were the clean lines of the aircraft. They should have tried to pull a high G turn in order to cut the corner on the 262s escape but this was the first time they had faced the German jet.

The Stormbirds repeated the same type of attack as before and even though the Russians had pulled together, they hadn't dropped to the deck. This would have been the only way to make Kurt's attack more difficult. It would have forced the jets to attack through the gunner's return fire. He used all four cannons this time but misjudged the angle of his shot. Three cannon shells hit the tail of the Il2 causing the rear of the aircraft to come apart. It dropped straight down five hundred metres into a pine forest and exploded. Another three Russian fighter-bombers crashed and every other Sturmovik was damaged. Kurt considered a third attack but then glanced at his fuel gauge. There was just enough left to get back to that sad excuse of a base. He ordered the Stormbirds to climb gently away from the combat and they did so, leaving the Russian fighters far behind them. He smiled at the ease of the victory knowing that tomorrow the battle would begin in earnest.

v

This was something Klaus had been longing for. The clearing of villages and the killing of partisans had confused him. One day they were hanging hostages and the next his squad were making sure that families weren't separated. Now they were going to attack a prepared Russian position and drive a hole through the enemy's lines.

His battalion was to take a stretch of forest on the main road between Tula and Orel. Not that there would be much left of the woodlands after the bombardment had finished. 21 cm Nebelwerfers were firing a massive barrage onto the countryside in front of them. The area had already been hit by 150mm artillery and a fighter-bomber attack. Klaus hoped the Russians would be so stunned that they wouldn't be able to respond. Then shells started to explode near the trench he was in. Soviet artillery was firing back. Soon shrieks and screams came from the jumping off position.

"Ivan has had months to prepare a warm welcome for us," muttered Rottenführer Hugo Sommer. "It's bloody obvious we would be going for Moscow this time."

"But we are over one hundred kilometres from the Soviet Capital," said Klaus.

"Have you ever had a look at a map? It's not that far for an armoured division. Hell, when we first hit Russia we were making thirty kilometres some days, and one day we went fifty!"

"Different times, Rottenführer," said Rainer. "Back then Ivan was on the run. Now they are ready, and the front line isn't just some thin crust to be punctured and its home free on the other side. The Russians have learned about defence in depth."

"We will still defeat them. I have never seen so much armour behind us," said Klaus.

"Ivan will have just us much waiting for us. Mark my words boys, this will be a hard fight," said Sommer.

The shelling stopped when German artillery responded to the Russian attack. Then the Nebelwerfers stopped firing. MG42s started hammering the tree line down predetermined corridors. A whistle blew and the panzer grenadiers of the 3rd SS Division went over the top. The battalion left their trench lines and dashed forward before some squads dropped to the ground. Others kept moving forward and then they took cover. One group covered the other while different squads sprinted forward. Klaus aimed his new StG44 assault rifle at the shattered tree line. All the riflemen in the battalion had been issued the new gun and it had dramatically increased everyone's firepower. The rifle didn't have the range of a standard 98K but then who could hit anything beyond four hundred metres anyway? He had to be careful with it as a good knock could damage the receiver. Still, he liked the weapon.

A Soviet machine gun started firing from the tree line, and then another opened up from a small rise. Klaus dropped to the ground and crawled forward to a shell hole. He popped up and fired short bursts at the winking lights that sent tracers towards his friends. SS troopers fell and screamed as the rounds tore at them. Obersturmführer Sauer ordered the men to throw smoke grenades and this worked momentarily. The breeze however, was too strong and it pulled the drifting white vapour apart quickly. The Germans had moved closer to the Russian trench line and Klaus noted that the machine guns were firing from block houses.

One seemed to be built into the ground from thick logs and earth, while the one on the rise was bigger and had been constructed from concrete and covered with soil. At least two machine guns were shooting from it. Four panzers rolled forward to help the soldiers. Two were Mark 3 flame throwers and the others were StuH42s with powerful 105mm guns. There was also a Brummbar assault vehicle with a 150mm gun. The three assault guns engaged the concrete bunker on the rise while the flamethrower tanks moved towards the earthen pillbox. An anti-tank gun fired and hit the Brummbar but the thick frontal armour defeated the shell. Three more anti-tank rounds broke up on the frontal plates of the assault vehicle before it found the Russian gun and blew it apart with a heavy shell. The StuH42s fired into the concrete pillbox heavily damaging it. Then Russian infantry burst from a small tunnel near the assault guns. Four men fired at the accompanying German infantry while two others threw bottles of burning fuel on the StuH42s. The improvised Molotov cocktails burst on the engine compartment. One of the men then dropped a grenade down the barrel of one of the guns and the resulting explosion caused the main weapon to become inoperable.

The StuH42s suddenly went into reverse, catching one of the Russians unaware and crushing him beneath its tracks. They continued on, flames and smoke billowing from the back deck of one of them for another hundred metres before slowly grinding to a halt. Most of the fire had gone out but the engine was making a grinding sound. The crew of the StuH42 then opened the hatches and jumped clear. They were coughing, and staggered behind their assault gun as smoke drifted from the fighting compartment. SS troopers ran up and shot at the Russians who had knocked out the vehicle, killing two of them. The others jumped back into their tunnel and disappeared.

Klaus and Rainer had followed the flame panzers as they attacked. Unfortunately broken trees prevented the vehicles getting closer than forty metres from the earthen bunker. Bullets pinged off the panzers' armour and Klaus imagined the noise inside would be unbearable. Still, it was better than being hit. A huge jet of fire sprang from the end of one of the panzer's barrels filling the air with the smell of burnt oil. Thick black smoke obscured Klaus' view for a second but when it cleared he could see the area around the bunker was blackened but not destroyed. The range was just too great. The panzers kept firing and they also sprayed the trench line with their machine guns. This allowed Obersturmführer Sauer to rally his men and lead them through the shattered trees and into the enemy trenches.

The canvas and board on the top of the trenches were burning in places and the area was covered in drifting smoke. Dead Russians lay over a SG-43 machine gun. The loader was missing most of his head yet his companion seemed almost untouched. Klaus thought it strange but didn't have time to dwell on the unusual sight as Sommer pushed him on.

"Wake up Killer, this is where it will get really interesting," said the Rottenführer.

A little further on down the trench three Russians came running. They were carrying boxes of ammunition and didn't have time to reach for the guns on their backs before a hail of bullets caught them and threw them backwards. The boxes they were carrying splintered with hits, and machine gun bullets as well as grenades spilled free. Rainer ran forward and grabbed some of the undamaged RG-42 grenades. They were a crude bomb but the SS all knew how to use them. Of course hits with bullets didn't set them off, they needed to be primed first. Rainer grabbed a few and then passed a few to the others.

"Remember, these bombs only have a 3.2 second fuse, about a second faster than our own," said Sommer. "You'll need to prime them first."

They spent a few seconds doing so while Adlar went along the trench in one direction and a trooper named Kohler went the other way.

"All clear," declared Adlar.

The squad proceeded without words, their weapons ready. Ahead they could hear a machine gun firing as well as the chatter of submachine guns. Sommer signalled the squad to ready grenades and then a rain of the bombs flew around the corner to land among the Russian soldiers. The crack of explosion was punctuated with the screams of men and then the SS squad charged. They were on the enemy before they knew what had happened. Automatic fire cut the surviving Russians down. A sheet of earth covered canvas had concealed a dugout and from it spilled more enemy soldiers. A big man with a flattened nose took Kohler in a bear hug and fell to the ground with him. A Russian officer came out with a pistol blazing and shot Hanno twice in the head. Klaus screamed and threw himself on the man, knocking the hand gun aside. He crashed into the side of the trench with the man swinging at him with his assault rifle but was too close to put any strength behind the blow. The Russian head butted him but Klaus was off balance and had dropped his chin. The officer's forehead ended up hitting his helmet instead of flesh and the man reeled away a couple of steps. Obersturmführer Sauer shot the man in the shoulder and the side with his Walther pistol and the Russian fell. An enemy soldier swung at Adlar with a rifle butt but the SS trooper went under the blow and chopped at the man's chest with a sharpened shovel. Klaus had seen his friend sharpening the implement the previous night and thought it was a stupid idea. Now as the blade cut open the Russian's chest he wasn't so sure.

It was blood and chaos but part of Klaus loved it. This was battle with the enemy of his people and he would kill them all. His StG44 was empty so he pulled out his SS dagger and Astra 900 pistol which he had won in a game of cards. The big Russian was choking

Kohler on the ground and the SS man's face was going blue. Klaus swiftly pulled back the Soviet soldiers head by the hair and cut his throat. Blood poured from the wound and the man grabbed at his leg. Klaus kicked him aside and shot a man running away in the back. He then dropped into the dugout where he saw a woman by a radio set. She had a bayonet in her hand and came at him. Klaus fired three bullets, which hit her in the neck and chest. Near her were some papers and a book burning on the ground. He stomped the fire out and looked around the room. Two other wounded Russians lay on blankets in long recessed holes in the wall. He shot both in the head and then re-emerged into the trench.

The battle was over. Hugo Sommer held a wounded Russian against the trench wall. The man was finding it difficult to stand upright and his face was covered in blood. Kohler stood against the other wall still covered in the blood of the Russian with the flat nose. He was rubbing his throat and his skin was the colour of cheese. Hanno was dead. Adlar was wounded in the leg and Rainer was bandaging the bullet wound. Then the wounded Russian officer muttered something and a grenade rolled from his hand. Sommer didn't hesitate. He swung the wounded Russian around and dropped on top of him. The two of them fell on the grenade with the bleeding Soviet soldier's body covering the bomb. The explosion lifted the two men off the ground but the Russian had smothered the weapon. His body had become a shield. Hugo Sommer didn't escape unwounded. His lower legs were peppered with shrapnel and one of his ear drums was ruptured. Even though the Russian officer was dead, Rainer spent some time kicking his body.

"I'll live," said the Rottenführer as they bandaged his wounds. "But the job's not done yet. Leave me Kohler and take out that bunker. The flame panzers can't reach it and this trench runs all the way there."

Klaus nodded at Rainer and they loaded up with grenades. The Obersturmführer went to gather more men but Adlar joined his two comrades and looked quickly at the target from the lip of the trench before dropping down into cover again.

"I think that we won't meet many Ivans getting to the bunker. This was their main position," he said gesturing at the dead.

Rainer nodded and then spat on a corpse. "We can do this."

Klaus licked his lips and nodded. His body was buzzing with adrenalin and he strongly felt the urge to kill. He checked his assault rifle, making sure it was clean but found it had been damaged. Looking around he spotted a Russian submachine gun. The Papasha never seemed to jam so he picked it up and grabbed a couple of the round magazines from inside the dugout. It stunk in there as the woman had voided her bowels on dying. Klaus looked at her body without regret. Everyone in this stinking country deserved to die.

"I'm coming too," said Kohler.

The man still looked shaky but Klaus nodded at his bravery. This is what an SS trooper was expected to do. Fight on even when wounded.

The way to the pillbox was littered with the dead. Some had been caught in the fire of the flame panzers and the twisted blackened bodies turned Klaus's stomach. He hoped he never died that way. There were wounded and he raised his pistol to shoot them but Rainer put a hand on his gun and then placed a finger against his lips indicating silence was necessary. Klaus nodded and lowered the Astra 900 which he was carrying in his left hand. Ahead the communications trench zigzagged. Two Russians were creeping forward, probably sent by their commander to check the area. Both sides spotted each other at the same time with Klaus and Steiner dropping to the ground as they fired. Adlar was still back around the corner but Kohler was too slow. He was hit in the cheek and neck and fell gurgling. His fire from the StG44 had hit both of the Russians and they tumbled away wounded. Adler rounded the corner and put a short burst into each man with his MP40.

The three surviving SS men slunk forward to the bodies, weapons ready in case either moved. Both of the enemy soldiers were dead and so they moved on slowly.

The trench went around another corner and ahead was the rear of the earthen pillbox. Firing could be heard from within and a single man with a SVT-40 automatic rifle guarded the exit.

Rainer had very quickly glanced around the corner with his shaving mirror and reported this in a whisper to his companions.

"Grenades and then a rush?" said Adler very quietly.

Klaus nodded and pulled one of the Russian RG-42s from his pocket and they all counted silently together. The two grenades landed around the open door with one bouncing just inside. There was the crump of bombs, then screams. The Russian near the door was lifted from his feet and hurled through the air. The SS troopers sprinted forward firing from the hip. Bullets poured into the pillbox and then Klaus was inside. He fired at everything until his gun was empty. At least ten enemy soldiers lay dead by the time he was finished.

Later, when the 2nd Battalion had driven passed them through the hole in the Russian line ensconced in their half-tracks, the company had gathered. There were only ninety of the original one hundred and fifty still standing. A few stragglers would drift in later but they had lost a third of their strength. Klaus felt exhausted but the Obersturmführer insisted they eat and wash before they rested. His commanding officer later approached him and he jumped to his feet.

"At ease, Moller," said Sauer. "I've just come to tell you what I told Stein and Vogt. You and your friends performed exceptionally today and I'm putting you all up for an Iron Cross First Class. You have earned it."

For a second Klaus didn't know what to say. He was going to receive a medal for serving his country. Pride surged through him and he spluttered his thanks. He was so pleased, his exhaustion fled momentarily. When eventually he fell asleep a smile crept across his face.

V

The thirty-two Royal Tigers moving forward at speed was an impressive sight. Wolfgang wondered if anything could stop them. Realistically, he knew the heavy panzers were not invulnerable but by the gods they looked powerful. There had been forty-eight but twelve had broken down on the drive from the assembly area.

The ground in front of them had been bombarded with mortars and lighter calibre artillery, in order to detonate mines. Four mine-clearing panzers also rolled in front of the Tigers to clear a path. Wolfgang was glad that the high command had listened on that front. The Tiger was too expensive to be put out of action by a mine. One of the Panzer Fours with the attached roller shook as a hidden bomb was detonated. Anti-tank guns started firing at the Tigers in batteries. Four shells hit the front of his heavy panzer in quick succession, all of them breaking up or bouncing off.

Wolfgang ordered the Tiger to halt and told Franz to target the culprits. Dug in 76mm guns fired together but again they had no effect except to cause the panzer to ring like a bell. The high explosive rounds fired from the main gun soon tore the Soviet position apart. There were trenches and pillboxes in front of the Tigers. Behind the panzers, SS troopers from the French Charlemagne Division clustered like grapes. They wore summer camouflage uniforms and were lucky enough to carry the new assault rifle. The ground underfoot was only lightly cratered and there was little cover except for the Tigers. Ahead lay one of the most fortified areas of the Russian lines. This was where the Royal Tiger was supposed to excel. Doctrine said the Tiger was a break through tank, but often it ended up being used as a defensive weapon or in counterattacks. Now it was being used as it was truly intended, to smash through enemy lines and clear the way for the faster panzers that could exploit the break through and move out into the open.

Ahead, a line of dug in T34s started firing. These were the new version with five crew members and a powerful 85mm gun. The larger turret gave them a higher profile but thicker armour protected the men within. However, nothing could stop an anti-tank round from a Tiger Two. The longer version of the 88mm gun was also extremely accurate and even though the T34s only had their turrets visible, they weren't moving. Immediately Franz started picking off the enemy panzers. A Tiger rocked as it was hit by an 85mm shell but it shrugged off the impact. The range was just over one thousand three hundred metres and the Soviets were having difficulty hitting the Tigers. One shell hit the ground in front of Wolfgang's Tiger and skipped like a stone in a pond. It hit the sloped armour next to the mud guard and deflected away leaving a long mark on the steel.

One of the Tigers took multiple hits and the armour started to come apart near the hull machine gun. The crew abandoned the vehicle just before a round punched through into the panzer's interior causing fire to roar out of the open hatches. The accompanying infantry ran for cover before the ammunition inside the Tiger exploded. The T34/85s were eventually all destroyed, though they had managed to knock out four Tigers. The heavy panzers then switched their attention to the block houses and pill boxes.

As the Russian fortifications started to come apart under the hammer blows of the big 88mm guns, Russian artillery started to fall. The French SS scattered and threw themselves to the ground and the heavy panzers were forced to trundle on alone. Wolfgang felt for the infantry as shells fell among them. There was little cover so the Frenchmen took heavy casualties. Screams and the high pitched whine of incoming rounds could be heard, even through Wolfgang's headset. Shrapnel pattered like iron rain against the side of the Tiger and, not for the first time, he felt grateful that he was inside a panzer.

Two hundred metres from the Russian trench line Wolfgang ordered his company to halt. He didn't want to take the heavy panzers among Russian infantry without the support of the SS troopers. He was forced to sit back and machine gun the line of sand bags that marked the Soviet position, while occasionally firing high explosive shells from the main gun at suspected concentrations of enemy soldiers. It was like hunting quail with an elephant gun. Eventually the Russian artillery stopped firing due to a Luftwaffe attack, though Wolfgang didn't know that at the time, and the SS troopers caught up. The Russians had been smashed by gunfire and pinned down by the panzer's machine guns, and were unable to fight back effectively. Soon hands were being thrown in the air and white flags appeared.

The French SS wanted revenge for their casualties but officers prevented a massacre. Orders were that Russian prisoners were to be shipped to Germany. There was a manpower shortage in the Reich and the days of letting captured soldiers starve to death was over. Battered and wide-eyed Russians were shepherded towards the rear. The wounded were shot out of hand. A few Soviet officers tried to protest but they were hit with rifle butts and then dragged to safety by their men. Wolfgang thought they were lucky to be alive and felt they were probably safe now.

Fourteen Royal Tigers threw back two Russian counterattacks later that day. A mass of T34s and T34/85s had come charging out of a small forest towards a column of half-tracks filled with troopers from the Charlemagne Division. The Tigers were being refuelled in a nearby village when they got frantic radio messages in bad German asking for help. Wolfgang's company were there in five minutes. The T34s were firing at the French who had scattered. Some of the enemy panzers had been knocked out by Panzerschrecks and were keeping their distance. Wolfgang halted in a hull down position and ordered Franz to target the T34/85s first. He had seen that the Tiger wasn't invulnerable to the newer Russian tanks gun and didn't want to take any chances. A lucky hit or multiple strikes from the 85mm gun could destroy his heavy panzer.

The Russians were disorganized and soon fifteen T34s were smoking wrecks. A few of the Russian tanks tried to flank the Tiger's position but Wittmann brought up his company and destroyed the attempt. Burning T34s littered the flat countryside in front of the woodland. Then the enemy were withdrawing back into cover. They had just reached the forest when twelve FW190s swooped in. The fighter-bombers plastered the Russian panzers with bombs and returned to rake the burning woods with cannon fire. The French SS were all on their feet waving and cheering as the Luftwaffe pounded the enemy. Wolfgang was glad of the help but wanted to get down among the SS troopers and say that it was the Tigers who had driven the enemy away. He smiled at his foolishness. It really didn't matter as long as the Russians were defeated.

In the end, the Tigers and the accompanying infantry pushed eight kilometres into the Russian line on the first day, breaching two defensive lines. More minefields and trenches waited in front of them on the next day, and the one after that. The Russians counterattacked relentlessly and their artillery pounded the German lines at night. The French SS took heavy casualties and the 101 Heavy SS Tiger Battalion didn't get off lightly either. Maintenance remained the worst problem with Tigers breaking down or being made unserviceable due to combat. In three days the unit was down to ten heavy panzers.

On either flank the other SS divisions were facing similar problems but were still making progress. The 3rd SS had gone the furthest as they had acquired a number of specialty vehicles to help deal with Russian fortifications. Obergruppenführer Theodor Eicke had a reputation for acquiring the best equipment for his division, even if he had to steal it. Wolfgang had met the man and thought him a brutal killer who seemed to hate Jews with a passion. Eicke may have been a bastard but he certainly knew how to look after his division.

Thoughts of home often intruded on Wolfgang. He realised he needed to concentrate on keeping his company alive and defeating the Russians but Larisa and her pregnancy often had him pondering the future. It was possible he would die in Russia and never see his child yet he wouldn't dwell on that. He had bought gold at highly inflated prices and ordered his wife to bury it at hidden locations. So far they didn't have much of the precious metal but it was enough to keep his family alive for a while if Germany was defeated. At the moment that looked unlikely. The Germany army was after all deep inside Russia and the Allies were locked in combat in the southern half of Spain. Bombers had stopped attacking into Germany and the divisions from the Baltic States, the Ukraine, Galicia and even Dutch and French SS divisions had joined the conflict in the East. As he

chatted with his crew he watched an artillery barrage drop on distant

enemy trenches and wondered if the war would ever end.

v

The landing craft bobbed and wallowed in the blue

Mediterranean Sea. Ahead the wide beaches to the east of Cagliari

beckoned. Tom couldn't believe that finally the Allies were landing on

the shores of one of the main protagonists of the War. Sardinia was

Italian territory after all. The British 6th Paratrooper Division had

landed in around Cagliari the previous night and the 20th and 24th

Brigade were already ashore and had secured the beachhead. The 9th

Armoured Regiment was also landing with the 2/48th Battalion. Tom

had seen its tanks being loaded into the Landing Ship Tanks (LSTs)

back at Gibraltar. The new Sentinels or AC4s with either 17 or 25

pounder guns had been driven aboard the ships by Australian crews

who were itching to use the powerful guns against German or Italian

armour.

The 2/48th Battalion splashed ashore and then gathered around the cafes and houses that lined the beach. Only a few buildings were damaged and all of the reports indicated the Italians defending the area had fled after a few shots had been fired. There were only three divisions on the island and all of them were suffering from low morale. One mountain regiment was based in the north and was resisting the American landing at Porto Torres. Paratroopers from the 82nd Airborne had landed during the night and become engaged in a fierce fire fight but the landing of the Big Red One in the morning seemed to have driven the Italians back. Of course Tom didn't know about this. He was more concerned with the sound of firing to the northwest.

Italian marines and an officer training school were based at the small town of Ussana to the north. The San Marco Regiment had been relocated to the island after the losses it had taken in Russia and the officer school held about five hundred men. Tom was to find out that these groups had gathered a few training P40 medium tanks, some trucks and a little artillery and had attacked the 6th Paratroopers in and around the airfield near the inlet. They had been held by the tough British soldiers but ammunition for the allied troops was running short.

The briefings had said the Island of Sardinia was one hundred miles wide by about two hundred miles long. It was mountainous in parts but split by a long plain that ran half the length of the island, stopping before at range of northern hills. The Americans were taking that end of the island while the Commonwealth took the southern end. Air support came from North Africa, though with the distances involved for fighter coverage the airfield at Cagliari had been made a priority for early capture. There were other airstrips on the island but this one was near the coast and therefore easier to take.

As his battalion walked towards the town Tom remembered what the German prisoner of war had said to him. There was always the chance of redemption. War took, but it sometimes gave you the chance to make amends. He glanced at the men trotting down the road with him. These soldiers were veterans of the desert, England, and now Spain. They were ten miles at least from the airstrip but as they passed a rocky headland to the southwest, a group of tanks drove up. The new Thunderbolt C4 Sentinels were a mixture of those carrying the 17 pounder guns, and the shorter 25 pounders. Tom guessed each platoon wanted a mix of anti-tank and anti-infantry capability. His company piled on to the armour while the rest of the Australians waited for other forms of transport. Now they moved quickly. The tanks drove passed a shallow inland lagoon following a main road that skirted the edge of the town. Dingo armoured scout cars drove up quietly to the column on more than one occasion warning of trouble ahead and suggesting different routes through to the paratroopers. A Staghound armoured car was found around one bend in the road firing at Italian soldiers who were ensconced in a number of low stone houses at an intersection near the Parco di San Michele, an old fortress from the 13th century. The Thunderbolts equipped with 25 pounders pushed forward and blasted the old houses. Tom almost felt sorry for any Italians left inside. Soon the walls of the building had collapsed and all opposition ceased. Then mortar shells started to drop around the column of Australian tanks. There was probably a spotter in the tower of the fortress. Tanks started to shoot at the structure but the walls were very thick.

Intervening structures and the range at which the Thunderbolts were shooting meant it was unlikely the Italian artillery spotter would be driven away.

The commander of the company of tanks decided that speed was their best ally and the Thunderbolts accelerated away. Luckily the mortar crew's aim was atrocious and not a single Australian was hit. The towers on the fortress were shattered as 6 inch naval shells fell on target. The Staghound armoured car had a command radio and had called for some support. Immediately the mortars stopped firing.

Now the Australians were coming upon small groups of weary paratroopers who waved at them as they passed. At one point a major signalled the leading tank to come to a halt before climbing up to have a word with the commander. The Australians then changed direction. The officer from the 6th Airborne stayed on the leading tank and directed the column around the edge of an industrial area where firing could be heard, then the company was told to dismount. The land was open here but a scattering of buildings marked an area of small farms. Lieutenant Harry Bremen warned his platoon that they were only two to three miles from the main airfield. A ferocious fire fight was going on somewhere in front of them and it looked like, at this particular location, the Italians were going to put up a fight.

A Carro Armato P40 medium tank fired from cover near a small white cottage but its shell bounced from the sloped armour on the turret of the leading Australian tank. Unfortunately, as it skipped clear it took off the major's arm at the elbow and sent him sprawling from the vehicle. The Australian armour spread out quickly and returned fire. A 17 pounder shell punched through the riveted armour on the Italian tank with ease, causing an internal explosion that killed the crew. A 90mm gun hidden under a camouflage net fired next and its heavy AT round tore the tracks off a Thunderbolt. The AC3 ground to a halt and its crew leapt from hatches which were quickly thrown open. Other Thunderbolts fired back and soon the large Italian anti-tank gun was knocked out.

Small arms fire had come from a number of buildings and Harry Bremen led his men forward bent over at the waist, as though they were pushing forward into a strong wind. The armour provided covering fire but men went down. Snowy stopped by a fallen tree and started firing short controlled bursts at the Italians from his Bren light machine gun. From the airstrip came a renewed volume of fire and Tom thought he saw men with strange American like helmets firing at the Italians. Then he noticed the unknown soldiers were using Sten submachine guns.

"Come on, the paras are attacking," roared Harry Bremen.

The Australians rose to their feet and charged forward yelling and screaming. The Italians broke and ran. Within hours the airfield was secure and later Tom watched as the first DC3 transport aircraft and then the new Hawker Typhoon fighter-bombers landed. Italian soldiers sat inside the main terminal with their hands tied behind their backs. It looked as though the battle for Sardinia was going to be a short one. What Tom was painfully aware of was that no chance for redemption had come his way. He guessed it wouldn't happen straight away but remained hopeful that the German prisoner was correct. His opportunity would come.

v

"Sardinia!" yelled Goering. "Why in the Hells would the Allies land there?"

"We believe it's a stepping stone," said Kesselring.

The leader of the Luftwaffe had joined Goering and Keitel at Carinhall to discuss the campaign to take Moscow when news of the allied landing had arrived.

"Are the Italians putting up a fight?" asked Goering.

"Some of them are, but not enough to make a difference. The island is likely to fall in a week," said Keitel.

"The Italian Air Force has tried to intervene and has reported some minor success, though at heavy cost. We believe Il Duce has ordered these attacks to stop, in order to conserve the strength of the Regia Aeronautica in case the next attack is on the Italian mainland. The Fw190 fighter-bombers we swapped for the long-range Fiat fighters were used on mass and sunk two transports and damaged a light cruiser. They just had the range to hit the American lodgements in the north of the island."

"Have the French done anything? After all, Corsica is just next door." said Kesselring.

"They said they don't have the strength. As a matter of fact, it looks like they are going to cut their island's garrison to next to nothing," said Keitel.

"Effectively handing Corsica to the Allies," said Goering rubbing his face.

"They believe it would be too hard to defend. They're probably right," said Keitel.

"Where will the Americans go next? If you are right, and all logic would suggest you are, then Sardinia, and probably Corsica are bases, but for what?" asked Goering.

"Italy or southern France," said Kesselring.

"Not northern Spain?" said Goering.

Keitel and Kesselring exchanged a glance. "We don't think so," said the Field Marshal. "If they did that it would be a lot of effort for a small reward. The fastest way to Germany is via France and if they hit

Italy they could knock an important ally out of the war. We need to be ready for either option."

"What have we got in reserve?" said Goering.

"The German Youth SS Panzer Division and Panzer Lehr are both ready but we sent the new 509th Heavy Panzer Battalion to reinforce the attack on Moscow. The two paratrooper divisions and the 22nd Air Landing Division are also available," said Keitel

"It won't be enough, especially if the Allies land in southern France. The French have one panzer division and only three hundred Bf109s scattered around their country, and another eighty Fiats, all of which are in the south. Their army has probably seven good divisions after what happened in Africa. Petain isn't blind and he will pull many of his best units to the Mediterranean coast," said Goering.

"We need to push on with everything we have in Russia," said Kesselring.

"I agree," said Keitel. "The fall of Moscow is our best chance to end the war on favourable terms."

"Yet we are losing ground every day in Spain and now another invasion appears imminent," said Goering.

"We must not step back now," mused Kesselring.

"They will not attack for at least a month, maybe longer," said Keitel.

"That is as long as you have. One month. If Moscow hasn't fallen by then we will need to bring more units back west," said Goering. "Now how far have we got to go?"

Chapter Eleven: July 1944

The 5th SS Panzer Division had been withdrawn as had the 1st and 5th Panzer Divisions. An Estonian SS panzer grenadier division and an infantry division had replaced the missing units on the northern flank of the attack towards Moscow but there was no replacement for the 5th SS Division. Wolfgang was worried. The attack towards the Russian capital had become a battle of attrition. His unit was at Chekhov only sixty kilometres from Moscow, yet he knew the 3rd SS further to the east was closer, at Barybino. Looking at the maps and from what he knew of the advance the plan to envelop the capital from the north and south wasn't working. Divisions seemed to be channelled towards Moscow and the idea of the two arms of the attack meeting behind the city seemed unlikely. If they were going to join anywhere it would be in Moscow itself.

Then there were the stories of the Russians counterattacking on other fronts. The offensive towards Leningrad had been defeated but the attack on German territory along the Don River was ongoing.

Not only were the Soviets applying pressure on other fronts but the losses from the attack on Moscow itself had been heavy. The Charlemagne SS Division was almost exhausted and the 101st Heavy Tiger Battalion was down to seven operable panzers. At least twenty were being repaired and another ten had been returned to Germany, so extensive was the damage to these Tigers. Eleven heavy panzers had been destroyed.

Wolfgang was exhausted himself and wondered how long his command could keep going. He tried to encourage the men to keep working. They were so close now and all of them believed that if Moscow fell the Russians would give up. Then they could deal with the Allies and the war would end. Wolfgang didn't believe in a Greater Germany, he didn't care about the Jews or Communists. He just wanted it to be over so he could be with his family. A letter had come just the other day and the doctor had confirmed Larisa was probably carrying twins. He had been so happy after reading those few lines, and then he had to get into his Royal Tiger and lead another attack. It was one of the few times when his mind hadn't been on the job. If Wolfgang hadn't led such a fine crew they probably would have died as he had almost lead them into a Russian ambush. Only Otto's gentle questions about reconnaissance reports caused him to stop and request that armoured cars check the patch of forest to their west. The Pumas were fired on by new IS2 heavy panzers. Wolfgang was glad he had listened to his driver. The 122mm gun on the Russian tank was very powerful and would have had no trouble knocking out a Royal Tiger from the flank. Hell, they could even take his panzer front on and have a fair chance of winning. The Luftwaffe was called in and pounded the small woodland, followed by an artillery barrage and an infantry assault. Five of the Russian heavy tanks were found burning in the shattered forest.

Now the remaining Tigers were being asked to attack again. This was supposed to be the last belt of fortified positions before the panzer grenadiers hit open country. Wolfgang certainly hoped that was true. Then perhaps his battalion would get a chance to rest and perform some maintenance. The Tigers advanced to a position a few kilometres east of the Moskva River. The 3rd SS had cleared a nearby patch of forest with artillery and a savage infantry assault. This allowed the Tigers to cross on a reinforced pontoon bridge. The 101st

SS Heavy Panzer Battalion had been moved further east to support the push to get behind Moscow and this was where the 3rd and 2nd SS were pushing hard. Vigorous counterattacks on the growing eastern flank by the Russians were a growing concern. The German attack was gradually losing momentum and they were still fifty kilometres from central Moscow.

The Russians here had been severely weakened and their fortifications were thin and hastily put together. The countryside was open and the soil hard packed allowing the Tigers to get into good firing positions and use the long range of their guns to destroy the Soviets. A weak attack was made by a group of KV85 tanks. This was easily beaten off with six of the Russian panzers being destroyed. The Panzer Fours of the 3rd SS then advanced with grenadiers in half-tracks towards Druzhba. That night Wolfgang took his Tigers through to the village of Dubovaya. The 3rd SS had travelled twelve kilometres in a day, one of the biggest advances in the campaign. The 2nd SS had swung in behind them and was to attack northwest in the morning, while the 3rd and the Tigers were heading almost west. The target was the brick airstrip of Bykovo ten kilometres away.

It dawned clear with a strong southerly breeze. Overnight there had been some light rain and the yellow grass was still wet as Wolfgang walked to his battered Tiger. The battalion had twelve working heavy panzers and this was the most that had been operational in a week. Around them the panzers of the 3rd SS had started their engines. Panzer Fours and Panthers were gathering in the distance. Nearby StuG3s were loading shells and even a few of the new Jagdpanthers with their long L71 88mm guns clanked passed. These new tank destroyers were supposed to equip heavy anti-tank battalions but the general of the 3rd SS, Theodor Eicke, had managed to get these as replacements for wrecked StuGs. Wolfgang thought there must be over one hundred and fifty assault guns and panzers in the area. Somewhere nearby the 2nd SS probably had another hundred, though those were supposed to head off in a different direction.

Ahead there was a rectangular patch of land bordered by forest and river. To the north there was an area of woodland about five kilometres wide, beyond which was more open country. It was here the 2nd SS was supposed to push forward. The events of the day were to prevent that from happening. The first sign of trouble was the sound of cannon fire. Panthers were shooting at something approaching from the west. Radio calls were soon heard reporting large scale Russian armour movements. Wolfgang got orders to take his Zug to the edge of the woods and scrub further south. One of the Tigers broke down on the one kilometre to the new position while in the distance the sound of continual gun fire could be heard.

Wolfgang led the remaining two Tigers through the trees running over small saplings and bushes until they emerged from the wood. There were already other German vehicles firing from cover. Eight Jagdpanthers were shooting into a mass of swirling panzers over a kilometre away in a field of wheat. It was hard to pick out targets due to the smoke and dust. Then suddenly a wave of Soviet armour turned towards the line of Tigers and Jagdpanthers. The T34/85s rumbled forward firing on the move. Their shells went high and soon Franz was picking off enemy tanks. His first shell went straight through a driver's observation slit before slamming into the rear of the T34's internal crew area. The enemy panzer veered sideways while burning furiously and clipped another tank, sending it out of control. Another round went through a turret that was turned sideways, igniting the propellant in a shell. Wolfgang didn't hear the screams but he saw the commander of the T34 try and drag himself out of the top hatch while flames roared around him. He fell back inside and disappeared as greasy black smoke poured from the opening.

At six hundred metres, the T34/85s stopped along a road that ran north south across the line of their advance. They all stopped together as Russian tanks finally had radios. A shell hit Wolfgang's Tiger on the hull but broke up on the heavy armour. A Jagdpanther lost a track but otherwise the 85mm guns of the T34s couldn't penetrate the German armour. Some of the Russian tanks closed the range and a Jagdpanther was knocked out as an 85mm shell caused pieces to flake off the steel plate on the inside, and the welds broke causing the steel to come apart.

With his head sticking out of the commander's cupola Wolfgang saw the crew abandon its vehicle and take cover in a hollow in the earth. Looking north he could see flaming panzers from both sides littering the battlefield. What he didn't know was the Russians had thrown their reserves into the attack to try and halt the forward movement of the two SS panzer divisions. The 6th Guards Tank Army had been shifted from the northeast of Moscow and told to halt the German advance. Eight hundred panzers of various types were thrown at the Germans in waves, with the heavy IS2s proving the most difficult to handle. The one hundred and twenty tanks the 3rd SS possessed weren't enough to stop them, so the 2nd SS were forced to change direction and assist their sister division. These panzers came through the forest from the north and caught the heavy Russian armour in the flank throwing it back towards the airstrip at Bykovo.

The Luftwaffe also had a hand in the destruction of the Soviet tanks, as Ju88cs equipped with a single 37mm cannon slung under the fuselage and Ju87s mounting two similar cannons, attacked the weaker rear armour of the Russian panzers as they retreated. Overhead, a massive dogfight between Fw190As and Bf109Gs raged as new Soviet LA7s and Yak fighters duelled. The German jets were absent but a newcomer, the Fw190D, made an appearance. The battle in the sky continued for most of the afternoon and Wolfgang did spot the odd plane fall, trailing long streaks of black smoke.

His Tiger had taken three hits from 85mm shells but was still operational. The heavy panzer battalion was scattered and now pushing forward across a field of burning panzers. He had never seen so many wrecked tanks and the smell of burning rubber and flesh was one which would never leave him. The Soviets had definitely come off worse than the Germans but plenty of Panzer Fours and Panthers sat smouldering in fields of destroyed sunflowers and wheat. Ahead, a Soviet collective farm was being assaulted by a new vehicle that Wolfgang had seen before when he had been testing the Royal Tiger in Germany. The Jagdhund was a conversion of the Skoda T25 Cheetah to a tank destroyer. It had 80mm sloped frontal armour and a L48 75mm gun and was supposed to be very quick to fire. The 2nd SS had replaced all of its StuG3s with the new tank destroyer and it had performed well in the battle.

Wolfgang eased his Tiger forward where it could cover the attacking tank destroyers and he soon found targets. A group of older

T34s charged from between the buildings to attack the Jagdhund. The Tiger's L71 88mm gun cracked as he ducked back inside the turret. Such was the power of the gun that if his head was outside when it fired he could be injured by its concussive back blast. A Russian panzer had its turret ripped off and what was left of the tank careered out of control into a building. Franz coolly picked off more of the enemy armour and only one Jagdhund was caught by a flanking shot through its thin side plate armour and destroyed. Then artillery lashed the battlefield, obscuring everything in dust and fire. This went on for twenty minutes as Wolfgang moved his Tigers forward. Eventually he stopped and asked for directions to the rest of his unit.

By nightfall the massive tank battle was over and the two SS divisions had to stop. They were down to thirty running panzers each and their crews were exhausted. The Russians had lost over seven hundred tanks and Wolfgang wondered if the losses worried them. The may have lost a tactical engagement but strategically they had halted the most threatening of the German thrusts on Moscow, at least for the time being.

The airfield was only three kilometres away but it might as well be the moon. Oberschutze Klaus Moller was lying in a ditch with his StG 44 in his hands. He was hiding at the edge of some parkland not far from the Moskva River. They were only twenty kilometres from the centre of Moscow and were probably the closest unit to the city. The northern arm of the German thrust was stuck at Dubna and Klin. The closest army on that front was still sixty-five kilometres from the centre of the capital. The 1st SS were at Podolsk, forty kilometres from the middle of the city. Far to the south the Russians were attacking, trying to divert German resources and take back the Caucasus. Klaus of course had no idea how thinly stretched the resources of his country were.

A drone approached from the south slowly. Black dots grew in the patchwork sky. Between the scattered clouds waves of Luftwaffe bombers appeared. Four-engined JU290s led the way, followed by HE111s and JU188s. Flak came up from the Russian positions but groups of FW190s dived down to hit the source of the ground fire.

Despite the efforts of the fighters, heavy bombers were hit. Klaus watched as one of the large machines flew over the German lines, disgorging men as it did. Parachutes blossomed as the aircraft rolled over and crashed next to the river. In the distance a rolling thunder began as sticks of bombs fell on known Russian positions. The artillery and reserve troops caught most of the bombardment, while rockets and howitzers hit the forward trenches. Klaus marvelled at the display. He believed the Luftwaffe must have used over a thousand planes, though the number of bombers was really three hundred. Then the sound ebbed, to be replaced by the shriek of a whistle.

The company rose from their trenches as one and Klaus ran with his squad. The exhaustion he felt was forgotten as adrenaline pumped through his veins. Soviet machine guns started to chatter but MG42s swamped their locations with return fire. The first platoon was caught in the open and at least four men tumbled to the ground in quick succession. A STuH42 clattered forward firing its 105mm gun and a strong point burst under the direct hit. Then a hidden anti-tank gun fired and the assault gun lost a track. More shells followed but they had trouble defeating the frontal armour. The crew were forced to abandon the vehicle and eventually a shell punched into the interior of the assault gun causing a fire. The Russian anti-tank guns were spotted and destroyed by a pair of Royal Tigers sitting back a kilometre from the attack. The heavy shells caused the grass to part as they flashed overhead, before smashing into the metal shields of the Soviet anti-tank guns and hurling them into the air with the resulting explosions.

Klaus ran on, only stopping to kneel and fire at some retreating Russians near a small farmhouse. One of the men tumbled to the ground wounded and Klaus sprinted forward and shot him in the head.

"Another one for Killer!" roared Rottenführer Hugo Sommer.

Klaus grinned and continued until a mortar barrage started to drop shells nearby. He could see the wrecked planes around the edge of the airstrip and the crumpled hangers. Flames licked from burning barrack blocks as German panzers raced forward onto the brick runway. Anti-aircraft guns fired back with quick firing 25 mm and 37mm guns. Men came apart as heavy cannon shells hit them, taking off arms and legs and tossing soldiers around like rag dolls. The Tigers arrived and the Russians ran. They had nothing to stop the heavy panzers today and the two of them rampaged across the airstrip followed carefully by a score of Panzer Fours.

The armour was forced to stop by craters. The Luftwaffe bombers may have destroyed the Russian artillery and reserves but it had also torn up the earth to such an extent that the Tigers couldn't continue. Klaus was riding on a Panzer Four by now and he saw evidence of the destruction caused by the bombers all around him. Mangled trucks and wrecked guns lay twisted and scattered. Bodies lay half buried and even T34s were tossed upside down. The road was also destroyed and the Panzer Fours channelled into the first of the outer suburbs of Moscow. Ahead an anti-tank ditch was destroyed by bombs but somehow a panzer managed to cross it, then it halted and started firing at nearby houses. These buildings were already crumbled wrecks destroyed by the Luftwaffe. A burst of machine gun fire caught two German soldiers coming out of the ditch and sent them tumbling back to the earth. The Panzer Four located the chattering gun and destroyed it but was then hit by a large calibre shell that tore its turret off. A squat ISU-152 sat back among the

rubble and fired its heavy machine gun, forcing the SS troopers to

take cover. After a while the massive gun fired again but the shell only

caught a single man near a tree stump. The blast would have killed

the soldier but the shrapnel shredded his body. Klaus and his squad

tracked along the trench until they found a point where they were out

of sight from the assault gun. They popped up and ran ten metres to a

house, bursting through the front door and into the structure without

stopping. An old man came out of the darkness swinging a wood axe

and Rainer shot him down with his MP40. Klaus then tossed two

grenades into the cellar and heard the screams of women and

children just before they went off. Stupid old man shouldn't have

attacked us then maybe I would have spared them, he thought. Then

he ran on.

Rottenführer Sommer pointed out the aim was to flank the

assault gun and destroy it but he told his squad to be cautious.

"It won't be unsupported. Ivan may have been hit hard by the

bombers but it looks like he is starting to recover. There will be infantry about. Also we might bump into civilians, but here everybody is your enemy," said the squad leader.

Klaus had no problems with this. Any Russian who got in his way would die, whether they carried a gun or not.

The back door opened onto a yard crowded with empty crates and rolls of fencing wire. Sommer glanced at the upper windows at the rear of the building.

"I wish we had time to clear the upper storeys," he muttered. "Could be a sniper or a machine gun up there and we wouldn't know until Ivan opened up on us. Still, we need to get to the assault gun," he said.

They dashed passed the pile of timber and wire to a back fence before peering out into the street through a small gap in the split palings. It seemed clear so they ran across the road to another building. Just as they reached the door a group of Russians came around the corner thirty metres away. Both squads saw each other at the same time and started shooting. Rottenführer Sommer killed two men but was hit himself and fell into a group of small bushes. Klaus had a grenade in his hand and pulling the cord, tossed it just behind the Russians. The explosion threw some of the enemy soldiers off their feet. Others were disorientated by the blast but an officer fired his pistol at the SS men before being cut down by a submachine gun blast.

Klaus looked around and saw that Sommer was dead, and Adlar Vogt was groaning and holding a shattered shoulder. Two of the dead Russian officers' bullets had hit him and bright blood was running from between his fingers. Schutze Rainer Stein pulled out his field dressing and started to tear away the shredded uniform. Klaus glance down the street and saw that it was empty. He decided to continue alone and see if he could knock out the assault gun. He thought such an act would win him great regard in his unit so he turned and started cautiously into the next house. This dwelling was a small apartment block like most others in this area, except not as high. A long corridor ran passed stairs going up the next storey. Ahead, a door stood slightly open and Russian voices could be heard from within. Without thinking he burst into the room with his automatic rifle at the ready.

A woman in her late thirties with brown hair tied in a bun stood huddled by the wall with two young girls. The children looked scrawny and their hair was caked with dust. A boy of perhaps ten stood with them. All had wide eyes. Klaus thought they looked unnaturally white and wild. The woman started muttering something. He understood the word please in Russian and perhaps mercy.

"Kill Stalin, Kill Stalin," the woman wailed.

Klaus could almost smell the fear and it was intoxicating. The woman crawled towards him and said something else before speaking again. He thought she was begging. It disgusted him and he pushed her away.

"You are all scum," he said and lifted the rifle. He shot the two girls first and noted the blood that splattered the wall behind them. The sound seemed to echo inside his head. The boy stood with his mouth hanging open. Klaus killed him with a single bullet between the eyes. The woman dropped, crawling to the girls and Klaus let her go. He thought of letting her live but then he remembered her snivelling voice and rage swept through him. He switched the rifle to full auto and fired a long burst, which chewed along her spine. She ended up lying on top of the dead girls covered in blood.

"That wasn't necessary."

Klaus spun and saw Rainer looking at him from the doorway. His face was twisted and his eyes were locked on the bodies.

"They are Russian," said Klaus.

"Maybe," said Rainer, "but you enjoyed it."

"I like killing the enemies of the Reich."

Rainer shook his head slowly and then headed for the rear of the building. He held his Russian submachine gun in front of him and refused to look at Klaus. He is weak and doesn't understand what needs to be done, thought Klaus. German needs to clean this country of vermin and those that couldn't stomach the job shouldn't be in the SS. This is what they would have done to us, given the chance.

The assault gun fired again and its shell smashed a building to rubble, two hundred metres from its position. Nearby, a Russian DShK heavy 12.5 mm machine gun fired down the street. Small arms fire from German infantry came back, chipping bricks and plaster from buildings but doing little more than that.

"We need to cross there," said Rainer pointing at a spot where an apartment block had collapsed across the road creating a jumbled pile of rubble and smashed masonry.

"There could be other Ruskis in the ruins," said Klaus. "I guess if we give it a few minutes and no others start shooting at our comrades we'll be safe."

Rainer nodded but didn't look at him. They made their way through the buildings in and out of shell holes. At one point it looked like they would have to leave the houses and chance the road. Klaus decided to blast a hole between the different dwellings instead, using a few stick grenades. The hole created was just enough to squeeze through into the next building and soon the ruins lay in front of them.

The small maze of rubble allowed them to cross the road unscathed but on the other side two Russians were laying a telephone cable. They were busy trying to splice a broken wire together and spotted Klaus as he slid down a rubble slope towards them. He fired his automatic rifle from the hip and the bullets caught both men in the body. Rainer also fired and the bodies jerked a few times before becoming still. Klaus cut the almost complete connection and threw the spool of cable into a shell hole. One of the Russians moaned and Rainer shot him once with a single bullet before crawling to a smashed wall and looking around.

"Nobody seems to have taken any notice of the firing," he said

Even though the area near the ruins seemed clear Klaus was worried the small arms fire might bring a curious Russian squad to their position.

"We need to move now," he hissed.

The assault gun then did them a favour. It backed down the street to a new location near an apartment where the top floor had collapsed into the structure. The Russians manning the heavy machine gun were now not in a position to support the vehicle with covering fire. A shell roared from the short barrelled gun and another building blew up in a shower of dust and bricks.

"How many grenades do we have?" asked Rainer.

The pair of German soldiers soon discovered they had four between them.

"This is not enough to disable the engine by throwing them on the back of the panzer. We'll have to drop them in through the hatch, or down the barrel of the gun," said Klaus.

Rainer nodded and bound his two grenades together while Klaus did the same.

"You better do this," said Rainer. "I'll cover you. Keep the grenades in one hand and a pistol in the other. Try and climb on the back of the panzer quietly so as not to spook them. There is a good chance the hatch is open."

Klaus almost objected, then he realised if he destroyed the panzer the glory would be his, if he lived.

He dashed from the building in which they were hiding and made the twenty metres to the ISU152. Then a burst of rifle fire chewed up the ground at his feet. Rainer started shooting with the StG44 that Klaus had left with him. He was glad now that his comrade had decided to stay back and cover him. Klaus hauled himself onto the rear of the assault gun trying to move quietly, as advised. He crouched behind the raised crew area and readied a grenade. Klaus decided not to pull the cord until he was sure the hatch would open as he didn't want to be left with a live explosive in his hand with a four and a half second fuse burning. He tried the left hand hatch first and found it wouldn't budge, so he tried the right hand one. This lifted a little so he tucked the pistol into his belt, pulled the cord and opened the hatch. The grenade dropped inside and Klaus heard a roar of surprise. The explosion occurred before he dropped the steel trap door shut but he had slid back enough from the opening that the blast and shrapnel missed him. For good measure he set the fuse burning on the second bomb and dropped it in as well, but this time he did slam the hatch shut. As the second grenade detonated Klaus jumped from the back of the assault gun and ducked inside a nearby doorway. He could see Rainer across the street through a window and his comrade signalled him to stay put.

The heavy machine gun continued to fire around the corner until someone fired a number of Panzerschreck rockets at its position. Other Russians were moving up but after the heavy machine gun was knocked out they ran head long into the advancing SS troops. A vicious fire fight ensued, followed by hand-to-hand fighting. Klaus missed most of this as the action swept down side streets, though he and Rainer had the opportunity to ambush a group of retreating Russians as they fled. Klaus fired at them until his new Luger was empty, while his comrade shot down the running troops with the automatic rifle.

Soon SS troops had taken possession of the area and Hauptscharfurher Hansen stood before him. "I believe we have you two to thank for the destruction of that IS," he said pointing at the smouldering enemy assault gun.

Klaus grinned but Rainer looked away. "It was mainly Killer's work," his companion said.

"Killer, eh! I bet there's a story behind that name," said the officer. "Well done anyway, I don't think that is the last of this. In the meantime, we need to get ready for the inevitable Russian counterattack so you better find the rest of your platoon."

"Yes Herr Hauptscharfurher," the two soldiers said in unison.

V

The Americans picked at the edge of Germany's aerial

defences without making the deep penetration raids of March.

Lieutenant Henry Richardson understood why, but it was still

frustrating. The loss rate for the heavy bombers during the spring

raids had become horrific. Until an answer for the depredation of the

German jets was found, it would be too costly to send the B17s and

B24s far passed the Rhine.

This morning the Yoxford boys were up early testing new

P51Ds. They wouldn't be accompanying the heavies to Aachen. Henry

was fine with that as he needed the rest. He had already flown to the

Rhine yesterday, except that time the target had been Cologne. The

jets had come out in force to oppose them and forty B17s had been

lost, as well as fifteen of the escort. The purpose of these raids was to

bleed the Luftwaffe by providing such a massive escort that the jets

struggled to have a clear run at the bombers. P47s and P38s could

almost fly to Cologne making it easier to saturate the sky with

fighters. Smaller attacks by medium bombers at the same time tried to dilute the German response but that didn't always work as they were often ignored. Then there was also the new prop driven fighter the Luftwaffe had introduced to make things interesting. The FW190D was a hot ship. It was fast, well-armed and had an impressive turning circle. In the hands of a good pilot it was extremely dangerous.

To the north of his flight the bombers were gathering on the East Anglian airfields. Marltesham Heath was packed with bombers lining up in the early dawn light getting ready to take to the sky. Suddenly a number of sleek twin engine aircraft shot by at low altitude.

"What were they, skipper?" asked 2nd Lieutenant Mac McConnell.

"I think they're jets," said Henry. "Follow me but hold formation."

The P51s dived after the Arado232s and started to close the distance. Ahead, the airstrip loomed and Henry realised what the Germans were up to.

"Oh my God. They plan to hit the strip while the bombers are getting ready to takeoff," he said. He pushed the throttle to its absolute limit and felt the engine surge. Ahead the first four jets reached the airfield. B17s were lined up in rows, their engines revving. The first bomber was trundling down the runway slowly building up speed when the Arado 232 released its bomb. The AB-250 bomblet dispenser held thirty SD-4 butterfly bombs. These were usually an anti-armour bomb, but it was also perfect for use against aircraft. The B17 was probably moving at about sixty miles an hour when the bomblets exploded around it. Two of the devices hit the wing blowing it off and shattering the fuel tanks. The B17 lurched sideways, a mass of flames and shrieking aluminium before smashing into the dispersal huts. The second jet dropped its bombs on a group of six bombers waiting to takeoff. The devastation was impressive with engines bursting apart and B17s being split in two. Then a bomb load went off and planes were torn apart with pieces flying hundreds of feet into the air.

An Arado flew into the blast zone and the pilot lost control. The jet flipped over and flew at full speed into a hangar on the edge of the field where it blew up. The curved roof of the large structure

bulged outwards before coming apart in a rain of fire and iron. The

next four jets caught a group of bombers still on the taxiway and

bracketed them with cluster bombs, with similarly impressive results.

B17s erupted in balls of smoke and flame. Henry saw a mid-turret

from a B17 fly high into the air before coming to rest on top of the

officer's mess. Everywhere there were exploding aircraft, smoke and

fire. The fully laden bombers were a death trap and men were

running from their machines and jumping into fox holes. Elsewhere,

pilots tried to guide their planes across grass fields away from the

destruction. In one case an out of control bomber went through a

high wire fence and onto a perimeter road before coming to a halt.

Finally Henry and his wingman caught up to the last four jets.

The range was still four hundred yards but he knew he couldn't wait.

The new N9 gun sight was definitely helpful and the fact he was

almost straight behind the jet was also useful. He fired a quick burst

from his six guns then adjusted his aim and fired a two second burst.

He saw pieces break off the Arado around its engine and starboard

wing. The plane dipped sideways and smashed into a line of trees at the edge of a straight section of country road. Henry winced as he knew he had killed a man. He hated the thought but looking at the carnage at the airstrip he knew he had no choice.

The second jet was hit by his wingman and dropped to the ground. It nosed into a small mill pond where it hit the low wall holding back the water and exploded. The other Arados dropped their bombs over the runway hitting a group of bombers that had switched off their engines and were in the process of being abandoned by their crews. Some of the B17s were trying to spread out and taxied haphazardly away from the other planes. Again, bombers were torn apart and fires raged as men ran for their lives. Henry felt his anger build. He didn't want to kill Germans but his countrymen dying by the score. As the last jet turned away he managed to cut inside its turn. The speed from his dive was dissipating and the jets were picking up speed as they were now free of any ordinance. This one had made a mistake and he fired. His burst hit the tail and the German panicked, throwing his plane into a tight turn. Henry followed him and caught the jet as it tried to climb away. The range was now about five hundred metres but Henry fired two long bursts. An engine flamed out and the Arado dived and turned hard towards the east. Allowing for some deflection he fired again and the jet flew through the stream of bullets. Henry saw the second engine explode and hoped the German would jump. Even now he just wanted to stop this man hurting any more Americans; he didn't want to kill him. The pilot didn't bail out and the Arado plunged into a field of wheat, exploding and setting the crop on fire.

"Great shooting, skipper," radioed Second Lieutenant McConnell. "That's your tenth kill."

Henry didn't feel like celebrating. He had just taken two lives and behind him hundreds of his countrymen were dead or wounded.

v

The group of high ranking Germans had gathered at Carinhall to discuss the attack on Moscow but Goering had wandered off topic. He pointed at Speer and wagged his finger.

"If we don't get these wonder weapons into production then the enemy's ability to outproduce us will eventually win them the war!"

"We have the jets," said Kesselring.

Goering spun on his heels. "They are not enough. The Stormbird is a defensive weapon. Granted, it has given us control of the skies east of the Rhine, but to the west allied aircraft reign supreme. Even in the east the Russians are able to contest airspace over selected areas of the front for extended periods of time."

"We are stretched too thin, my Führer," said Kesselring.

"Do you think I don't know that!" snapped Goering. "I watch the numbers. Luftwaffe strength has fallen below five thousand serviceable aircraft for the first time in over a year!"

"Yes, but we have many more jets in the sky and new piston engine fighters are making their way to our pilots," said Kesselring.

Speer chimed in. "And many of those are the Arado bomber."

"But this cannot win us the war. When is the A4 going to be ready?" asked Goering.

"September, probably late in the month. The plan is to launch one hundred against London in the first attack. Since the British have started bombing by night we have dispersed production. Their raids are still not much more than a few hundred planes at a time, but they are growing. They mainly use the American B24, but a few new machines called the Lancaster were recently shot down by flak."

"The lack of interference to our production facilities is something I do thank the Luftwaffe for," said Goering in a softer tone. "However, it won't win us the war. The super bomb is still years from becoming a reality, and our enemies must be working on their own. We need to have countermeasures; some way of striking back just as hard if they ever make one."

"My Führer, the A4 can carry chemical weapons," said Speer. "We are working on proximity fuses that will spread the payload at one thousand metres and we are increasing our stockpile of Sarin, but we have plenty of Tabun and it's almost as good."

Goering nodded grimly. "Alright, we will prepare some rockets with these agents but we won't use it unless provoked by an allied use of chemical weapons, or the detonation of a super bomb. Actually, at some stage we might have to send them a warning."

"In the meantime, work on the Sparrow jet fighter continues apace. We are not making it out of wood as the gluing problems were slowing the project. The fuel load has been increased and the plane is projected to be ready by February next year," said Speer.

"Galland and Molders think it's a waste of time," said Kesselring.

"They know nothing about production costs," snapped Speer. "Imported, unskilled labour can build these planes and they are cheap."

Kesselring put his hands in the air as though surrendering and Speer frowned.

"These are still defensive measures. Even if the new anti-aircraft rockets eventually work, they protect us but they don't help us attack," said Goering.

"The E50 and E75 project will probably give us top quality cheaper panzers by mid-1945," said Keitel.

"I haven't heard of these," said Field Marshal Manstein.

"They are a project close to my heart," said Speer. "Cheaper, more reliable panzers which retain all of the best aspects of our present vehicles. The E50, or Jaguar is the closest to being finished. I'm determined to keep it to the proposed weight of 50 tonnes. It will have the same gun as a Royal Tiger and slightly improved armour over the Panther. The Maybach nine hundred horsepower engine will make it quite fast for its size. It will also be more reliable. We are also working on more powerful engines."

"But it is at least six months away," said Goering.

"Well, that is why Moscow remains the key," said Field Marshal Model. He stood to the side of the room and was visibly frustrated by the discussions on projected weapon systems. As the commander of the northern pincer in the attack on Moscow, he was here to see what extra resources he could get for his army group.

"Agreed," said Goering. "It will cut off a major transportation hub as well as take a huge manufacturing centre. It is also an important symbol. Perhaps, with its capture, Stalin will seriously negotiate with us. So far talks with Molotov have not been fruitful.

They still talk of making the Dnieper River the border in the south and handing back Leningrad in the north. They want us to give back the Crimea and the oil fields! It's a joke."

"Without US support they would have surrendered already," said Keitel.

"I know," said Goering. "Their oil from Baku stopped flowing for a while, but now our bomber raids are too expensive in terms of planes lost. So, we mine and attack Astrakhan and attack shipping on the Volga, but with US tankers they are now up to seventy-five percent of their pre-war production. Our own oil from Grozny has only just started to flow west and our hold on the Caucasus north of the mountains is far from secure."

"It has increased our oil stocks by another six percent," said Speer.

"Yes, but for how long," said Goering.

"This is not why I came here, my Führer," snapped Field Marshal Model. "I need to know what you want done about Moscow. We still haven't taken the city and our losses are heavy."

Goering turned, his face red. "Your talent for blunt speaking is well known, Herr Model, but without oil, new panzers and jets, your army would be destroyed."

There was an uncomfortable lull. Goering took a deep breath and turned deliberately to Field Marshal Manstein. "What is the current situation?"

The handsome general picked up a short pointer and moved to a large map of Moscow and its surrounds. "The 3rd SS have made the deepest penetrations into the city from the southeast. The 1st SS have just closed up to the outer suburbs and the Charlemagne Division are supporting them. To protect their flank the 2nd SS and the 101st SS Heavy Panzer Battalion are trying to fend off vigorous Russian attacks. We are about to pull the 1st SS from the city and replace them with the 4th SS Panzer Grenadier Division. The panzer divisions are not suited to city fighting and their remaining panzers would be helpful in holding back the Russian attacks on their eastern flanks. I do have to report that these units are exhausted and have taken heavy casualties."

"They must push on, Herr Field Marshal. I have nothing to replace them with. They are Germany's finest and it is essential they use all their willpower to find a way forward," said Goering.

Model then stood up and walked to the map. "We have moved a number of weakened panzer divisions from the front line. The 1st, 5th, and 20th Panzer Divisions have been pulled back and replaced with infantry formations. The 78th Sturm Division has been sent forward to take their place. We have captured the main railway station at Zelenograd and pushed another ten kilometres further before our units became bogged down in the trenches and wire that the Russians placed in the outer defences of their capital. The countryside here is more thickly forested and not as suited to armour as the southern thrust was, hence the switch to infantry divisions. Khimki is the next target and we plan to hammer it with the heavy bombers tomorrow, launching a full attack."

"I'm not seeing a joining of the two thrusts behind the city in any of this," said Goering.

"Russian counterattacks and lack of resources have led us to a position where both thrusts will now meet in the city," said Manstein.

"Urban fighting is costly and the Russians always seem to have more men than us. It's lucky we have the Baltic States and the Ukraine on board, supplying us with soldiers. Now the question is what the Allies will do?" said Goering.

"Reports from Arado jet reconnaissance planes show a build up before Madrid and a concentration of shipping in Gibraltar and Cartagena," said Kesselring. "We don't have long and they will land somewhere."

"Yes, but will it be southern France, or Italy," said Goering. "We need to take Moscow in the next two weeks. Redouble your efforts gentlemen. The fate of the Reich depends on Moscow being taken."

Chapter Twelve: August 1944

The armoured car drove slowly through the streets of Ariccia. The M8 had to carefully navigate around the tight bend in the street to reach the outskirts of what once would have been a pretty town. Sergeant Charlie Winklen watched the roofs of the surrounding houses in case a German or Italian sniper had stayed behind with orders to cause further casualties. The 4th US Armoured Division had come ashore two days after the initial landings at Anzio, following on from the 29th US infantry, the 2nd NZ Motorised and the 9th Australian Motorised Division. The 101st Screaming Eagles Airborne Division had landed the night before the attack, with the 2nd Brigade of the 1st British Parachute Division landing slightly to the south of the lodgement.

The Italian 47th Infantry Division folded almost immediately, having recently returned from Northern Russia where it had suffered heavy casualties and was still reforming. The attacks of ferocious paratroopers followed by American tanks had led to units surrendering on mass. Now the road to Rome seemed open. Only small units of Italian paratroopers and some hurriedly moved detachments of the 3rd Blackshirt Division stood in their way.

Rumours abounded of trouble within the Italian government, but at the present moment none of that mattered to Charlie. Aerial reconnaissance had suggested armour was moving towards the front and the divisional commander wanted to know if it was German or Italian. Charlie knew the Australians and New Zealanders were pushing on/towards? Rome closer to the coast and the 29th was moving south towards Latina. The 4th Armoured was to skirt north passed Lake Albano and then plunge on top of Rome itself. He had heard another US division was landing tomorrow, to be followed by a British unit, though he didn't know which ones.

Thick stone walls ran along both sides of the road before opening onto a side road that gave Charlie a view of the surrounding countryside. The land here dropped away towards a wide, fertile plain dotted with olive groves and forest. To the east the land climbed over a thickly wooded slope towards the rim of the volcanic lake which lay out of sight. Ahead, a spur jutted out from the hillside through which the road made its way into a cutting. Charlie listen carefully and noted a grinding sound.

"Back up," he yelled to his driver.

The M8 sped back along the gravel and had just reached the cover of a red brick wall when a tank appeared. Charlie soon spotted two more and picked up his radio.

"Foxtrot Charlie, this is Little Fox. A P43 Italian tank and two P40s advancing on the main road between Ariccia and Albano Lazaile. On the old aqueduct. Wait, there is another P43 with an even longer gun, must be a new model, and there is infantry with them, probably a couple of companies," he said into the radio. He waited for the response and then acknowledged.

"Right boys, back to that company of infantry with the M10s. Things are about to get hot. They are too close for air support to get them in time so our troops will have to do it the old fashion way."

The M8 drove quickly back to an advancing company of troops who were standing around their half-tracks consulting a map. Charlie jumped down and made his way straight towards the ranking officer who happened to be a major. He quickly gave his report and the major stood tall and stretched.

"We can't stop them at the aqueduct so we will meet them in town. Lieutenant, get onto those M10 tank destroyers and tell them to move their arses here pronto. Also break out the bazookas. We will set up a defensive position just back from the main square at the T-intersection and along the side streets. Tell the men to hurry. It sounds like those tanks are close," said the officer.

The Italians drove across the road on the top of the ancient aqueduct and into the town square. The enemy tanks and infantry started to spread out just as the Americans began to fire from a tower which blocked the exit to the south. Machine gun bullets lashed the Italians and the P40s fired back with their 75mm guns. Masonry showered the area and men screamed. From the top of a building on the other side of the square, a rocket lanced down from a bazooka. It hit a P40 on the turret and the tank burst into flames.

Men were running everywhere and bullets ricocheted off armour.

Charlie had backed his M8 down a narrow lane behind the Italians and now wondered what to do. He was hidden around the curved side of a tall building but behind him the road narrowed to a pedestrian pathway. He knew there was a lane across the square that curved around under the aqueduct to a lower level of the town. Charlie could have abandoned the M8 and retreated by foot but he felt that would be a type of defeat, and decided to try and save the armoured car. Crossing the square at high speed would be dangerous but perhaps, with the element of surprise, they could do some damage on the way.

He told Private Patterson to drive rapidly behind the Italian tanks. His driver put his foot down and the M8 shot forward hitting an Italian rifle man who was too slow to get out of his way. Charlie was firing with the Browning .50 machine gun at anything that moved. The gun jerked in his grip and the movement of the armoured car made it difficult to hit anything. When they were right behind the second P40 tank Charlie told Patterson to stop. The M8 rocked to a halt and the he yelled at Private Occleshaw to fire. The 37mm anti-tank shell went through the thin armour at the back of the tank and the engine immediately caught fire. Then Charlie screamed for them to drive. It all happened so quickly that the Italians were too stunned to respond. The M8 then charged out of the square and around the sharp corner and under the aqueduct.

Unfortunately the armoured car had to slow to go around the bend and there were Italians above them on the aqueduct. As they came out from under the bridge like structure the men above them threw dropped grenades. If Charlie had thought to stop under the aqueduct it wouldn't have mattered and if the M8 wasn't open topped it wouldn't have mattered. But it did. Three grenades dropped behind the car and one landed in the crew compartment. Charlie just had time to yell a warning and jump out of the vehicle when the grenade exploded. Other explosions occurred behind the M8 and he was shielded from the shrapnel. The one which exploded inside the armoured car occurred in a cramped space and killed his crew. Charlie had no time to grieve, for the Italian soldiers were aiming their rifles and submachine guns at him. When the smoke cleared they would gun him down. Next to him was a garage door but it was locked. He drew his pistol and shot the rusty mechanism, half expecting the bullet to bounce and wound him. He was lucky and forced the door open just as a burst from a Beretta Model 38 submachine gun was fired in his direction. The bullets chipped rocks behind him as he plunged into the darkened garage.

In the gloom he tripped over a motorcycle. Cursing, he stood up and examined the machine. It seemed to be in working order though there were no keys. Smiling he pulled out his small knife and looked for the wires he needed. A quick cut and he was touching them together while he kicked the bike over. Charlie prayed there was fuel in the tank. The Italians would be sending at least a squad after him and they didn't have far to come. The Moto Guzzi GT20 came to life with a roar and he jumped on the back. Gunning the motor, he shot from the garage out onto the street where he almost crashed into the wall on the other side of the lane. Hearing shouts he turned the machine and sped down the narrow roadway as bullets chewed up the bricks around him. The lane was straight for over one hundred metres and Charlie was certain he would die. He had just made the corner when a bullet hit the rear tyre throwing the machine off balance. Charlie hit the brakes and managed to perform a controlled crash that took most of the skin off his left arm. He rolled around the corner, and coming to his feet, took off at a run down the descending lane.

Behind him the battle raged around the town square and surrounding streets. The American soldiers held the Italians to a narrow strip of buildings adjoining the aqueduct. The P43 tank with the 75mm gun had survived a number of hits on it frontal armour from bazookas and the P43bis tank sat back a little and blasted buildings with its 90mm gun. M10 tank destroyers eventually pushed forward to engage the Italian armour but were forced back by a sustained mortar barrage.

While the battle raged, Charlie continued to try and skirt around the fight in order to make his way back to the American lines. The streets were strangely empty so he slowed his pace and started to walk. He was shaking and fell to his knees. The death of his crew suddenly overwhelmed him. Before he had been trying to stay alive but now he relived the moment and cursed his decision to save the M8. If they had abandoned the armoured car then maybe his men wouldn't have died. They were his responsibility and he had failed them. He should have realised that there would be Italian soldiers on the bridge. He took risks and the men under his command had been killed. When he returned to the army Charlie decided he would ask to be reduced to the rank of private. He wasn't fit to lead men.

v

Rommel joined Manstein at the situation map. The two field marshals had driven to Carinhall for the conference and had arrived early. Both were curious about the Italian situation though neither of them commanded troops there.

"Rome will fall," said Manstein, "And then they will cut the country in half."

"I thought the situation was stabilising. The capital hasn't been taken yet," said Rommel.

"What the map doesn't show is the political situation. Mussolini has been arrested and it looks like the new Italian government is trying to change sides. Of course, it has been mishandled, so German units have been able to disarm most of the

Italian Army. A few divisions have sworn to fight on and there is even talk of an Italian SS division, though that's a fair way off."

"I know the 1st Paratrooper Division landed at Monte Cassino and the 22nd Air Landing Division were flown straight in to Rome, but what about the rest of the operational reserve?" asked Rommel.

"The Panzer Lehr are holding back the ANZAC Corps while the 116th Panzer is trying to keep the Americans in check. The German SS Youth Division is just arriving and trying to hold the Allies back from cutting across the neck of the peninsular but the enemy are flooding ashore," said Manstein. "What impressed me is they started in the middle of the country. For a while I thought the Allies might invade Sicily and start at the bottom, but that would have been stupid."

"And Madrid is about to fall," said Rommel gloomily.

"I've heard. It seems we are just stretched too thin with the huge effort to take Moscow, and now it looks as though the Russians are about to make another attempt to take the Caucasus."

"We have to call off the attack on Moscow," said Rommel.

"It was our one chance to win the war," said Manstein. "Now it looks like the best we can settle for is a draw."

"The war will be a long one if that is the case."

The conference decided to scatter the forces before Moscow and to pull the line back twenty kilometres in order to straighten out some of the bludges and save troops. The panzer divisions were moved, with some being sent west and others going to southern Russia. Goering barely said anything. He sat slumped in his chair while generals discussed what was best to do. Keitel, the lap dog, as Rommel thought of him, tried to cheer the Führer.

"It is not hopeless; we can try again for Moscow when the situation stabilises," said Keitel.

Goering's head slowly turned and he stared at the field marshal through blood shot eyes. Rommel wondered if his leader was exhausted or back on morphine. "This was it! The Allies grow stronger every day. Our chance is gone. Now we can only exhaust them and hope they become too weary to continue. The cost of blood to our people will continue to grow! In the end we could still lose. We had to

348

take Moscow to have any chance of winning and we came so close, but I won't lose the oil fields!" yelled the Führer.

For a moment there was silence before Speer spoke. "I can increase production if we keep the skies clear over Germany, and we can keep moving industry further east. We must increase the involvement of our remaining allies. The loss of Italy will hurt but we need to ask more of the Bulgarians. Maybe they can take over occupation duties in Greece. Yugoslavia has only sent one motorised brigade to Russia; they need to increase that to at least a corp. We need to rearm and energise the French. The line needs to be held in Spain and Italy while Russia's oil fields need to be hit again."

Goering seemed to come out of his despair. "We have to work on our wonder weapons. The Allies still don't have jets and we are working on a second generation, then there are also the new U boats. The rockets will rain down on London in response to their bomber attacks on our western cities."

"It is essential to find a way to strike the USA," said Kesselring.

Again there had been silence for a few heart beats as that statement sunk in.

"You are right," said Goering. "The war hasn't even touched the American continent yet and that has to change."

v

Redemption had become an obsession for Sergeant Tom Derrick of the Australian 9th Division. So far Italy had not offered him his chance, though it had tried to kill him more than once. The coastal plain was flat and open, and the arrival of an elite German division had slowed the ANZAC advance on Rome. The Americans were said to be only twelve miles from the centre of the city and had taken the countryside around the Parco dei Castelli Romina. Now that the volcanic lake had been taken, the 4th US Armoured had pushed on to Caimpino. The Americans were almost in the suburbs but the arrival of the 22nd Air Landing Division from Germany had slowed their rush. The collapse of the Italian Army meant there were holes in the front. The 3rd US Armoured were already at Sora, almost halfway across the peninsular, and the 29th US infantry had reached Cassino where their leading elements were already in combat with German Paratroopers. US airborne troops had marched by foot along the coast as far as Fondi and had yet to meet any serious opposition, and the British 6th Paratrooper Division was fighting Italian Blackshirt units that had refused to surrender at Colleferro. The main problem the Allies were facing was supply, with most of the food and ammunition having to come ashore at the small port of Anzio or over the beaches. The ANZACs were supposed to take the harbor of Ostia that served Rome. The Allies knew it was a small port but every improvement would help and there was also an important airstrip in the area.

Overhead, aircraft duelled. Tom watched and remembered the fighting between the Italian Air Force and the Americans over the previous week. The Regia Aeronoautica had thrown every available fighter at the bridgehead, with the FW190s they had swapped for long range Fiats proving particularly effective. The problem was compounded by the distance the P38s and P47s had to fly to support the landing from Sardina and Corsica. The eight-hundred-mile round trip, plus time above the target, strained both the pilots and the range of the machines. The B25s and B26 medium bombers attacked troop concentrations but were attacked by RE 2005s and Fiat G55s. Tom had seen the wrecks of at least eight of the bombers in the last two days. Even now he could see one that had crash-landed in the fields before him.

The M3 half-tracks drove slowly over the sun-baked fields. About three hundred yards in front of them fifty tanks moved unhurriedly towards the distant airstrip. Suddenly the armour turned to the northeast and sped up. Ahead, Tom made out small dark shapes moving towards them from the forests around Pratica di Mare.

Lieutenant Harry Bremen was staring through his US Westinghouse binoculars at the approaching tanks. "Damm, Panthers and some type of tank destroyer that I've never seen."

The Panzer Lehr Division had sent its panzer regiment to counterattack the ANZACs in strength and now the AC4 Sentinel tanks of the Australian army equipped with 17 pound guns and the AC3 Thunderbolt tanks with 25 pounder guns would meet the Panthers head on. At one thousand five hundred yards, the Germans drew first blood when a Sentinel equipped with the shorter 25-pound gun slewed sideways and smoke started to pour from the hatches. Tom saw men coughing and retching as they pulled themselves from the vehicle and fell to the brown earth. There were probably sixty Australian tanks in the open as well as a number of Achilles tank destroyers. The Germans seemed to have a similar number of vehicles.

The range closed and soon Tom could see the L on a black shield on the Panthers and squat tank destroyers. The Jagdpanzer with their L48 75mm guns stopped and started firing from the edge of the conflict zone. The Panthers' longer guns easily defeated the armour of the Australian tanks but the superb 17 pound guns could also punch through the German armour. Anti-tank rounds from the 25 pounders weren't as effective and as HEAT rounds were still being developed and many of the Sentinels were ineffective until they could take flank shots.

The M3 half-tracks stopped and the Australian infantry jumped out and dispersed. Tom ran forward with Snowy, Stan and

Harry. His white-haired friend carried an MG42 and the officer an Italian Beretta Model 38. Harry said it was more powerful than the Owen and almost as rugged. Tom used the Thompson and swore by it. His MP40 was out of ammunition anyway and he supposed it was what you were used to. Around them, tanks smouldered or burnt and a Sentential tank without a turret poured greasy black smoke into a clear sky. A small farmhouse surrounded by trees burnt and near it sat a Panther with two holes in its frontal armour. It wasn't on fire, so Tom slowed.

"Where's the crew?" he yelled above the sound of the flames.

An MP40 fired from a group of shrubs and Stan screamed. The rest of the Australians dropped to the ground and Harry opened fire with his submachine gun. Men in black uniforms darted among the bushes around the farmhouse, firing with pistols and other small arms. Then Snowy turned the MG42 heavy machine gun on them. Some Germans jerked and fell and others threw their hands in the air. Before Tom could speak, his lieutenant gunned down the surrendering panzer troops.

"Don't even say it," said Harry meeting his sergeant's gaze.

Around them tanks exploded or fired at unseen targets. Tom could make no sense of the battle. He wasn't to know that even the Puma armoured cars of the Panzer Lehr's reconnaissance battalion had joined the battle, firing with their high velocity 50mm guns at half-tracks or the side armour of the Australian tanks. German infantry were also moving forward into the conflict area which was only about two miles wide and three miles long. Neither side dared use air units or artillery in fear of hitting their own troops.

A Panther stopped nearby and fired at a Sentinel that was only a few hundred yards away. Its commander was in the cupola speaking into a radio and was obviously taking the chance of sticking his head out of his tank in order to see well. Harry jumped from the bushes and shot the man with a single burst before running forward. He then ran onward with a grenade in his hand, but the Panther accelerated away and spun in a tight circle throwing up earth as it did. The Harry threw the grenade but it bounced harmlessly from the turret and exploded in the field. The Panther stopped and the machine gun swivelled. Then the panzer shuddered as an anti-tank round hit it in the engine. The crew members started to hastily evacuate the Panther and were cut down by the Australians before their feet had even hit the ground.

Three Sentinels charged passed Tom and his squad, but one of them lost a track and came to a screeching halt. Two shells hit the tank in quick succession and it started to burn. Men tried to pull themselves from the hatches but the fire grew quickly. Tom didn't hesitate. This was redemption. He would pull these men free and save them from a horrible death. Charging across the hard packed earth he saw a man with sandy hair trying to pull himself from one of the forward hatches in the hull. As he ran flames licked around the man. The soldier started to scream. Tom was only twenty yards from the tank when the man slipped back inside. Dirt whipped up around his feet and he realised someone was shooting at him. Behind him he heard the scream of Snowy's MG42 and the noise of a submachine gun.

Reaching the tank he pulled himself aboard and looked into the flames. Inside, the blackened man writhed in the fire. Tom was horrified and leant away. He hesitated for only a second before sticking the muzzle of his Thompson in the hatching and squeezing off a long burst. The screaming stopped. This wasn't redemption; he was an executioner. Tom fell to the ground next to the tank with tears streaming down his face. Harry ran up next to him and started to pull him back to the bushes near the farmhouse.

"Come on mate, it will be alright, we'll get through this," his friend said. Harry kept whispering soft words in his ear until they were back in cover. Tom didn't hear the reassuring words. All he could see was the twisted and blackened face of the man in the tank.

v

The ME262B had two seats and Oberleutnant Kurt Osser sat in the rear position. He thought he would be unhappy in a training role but now understood that the enforced break from combat was exactly what he needed. His last mission had been over Cologne and it had been the first time he had used the R4M rockets. Kurt was impressed by their performance. He was able to fire the projectiles

from a thousand metres in a battery of twelve rockets and then he

could fire another twelve a second later. At that range, the twenty-

four rockets would saturate an area of about thirty metres square.

One or two would be almost certain to hit a bomber and one was all it

took to bring a B17 down. In his last mission, he was firing at B25s and

at least four of the projectiles hit, blasting the enemy machine out of

the sky.

His one hundred and eighteenth kill looked like it would be his

last for a while as the Luftwaffe was expanding its training regime. A

number of aces had been pulled from different parts of the front line

to spread their expertise among the training pilots. The Jesau airfield

was large and had a concrete strip. Konigsberg was only sixteen

kilometres away but he had managed to visit the historic Baltic port

just once since he had arrived here. Flying was over pine forest or the

nearby sea where it was safe to drop bombs on

lashed-together barges or to strafe them with cannons. The weather

was pleasant enough in late summer except for the mosquitoes. The base itself concentrated on turning raw pilots, who had been through the early training program, into jet pilots. There were at least twelve of the ME262Bs located here as well as ten of the single-engined machines. There were also eight Arado232 jet bombers, as well as a small experimental unit, trying to solve the problems with the Heinkel 162.

The newest fighter was fast and promising but still had a number of teething issues. The one that concerned Kurt the most was the ability of the simple ejection seat to misfire. The engine sitting right behind the pilot made it necessary for the device to work or there was no way out of the machine if it was hit, or the turbine flamed out. It was the same with another strange machine which sat in a large hanger off the runway. This aircraft was prop driven but had engines at either end of the machine. Kurt thought it looked like a porcupine with its long nose. The Dornier Do 335 was being tested for future operations as both a night fighter and a fast fighter-bomber. Kurt had spoken to the test pilots who had nothing but praise for the aircraft. Two more Do 335s, which had been converted to twin seater machines, sat on the concrete just forward of the main hanger most of the time. One of these had been fitted with a radar set and had wing cannons as well as the centrally mounted guns.

"Ease back over the town Oberfahnrich Braun, and remember to be careful with the throttles," said Kurt.

The ME262 curved gracefully away from the Vistula Lagoon and angled towards the airstrip. Kurt thought the young pilot was handling the aircraft well and didn't think it would be long before he would be at a front line unit. Many fighter Geschwader were now totally armed with jets. The He 162 would be used against enemy fighters and fighter-bombers and could operate from grass strips. With only two 20mm guns it would struggle to take down a heavy bomber. The FW190Ds were important and used to cover airstrips and operate from rough locations, and the Bf109s were being sent to Germany's allies. Kurt had heard that a major effort was being made to reequip the French Air Force. Germany's western neighbour had plenty of pilots but few aircraft, and his country was now producing an abundance of planes.

Kurt wondered how the war would progress now that the Americans were in Italy and Madrid had fallen. The defeat of the US heavy bomber campaign had given Germany a chance but he knew the Amis would be back. He had heard rumours of a bigger and faster American bomber which could fly higher and carried an even more effective defensive armament. What Kurt was relieved about was that Germany's enemies had yet to develop a jet to match the 262. The British had a jet but only a few examples had been seen. One had chased an Arado 232 reconnaissance machine over the channel. The story was that it slowly made ground on the German jet but the Arado had reached a bank of heavy cloud before the British plane reached them. He remained hopeful that Germany would win the war and that it would maintain its lead in aircraft technology.

v

The Russians' counterattack south of Moscow had been stopped by the Charlemagne SS Division with the help of the 101st SS Heavy Panzer Battalion. Ahead of Wolfgang the forest burned and T34s smouldered. He sighed and wiped his brow. Hauptsturmführer

Michael Wittmann stood next to him with Hauptsturmführer Rolf Mobius to his right. The three company commanders were gathered next to a half-track that had recently returned from a reconnaissance mission through a forest to the north of the town of Moshchanitsy. The weather was hot and a wind blew from the south fanning the forest fire.

"The Unterscharführer says he could hear engines beyond the forest but he couldn't get passed the fires," said Wittmann.

"Don't they ever stop?" asked Mobius. "We have just destroyed over eighty of their panzers."

"The Russians seem to have an inexhaustible supply of men," said Wolfgang. "And now the Americans are supplying them with armour."

All of the burning tanks that sat scattered before the three officers were Shermans from the USA. M3 half-tracks and even a few M8 armoured cars lay wrecked and the 101st had taken possession of four of the popular Willys MB jeeps. The mechanics had told Wolfgang that they were tougher and easier to fix than the Kubelwagen.

"We will need to wait until the fire moves on or dies down and check out the Russian positions. We don't want to get surprised," said Wittmann.

"I'll take my Tiger down that way after dark and have a look around on foot," said Wolfgang. "That's if I have the fuel. At the moment I have enough to move maybe two kilometres."

"I'll get my crew to siphon some out," said Wittmann. "My Tiger needs its track fixed before it can go anywhere and I'm waiting for other parts as well."

"We have four working Tigers then," said Mobius. "At this rate the unit will be ineffective by the end of the week."

"The French have over twenty-four working Jagdpanzers, four with the long L70. The others all have the 75mm guns with the shorter L48 guns. They will have to hold the line until we get back up to strength," said Wittmann.

We need to be withdrawn, thought Wolfgang. The men are beyond exhausted. This rubbish that the willpower of the German soldier will keep them going is criminal. Men are dying from simple mistakes because of their tiredness.

"I'll send some of my boys over with a few cans, Michael, to collect the fuel. In the meantime I'm going to try and grab a nap," said Wolfgang.

It was a cloudy night and the wind had dropped to a gentle breeze. Ahead, the sound of noisy T34s could be heard but Wolfgang believed they were over three kilometres away. The road through the forest was narrow and he ordered his Tiger to halt near a stand of fallen trees. The fire had burnt patches of the woodland, leaving other areas completely untouched. This stretch of road was pristine, with shrubs and alder lining the verge. Wolfgang crept ahead with big Hans, the loader. He held his Walther P38 in his right hand while the enlisted man carried an MP40.

He could hardly see anything except a thin slither of gravel in the middle of the track. Trees hung overhead and the cloud cover blocked out the light of the stars and the moon. He thought about going back and getting a flash light but then decided shining a light

364

around would give away his position. Wolfgang thought he heard a sound and he stopped to listen. Hans seemed to be breathing unnaturally loudly and it distracted him.

"Wait here,' he whispered and crept further down the road.

Ahead, there was a fallen tree next to the gutter and some burning timber back in the forest. He caught a glint of metal and raised his pistol. The burst of fire from the Russian gun threw him back over the fallen tree, into a shallow gutter. Hammer blows had hit him in the left leg and hip. He didn't know how many bullets had hit him but he felt shock flow from the wounds and numb his brain. A man ran up to him and Wolfgang glimpsed the shadowy figure pointing a PPS-43 submachine gun at him. Then there was another burst of fire. The Russian's arms flew wide and with a grunt the man fell across his body. Hans ran forward shouting but then there was more fire, this time from a rifle. The loader's head snapped back and he fell on the road. Wolfgang felt around for his pistol as his senses started to return. He touched the Walther's barrel and pulled the weapon into his hand.

A Russian came around the fallen tree at the run, calling out to the man who lay on top of him. Wolfgang's understanding of the language thanks to his relationship with Larisa allowed him to comprehend every word.

"Sir, are you alright? I got the Nazis. The others will be up soon." The man started to pull the unconscious body off Wolfgang, who raised his pistol and fired it into the soldier's face. He got off two rounds, one of which went through the unfortunate Russian's cheek, the other hit above the left eye. The man fell sideways and didn't move. Then a fire fight erupted around him with men shooting from a variety of small arms. This was interrupted by the sound of grinding tank tracks coming from the south. The flat crack of an 88mm gun reverberated through the forest and Wolfgang knew the skirmish would be resolved by his side. Consciousness was slipping away as hands lifted him from the ditch.

"Bring the Russian too," he croaked. Then darkness enveloped him.

v

This raid was flying over Verdun and Metz, before turning east to attack Stuttgart. The direction of the mission took it over France for at least one hundred miles, in order to confuse the German fighter command about the actual target of the raid. It was thought that France had no appreciable air defence anymore, so no opposition was expected until the B17s hit the border of the Reich. Unfortunately, three French fighter groups had just been reequipped with Bf109 G14s with a MW50 boost. The aircraft was given a 20mm nose cannon instead of the heavy 30mm cannon and some models had heavy machine guns mounted under the wings. Lieutenant Richardson was flying top cover above four hundred B17s, as a swarm of fighters approached from the southwest.

As he watched, the Bf109s continued to climb before breaking into two groups. He saw the 354th Fighter Group dive down towards the enemy fighters and then heard orders for his squadron to attack the second mass of Bf109s.

"They are French," said someone over the radio before the voice was told to stop the chatter.

Henry was surprised as he didn't think France wanted to get involved in any more fighting. He supposed they were allies of Germany, but all the stories said that was only reluctantly.

The Bf109s were heading away from the P51Ds but then the enemy formation half rolled on their backs and came diving towards the 357th. The two formations swept through each other and Henry had a clear view of the enemy's markings. The large red, white and blue roundel and the striped tail section showed the plane was clearly not German.

It was a miracle that no aircraft collided. Guns spat flames and engines screamed, yet in that first rush, not a single plane was hit. The French pilots worked as a team. They hadn't flown the Bf109 long but they still had hours of flying time under their belts and were well drilled. If anything, they were even more aggressive than the Germans. A P51 was hit and a pilot threw himself from his burning aircraft just before it exploded.

Henry called to Second Lieutenant McConnell. "You with me Mac?"

"Still here, sir," his wingman answered.

They turned on a group of four Messerschmitts which seemed to be heading towards the bombers. As they closed, one of the enemy must have spotted them for the flight broke into two sections and half-rolled towards them. Henry turned towards the pair that had curved east and fired at the leader. It was a difficult deflection shot with the Bf109 heading towards him at an angle. The groups went passed each other and started to turn. Henry pulled in hard and felt the g-force build. Concentrating on staying conscious, he stayed with the Bf 109 in front of him and eventually his sight drifted over the enemy pilot's cockpit. His finger started to come down on the trigger but he hesitated, as he didn't want to kill this man. To take a life was such a terrible thing. A wife would mourn the pilot, or perhaps a mother. Somebody's life would be devastated.

The aircraft half-rolled, turned and was gone. He followed the Bf109 as it sped back towards another P51 which was trailing a thin stream of white smoke. The aircraft tried to escape but it was sluggish. Henry realised what was going to happen and rolled his plane on its back and headed down towards the wounded American aircraft. The Bf109 curved around behind the P51 and closed the distance with the damaged plane. At one hundred yards, it started firing and Henry saw the plume of flames from the P51. Then there was an explosion.

"What have I done?" said Henry.

"Sorry, sir?" said a confused McConnell.

Determined to make up for his mistake Henry kept following the French Bf109 but his wingman screamed a warning. "Red One, we've got two on our six."

Henry cursed and broke right before using the speed he had built up in the dive to climb quickly. The two French planes flashed by and he half-rolled and went after them. The enemy planes then went into a hard turn to port and Henry followed, firing bursts at an angle from three hundred yards. He saw pieces break off the rear of the second machine and a body jumped clear. Even after all that had happened he felt a sense of relief when the enemy pilot's parachute opened.

The sky was empty except for Henry and his wingman and they climbed slowly back towards the bombers. The image of the exploding P51 was etched in his mind and the dilemma of killing men, or taking the chance that fellow Americans would be killed, rolled around in his thoughts. Flak started to explode around the B17s as they crossed the Rhine. Henry tried to clear his mind as soon he would be facing jets and he needed to concentrate.

V

Rottenführer Klaus Moller was still angry. Yes, he had been promoted two grades and wore an Iron Cross First Class medal and a Tank Destruction Badge, but he was no longer fighting in the heart of the enemy's capital city. Rainer Stein was still with him, though that was little consolation, as the man had shown himself to be weak. He wasn't sure of the replacements in his squad either. The four men who had used to be guards at the Dachau Concentration Camp were hard, capable men but the ex-navy men weren't true National Socialists. They were competent soldiers, all having come through the SS training course before being allocated to various divisions after the comb out of the Kriegsmarine six months ago. He had heard of the eighty thousand men moved to the SS army and ten thousand had volunteered to be part of Germany's elite force. This was a good sign but to be in Totenkopf you needed to be able to undertake any task to ensure German victory, even those other men considered distasteful.

The 3rd SS Division had been moved from Moscow to the Don Bend to rest and reequip, after the losses during the brutal summer campaign. New Panthers were being unloaded at the train station next to the billets of the division, as well as Skoda T25s. The Panzer Four seemed to be appearing less and less. Puma armoured cars and replacement half-tracks as well as trucks stood ready for their new owners by the tracks. Even the small assault group had received Brummbars and StuH42s. The 3rd SS was being rebuilt and Klaus was determined his small squad would be ready to destroy the Soviet Army when the time came.

In the meantime, the division was tasked with moving more-able bodied Russians back to Germany to work on the farms and fields, and in the factories. Klaus had undertaken this task before when Rottenführer Sommer was still alive. He could see it was necessary but he would have preferred to be fighting. The village of Golovka had been built at the juncture of a small river, and what in Germany would have barely passed for as a creek. It was over thirty kilometres from the main road and one hundred from the comforts of Rostov on Don. Klaus' company had been sent this way with a pair of armoured cars and a dozen trucks to find able-bodied men and women to send back to Germany. As the area was isolated, it hadn't been investigated before. There were a string of villages in this area which had barely seen the war and had probably gone through the occupation unscathed. That was all about to change. The company was following the Kalitva River north, scooping up healthy workers as it went.

The trucks rolled into the centre of the village near the creek and SS soldiers spilled from their vehicles, immediately yelling for people to hurry to the open area in front of the village's only stone structure. Families were pushed and prodded into the open area while Hauptscharführer Hansen organized the selection of healthy

Russians. The Untersturmführer who commanded the adhoc group watched proceedings from the turret of the Puma armoured car. Men ran from door to door screaming and waving weapons as scared Russians made their way to the collection point, where a medical orderly made his selections.

Klaus and his squad made their way down a dusty side street to a group of ramshackle wooden houses near the creek. The door to the nearest structure was shut, so he kicked it in and burst inside. Huddled under a table where two children, a boy of about ten and a slightly younger girl. A man stood before them and a woman of some indeterminable age squatted near the fireplace.

"Bring them all out side," Klaus ordered.

His squad dragged them all in front of the house where another older couple waited under guard.

"This is all we could find in the other dwelling, sir," said Schutze Richler, one of the ex-navy boys.

"Vogel and Werner checked the trees along the creek. Might as well take the woman and the male. Leave the kids and the old ones," ordered Klaus.

The squad started to pull the woman away, when the girl started to cry. The younger man began yelling in Russian at Richler who looked embarrassed.

"We can take families, can't we, sir?" he asked.

"Only if there is no one to look after the children," said Klaus.

The Russian then grabbed Richler's arm and tried to pull the woman away. The SS man lost his balance and fell and one of the ex-concentration camp guards laughed. Klaus stepped forward and pushed the Russian away, but the man spat at him. He wiped the spittle from his jacket and hit the man with the butt of his rifle. The Russian staggered back towards the wall of the house where the rest of the family stood. They were all crying or yelling now. Klaus cocked his weapon and they fell silent.

He turned to his squad. "We don't argue with these scum. They follow our orders, instantly or they suffer." He turned and fired a short burst from his StG44 into the wife and husband. Wood chipped from the wall behind them as they both jerked and fell. The children and the older couple screamed with the old man holding his hands over the little girl's eyes. The next burst was longer, and then there was silence. The family were slumped against the wall with the old lady moaning softly.

"You didn't have to do that," said Schutze Muller, a tall blond man who had once served on a shore battery in Norway.

"You navy boys have never got your hands dirty. This is the war in Russia. These people murdered Germans in East Prussia. They raped and killed nurses!" yelled Klaus.

"Not these people," muttered Richler. "I doubt if they have ever been more than a few kilometres from this village."

Klaus took a deep breath. "First, you address me as sir. Secondly, the Slavs are rats who would spread the disease of Bolshevism across Europe. They tried to and we stopped them. For some reason, our present Führer decided we need them. Fine, they can live, but only if they follow our orders without question. Any resistance must be crushed."

Two of the men from Dachau were nodding while Vogel drew a pistol and shot the old lady through the head. "I'm with you sir," he said looking with narrowed eyes at the ex-navy boys.

Another squad led by Hauptscharführer Sauer came trotting down the road to the group. "Everything alright Rottenführer?" he called.

"Had a little bit of trouble sir, but we dealt with it," Klaus answered. "Unfortunately, a couple of possible workers were killed in the process."

Sauer frowned. "Well, write it up for me later. Should we take any further reprisals?"

"This village needs a lesson, sir," Klaus said, smiling. "Of course, it is up to you and the Untersturmführer."

Sauer nodded. "Burn the place."

Chapter Thirteen: September 1944

The JU390 approached the coast from the east. Twelve of the huge six-engined bombers had set out from an airfield in northern Spain, but two had returned with engine trouble. The Ju390s had cruised across the Atlantic at an altitude of five kilometres, which was near their service ceiling. In the thinner air it had meant less fuel had been used. One hundred kilometres from the coast of America they had dropped to only one hundred metres above sea level. The JU390s were counting on flying under any radar coverage and taking New York by surprise.

Each plane carried only six bombs, but in this historic mission the tonnage of explosives didn't matter. It was the fact they were striking at the enemy who thought they were untouchable that counted. The problem with the attack was that the strength of the defence was unknown. Hell, even the weather over the target was a guess. Yet this first attack was unexpected. The Americans had no idea of the existence of the JU390 and had not suffered an air attack on their country since they had entered the war. All that was about to change.

The radar at Sandy Hook briefly detected the JU390s before they dipped under its coverage, but the operators thought it was a glitch caused by atmospheric conditions and said nothing. Fighters from Mitchel Air Base were grounded due to low cloud with only two P47s in the air doing test flights. The JU390s came over Brighton Beach at low altitude and continued via Midwood and Park Slope before recrossing the river at Brooklyn Heights. The heavy bombers were now gaining height to avoid the tall buildings. Here, two planes headed for the docks near Times Square, while the other eight aimed for shipping at Newport and port facilities just west of Washington Square Park. The American defences still weren't aware of the impending attack, though people were pointing and staring at the strange aircraft. The Ju390s flew along the river and lined up on ships waiting at piers near W 23rd street. Major Werner Wagner's lead bomber dropped all six bombs along the docks in the area, killing eighteen workers and wounding another dozen. He had been aiming at two Liberty ships which had been loading trucks to take to Spain. The warehouses were filled with vehicles, many of which were destroyed. The second bomber, following close behind his leader, was more accurate and both ships were hit and caught fire.

The other bombers attacked shipping at Newport, with a destroyer suffering a hit hear the bridge, which caused a large fire. Now the air defences woke up and three inch guns started firing, though their shells went high. Bofors guns started shooting, with some of their shells hitting the taller building, punching through windows and concrete with one shell killing a spectator on a nearby roof. The highest casualties were caused at the Hudson yards where trains and carriages were crammed in side by side. A bomb exploded next to a taxi on 10th Avenue killing the driver and passenger, and three people standing on the sidewalk. Trains were derailed and destroyed, and workers were ripped apart by the explosions.

At this time, frantic radio calls reached the Mitchel Airbase and fighters were scrambled. Two P47s flying over Queens were told of the attack and turned west. The heavy bombers had finished their attacks and were climbing away, though two rear gunners sprayed

the crowded street below with their 20mm guns, causing more

casualties. New Yorkers were now hearing air raid sirens and some

were scurrying for shelter. Others still stood in shock, looking at the

German planes as they turned southeast.

Lieutenant Mulcaire and Lieutenant Simons had dived from

ten thousand feet and were scanning the sky for the German aircraft.

It wasn't long before they spotted three JU390s over Brooklyn. The

German bombers also saw them and closed their formation. The P47s

dived at the rear machine and opened fire at four hundred yards.

Most of the rounds went low until Simons adjusted his aim and saw

bullets chewing into the JU390's twin tail. He lifted his aim again and

saw pieces flying from the inner port engine when return fire from

the rear 20mm cannon tore through his cockpit, killing him instantly.

The P47 then nosed over and dived into an apartment block at the

corner of Bergen Street and Bedford Avenue, killing eight people.

Lieutenant Mulcaire saw his companion die and swore under

his breath. He and Dave had been good friends, and he was going to make the German pay. The JU390 was trailing smoke and had fallen back a little from the other two machines. He dipped under the huge bomber and raked it from below with a long burst. The eight heavy machine guns ripped through the cockpit and forward areas, killing or critically wounding both the pilot Hauptmann Han Guhr and his co-pilot. The plane staggered and rolled slowly to the side, quickly gathering speed and losing height before ploughing into the shallow water just off Bergen Beach. There was a gigantic explosion of spray before the aircraft sunk out of sight. Nobody had managed to bail from the stricken aircraft.

Lieutenant Mulcaire pulled his aircraft up into a gentle climb. He looked around for other targets but had lost sight of the German bombers. Sighing deeply he flew the P47 back towards the Mitchel Airbase. The first air raid on American soil was over.

The A4 rocket flew from its launcher near Veurne in Belgium leaving a cloud of smoke and dust before climbing swiftly though cloudy skies. It shot upwards over the North Sea, gaining altitude as it accelerated to its top speed of five thousand kilometres per hour. With a range of three hundred and twenty kilometres the rocket climbed to over eighty kilometres before the engine shut down. Then the rocket fell back towards its target. When the first rocket struck London, it did so without any warning. There was no air raid siren and no whistle or shriek, as there was with a bomb. The double crack of the supersonic rocket was followed by a brief rush of air, then the explosion.

One hundred and twenty A4s were supposed to be fired on that late September day. The Leitstrahl radio guide beam was to help with the accuracy of the rockets, but the system was experimental and only worked for the rockets fired from the Belgium border area. In the end, only seventy-eight rockets were launched with five of those exploding on re-entry. Twelve A4s were destroyed on a train just outside Ghent by British fighter-bombers. The pilots never knew what they had destroyed as the rockets had been hidden under canvas and the massive explosion that occurred when the war heads detonated, caused the British to think they had destroyed an ammunition train.

Of the rockets directed at London, fifty-two struck within the city limits. Eight hit within a kilometre of their aiming point, which was London Bridge. The sudden explosions all over the capital startled the English population but despite this, casualties were surprisingly light. Only one hundred and two people were killed in London with eighteen of those being on a double decker bus which was unlucky enough to be within twenty metres of a rocket strike. The vehicle was torn apart by the impact with one of the wheels being found one hundred and twenty metres from the point of the explosion.

Ten rockets were also fired from the German-occupied coastal strip in Normandy. The target was Portsmouth and the dockyards. The town was a much smaller target than London and two rockets flew over the area with one landing on Southwick House, a manor in a village of the same name. Unfortunately for the Allies, the house had become an important headquarters for the Royal Navy, and Admiral Ramsay and his staff were in the process of expanding facilities at the historical mansion when the rocket struck. The A4 hit the picturesque old building just behind the colonnades at the front of the building and the detonation caused the stone structure to collapse. Only two junior officers survived the explosion.

The Gunwarf Quays were hit by another A4, which landed in the water directly between two Vosper 70ft motor torpedo boats. The explosion lifted both into the air and broke their hulls in half. One landed in three pieces on the jetty and the other disintegrated. Only four crew members were on board at the time and none survived the ordeal. The attacks on Portsmouth turned out to be the most effective A4 strike of the day, with the final rocket landing on the southwest wing of the Portsmouth Naval Prison, killing twenty-two inmates and three guards. Two dangerous prisoners also took the opportunity to escape and remained on the run for three weeks until caught by military police on a farm near Winsford, just north of Exmoor National Park.

In all, the A4 attacks killed two hundred and five people that September afternoon. The face of warfare was changed substantially, as there was no way to defend against a strike by a ballistic missile except to hit them before they were launched. Unfortunately for the

Allies, the A4 was fired from mobile launchers that were easy to hide and the production facilities for the rockets were deep in Eastern Germany. For the time being it looked as though the English would just have to absorb the blow. The next target would be the Russian capital, as fifty of the missiles were sent east.

"The raids were a success, my Führer. We lost a bomber but the American press has gone crazy. There were signs that the US government tried to suppress news of the attack by the heavy bombers, but too many people saw them. Attacking in daylight was risky but it has paid off," said Kesselring.

Goering stood looking at the map of the eastern coast of America with glittering eyes. The leader of Germany was clearly overjoyed that the Luftwaffe had finally managed to strike back at the Amis.

"And you want to hit Boston next?" asked Goering.

"Yes, within the next day or two. We have a U boat off the coast monitoring the weather and we are just waiting for clear skies. We need to strike before the Americans organize their defences."

"I agree," said Goering. "The Ju390s are expensive and we don't have many of them. The opportunity to hit the USA during daylight hours won't last long."

"Then we will switch to night raids," said Kesselring. "These won't be as effective but they will force the Americans to divert resources to defending their homeland. Their public will demand it, as will their press."

Goering smiled. "That is one thing you have to love about democracies, when the fourth estate screams, politicians jump."

"Then there are the first photos from the V strikes. Goebbels has renamed the rockets as 'vengeance weapons'. The jets have returned and we are pleased with the hits on Portsmouth. Even though we struck London many times, we think the accuracy of the new weapon could be better."

"I knew they couldn't destroy a factory or blow up a warship, except by accident," said Goering. "These weapons are to inspire terror, though even here I doubt they will cause the British to sue for peace. It is just another straw on the scales."

"A very expensive straw," grumbled Speer who had stayed quiet up until this point.

Goering wagged his finger at the Minster of Production. "My dear man, the rocket is our insurance in case the Allies make the super bomb before we do. On that note, how is that project coming along?"

"Slowly," said Speer. "It looks as though the creation of an atomic bomb will be hugely expensive and is currently beyond our means. Advances have been made, with the production of heavy water in Norway. We are working on isotope separation and there has been some progress in this area, though if you want to make this bomb, we seriously need to increase the resources dedicated to the project. It will also be necessary to centralise the administration of nuclear research."

"Do it," said Goering. "If we could put a super bomb on a rocket, we could end the war. Continue with the rocket development, either for striking enemy armour or for blasting American bombers from the sky. We cannot win this war with numbers. Technology will be the key. The A4 loaded with saran gas is our defence against a super bomb from the USA and if we can make our own, then at least we can destroy Russia."

"In the meantime we need to hold the line," said Kesselring, both in the sky and on the ground."

"Precisely," said Goering. "And strike back where we can. That is where the Brandenburgers can come in. It is time our special forces landed a blow, and this is where I want them to strike." Goering's hand came down hard on the map, his palm slamming down on the eastern coast of the USA.

Notes: I have tried to stick to the true historical introduction of new types of aircraft and tanks as much as possible allowing the Germans to bring some items forward a little due to better organisation of their industry and little disruption from bombing.

Also removing Goering from controlling the Luftwaffe means that the competition for resources is rationalised somewhat. The lack of a Final Solution frees up assets for the Third Reich. In the end though, Germany was limited in its production capacity due to access to oil and minerals. This cannot be ignored.

I have also allowed Italy to be a little more effective, especially their air force, particularly as some of their later fighters were good aircraft.

Goering himself showed that he could exhibit great energy on occasions, such as at his trial at Nuremberg. He could also show great ignorance and behave in an emotional and illogical way. He was not a fool as some modern writers such as James Holland have tried to paint him as.

Germany under his leadership may have allowed greater autonomy to its generals. The General Staff certainly wouldn't have had to put up with the micro management of the army as they had to do under Hitler.

In the end, it would have been a very different war.

Made in the USA
Columbia, SC
11 February 2018